Praise for MARTHA WELLS

"A rollicking adventure yarn with plenty of heart –
Emilie & the Hollow World shouldn't be missed."
*Ann Aguirre, bestselling author of the Razorland
and Beauty books*

"Emilie is the best kind of adventurer – curious,
courageous, stubborn, resourceful, and quick to make
friends. I can't wait to see where she goes exploring
next."
Sharon Shinn, bestselling author of the Samaria series

"Wells... merrily ignores genre conventions as she spins
an exciting adventure."
Publishers Weekly (starred review)

"It's a stunning achievement that is utterly captivating,
effortlessly drawing the reader into the story."
SFSite.com

"Grit, glamour, guts, glory, grandeur, and delicate, subtle
moments of unexpected trust, great dialogue, and
deliciously revel~~ations~~"
Dear Author

MARTHA WELLS

EMILIE &
THE HOLLOW
WORLD

STRANGE CHEMISTRY

An Angry Robot imprint
and a member of the Osprey Group

Lace Market House
54-56 High Pavement
Nottingham NG1 1HW
UK

4301 21st Street, Suite 220B,
Long Island City,
NY 11101
USA

www.strangechemistrybooks.com
Strange Chemistry #9

A Strange Chemistry paperback original 2013

Cover by Amazing15.
Set in Sabon and P22 Arts & Crafts Hunter by Argh! Nottingham.

Distributed in the United States by Random House, Inc., New York.

ISBN 978-1-908844-49-1
Ebook ISBN: 978-1-908844-50-7

Printed in the United States of America

9 8 7 6 5 4 3 2 1

To Jennifer Jackson:
another one she never
gave up on.

ONE

Creeping along the docks in the dark, looking for the steamship *Merry Bell*, Emilie was starting to wonder if it might be better to just walk to Silk Harbor. So far, her great escape from Uncle Yeric's tyranny hadn't been great, or much of an escape. It's going to be embarrassing if I don't get further than this, she thought, exasperated at herself.

Emilie reminded herself failure wasn't an option. She scrambled behind a row of barrels, her boots squishing in foul-smelling muck, and squinted to get a look at the slip numbers next to the pier entrances. It was a cloudy night, the half-moon mostly concealed, and this end of the docks had only a few widely-spaced gas lamps. At the other end there had been tap houses and inns, and more people to blend in with, sailors or dockworkers heading for home and passengers waiting for the ships with a late boarding. This boardwalk was empty except for the occasional armed watchman, and if Emilie was stopped, she couldn't very well say indignantly, "I'm not a thief; I'm a stowaway, thank you very much!"

And she had to leave the city tonight; Uncle Yeric was a penny-pincher, but he might very well hire a hedgewitch to track Emilie with magic. Uncle Yeric and Aunt Helena would never lower themselves to hire a hedgewitch under normal circumstances, but considering what they thought Emilie was running off to do, they might make an exception.

Emilie had passed the gas-lit graving docks and the warehouses, looming dark and quiet. The hydraulic tower and the smaller pumphouse, its chimneys still billowing smoke against the night sky, made a good landmark; at least she knew she was in the right place. The *Merry Bell* and the other short-range steamers should be down here somewhere.

If Emilie hadn't spent money on food, she would have had enough to get to Silk Harbor by buying passage on the coastal ferry, which had departed late this afternoon. That had been her original plan.

She had formed the plan very carefully, stealing the newspapers out of the scrap paper bin to study the steamship lists and to learn where the passenger ferries berthed and the best route through the city of Meneport to reach the harbor. But none of the newspapers, or the storybooks that featured romantic heroines thrown out by their evil stepmothers (or stepfathers, or stepuncles) to make their own way in the world, had mentioned how painful starvation actually was, how once past the stage of acute pain, it made your thoughts slow and your body weak. It had taken Emilie two days to walk to the city, and by the end she had been footsore, exhausted, and so blind with hunger that she had stopped and bought a pork pie at the first shop she saw. It had fortified her for the walk across the city to the port, where she had succumbed again and bought a sausage roll and tea. Then she had found the booking office for the steamship lines and discovered that she was half the passage price short. If Emilie had had any inclination to see herself as a romantic heroine, this experience would have cured her of it.

I'm not a heroine, she thought, blending in with the shadows as she ran lightly to the next stack of cargo. I just want to live where I choose, like any reasonable person. She spotted a posted brass plate with the number eight on it. Finally!

The *Merry Bell* was a passenger steamer that made the short trip up the coast to Silk Harbor every other day, and it was due to leave at dawn. From what she had heard in the shipping office, it would carry a number of passengers, few of whom would bother with staterooms, since the ship would be docking before nightfall. Everyone would be sitting in the lounges or wandering the decks, and it would be easy for Emilie to slip in among them once the steamer was underway. That was the plan, anyway. She only hoped the state of her clothes, a somewhat-the-worse-for-wear shirtwaist, jacket, and bloomers, with stockings and walking boots, didn't call attention to her, especially if she had to swim in them. She didn't have any luggage, either. Before she had left she had made up a small bundle of her belongings and posted it to her cousin Karthea on the overland mail, so no one would see her leaving the house with a bag.

Emilie stepped out from behind the crates and took a careful look up and down the dock. A light mist had come in, clinging to the infrequent gas lamps, and the only movement she could see was far down the boardwalk. Her heart pounding, she darted across the wide expanse to the pier's entrance.

The walkway was roped off, but that must be the bulky stern of the *Merry Bell* tied up at the end. In the dark all she could see was the shape of a long steamer with two stacks and a paddlewheel, with a closed promenade along the second deck. A few lights shone from cabin windows, though there was no movement out on the decks. Only the crew should be aboard now, and most of them sleeping. Hopefully.

Now Emilie had to figure out how to get onto the thing. She expected that trying to sneak up the gangplank would be impractical. She was going to have to swim, but first she wanted to see if there was a ladder or net she could use to climb up the hull. She ducked under the ropes blocking the pier and started cautiously down toward the ship.

There was something lumpy between the end of the gangplank and a stack of crates, barely visible in the dark. She thought it was a tarp thrown over a piling. When she was barely five steps away, it stood up.

Emilie flinched back with a smothered curse. The looming figure became a bearded watchman in a battered gray coat. In a voice rough with suspicion, he said, "Hey you, what are you after here?"

Emilie backed away. She should have had a story. "Um, I just wanted to look at the ship. I'm not a thief." She realized a heartbeat later that it was the wrong thing to say. He hadn't accused her of being a thief, just implied that she was a trespasser. Now that she had blurted out the word "thief" like a guilty… thief, he was going to think she was one.

"Having a look at the ship in the dark?" He came forward, still looming, and even more suspicious. "Wouldn't be waiting for the mail, now, would you?"

"I'm not expecting any mail," Emilie said, trying to sound innocent. Maybe if he thought she was daft, he would let her go.

It did give him pause. She couldn't read his expression in the dark, but he said, in a different tone, "Are you with old Migiltawny's crew?"

Emilie considered the odds. The only choice was between yes or no, and one or the other had to be right. She took a chance. "Yes," she said brightly.

"Migiltawny the dock-pirate!" the man roared. "So you're his look-out!"

"What? No!" *Oh, hell*, Emilie thought. "I didn't know that. I mean, I'm not here for that. I'm not a pirate, either!"

"Oh, you aren't! Let's have a look at you." He flipped the slide on a dark lantern that had been concealed by the crates, and in the light he looked bigger and more threatening than before. Emilie started back and he grabbed for her arm.

She wrenched away, heard her jacket rip as she twisted out of his grasping hand, and bolted back up the pier. He didn't chase her and for a moment she thought he would let her go. He had to see she was a young girl, though it would be hard to tell how young in the dark, and she thought herself an unlikely prospect for a mail thief or a dock-pirate. But as she reached the pier entrance a piercing whistle split the air, and she heard pounding footsteps. Two more watchmen ran toward her from down the dock.

Emilie stumbled to a halt, looked wildly around, and took the only route left: three quick steps to the edge of the pier and a dive into the dark water.

The cold was a shock; Emilie gasped and swallowed foul salty water. She choked, coughed it up and started to swim away from the pier.

Behind her the men shouted and light shone on the water as they brought lanterns out. Emilie took a deep breath and went under. She swam as hard as she could and wished she could afford to get rid of her boots. If she ever got the opportunity to try to pass herself off as a legitimate passenger, she couldn't do it barefoot.

She surfaced when her air ran out, close to the pilings of the next pier. She clung to one and looked back at the *Merry Bell*, and was startled to see its decks lit by a dozen or more lamps, with crewmembers running back and forth to gather near the gangplank. She groaned to herself. Running away and then jumping dramatically off the pier probably hadn't helped convince them she wasn't a mail-thief-pirate-robber, but she couldn't tell them the truth, either. She had no idea what they did to stowaways. *It probably isn't as bad as what they do to pirates,* she thought.

This plan was turning into a disaster, and it was all her own fault. The *Merry Bell*, as disturbed as a trodden-on anthill, was out. She would have to look for another day steamer, or wait until the coastal ferry returned late tomorrow and try to sneak aboard it. In the meantime, she needed a place to hide until they grew tired of looking for her, and convinced themselves there was no gang of robbers ready to descend on them.

She should be better at this. Her mother had been a runaway too, and Emilie had never been allowed to forget it. Obviously it didn't run in the blood. Uncle Yeric would be so surprised. She paddled to the end of the pier, trying not to splash too much, and looked for another ship.

There was one two piers over, the decks lit by several lamps. Her teeth already chattering, she paddled toward it for a better look.

It was large, made of flashy bright coppery metal, but shaped like a round, top-heavy tub. Its hull was bulbous, and widened out to support platforms along the main deck. There were four decks, and it had three smokestacks, but they were set side by side across the width of the ship. There were no windows on the upper decks and few doors, though there was an open promenade. Some of the windows were lit, and she saw two men walking along the third deck, just turning into an open hatch. There was no gangplank down, and as she drew closer she saw the ship wasn't tied up to the pier, it was standing at anchor a short distance from it. The name on the bow was the *Sovereign*.

Emilie threw a look back at the dock. More men were gathering with lamps, agitated shadows searching the crates and barrel stacks, darting into every corner. Swearing to herself, Emilie swam toward the other ship.

She had to swim out and around the bow, to get to the side facing away from the lighted pier. I can't do this much longer, she thought. If there was no way to climb up to the deck, she was going to have to find a piling to cling to. The cold water sapped her strength, and she didn't think she could swim anywhere else after this, not without a rest.

But, for once, the first time in three days, luck was with her.

The ship had a cradle for a launch or lifeboat that had been lowered down the side, and sat just above the water. The boat was gone; someone must have taken it to go to shore. The cradle had a small platform with a ladder leading up the side to an open gate in the railing.

Emilie didn't know how exhausted she was until she tried to climb up onto the platform. Her soaked clothes weighed twice as much as she did, at least, and her arms ached with the strain by the time she dragged herself onto the narrow metal shelf. She lay there for a while, breathing hard and dripping, rivulets of water running away across the platform. But it was warmer out of the water than it was in.

After a time her breathing returned to normal, and

the metal platform began to feel cold and very uncomfortable. She sat up and started to wring out her clothes as best she could. Listening hard, she could still hear muted commotion from the docks, but she had a refuge for the moment, and that was all that mattered. She could stay here until the men on the dock stopped looking for her, then swim back to shore.

She heard the *putt-putt-putt* of a small boat motor. "Oh, no," Emilie muttered weakly. Out of the kettle, into the coals. What were the chances that it was this ship's launch, returning? After the events of the past night, she thought the chances were rather good.

She had had time to rest and to let several pounds of water drain out of her clothes, so tackling the ladder wasn't as difficult as it would have been earlier. The motor boat was drawing closer somewhere out in the dark, and that spurred her on.

She dragged herself up onto the polished wooden planks of the deck, and staggered upright. She started toward the nearest hatch: a heavy door with a thick crystal porthole. It stood open a little, and she cautiously peeked inside. It led into a wide interior corridor running parallel to the deck, lined with fine dark wood, the floor covered with a thick patterned carpet. An electric ceramic sconce about midway down provided wan light, enough to show her the richness of the brass fixtures and fittings. This must be someone's private steam yacht, she thought, startled. Not a good place to be caught if she didn't want to be mistaken for a thief again.

Emilie heard the boat motor sputter and turned. The launch was entering the slip, the light on its bow giving her enough of a glimpse of the occupants to see that there were several figures in dark clothing aboard. This isn't the best place to hide but it's the only one I've got, Emilie thought. She wiggled through the doorway without moving the hatch and started down the corridor.

She was still dripping, but fortunately the dark pattern of the carpet didn't show it. Anxious and feeling exactly like the unwelcome, uninvited intruder she was, she took the first turn to a cross passage.

The lights were brighter here which made her feel horribly exposed. She hurried past cabin doors, but they were all closed, and she was afraid to walk in on someone sleeping, or worse, awake. She passed a narrow stairwell, hesitated, then decided to stay on this deck.

Then the passage opened out into a lounge. It had deep upholstered couches built back against the walls, glass-fronted bookcases, and a white porcelain heating stove. There was a partially open door at the back. She hurried over to peek inside, and saw it was a steward's cubby, with a gas ring, a tap, and storage cabinets. As a hiding place, it was a good possibility. Surely it was too late at night for someone to want to sit in the lounge and call for a steward.

Footsteps sounded from somewhere nearby, and Emilie whipped into the cubby and pushed the door nearly to, leaving a slim gap. She crouched down on the tile floor, wrapped her arms around her knees, and tried to make her breathing silent.

Two sets of footsteps drew near, and she heard a man's voice say, "Lord Engal, I wish you wouldn't do this." It was a light voice, with a cultured city accent.

"You mean proceed with the expedition, or trust Kenar's word, Barshion?" another man, presumably Lord Engal, answered. His voice was deeper, with the same accent, and Emilie immediately pictured a much larger man. He sounded amused and dismissive. Emilie thought of Uncle Yeric, not in a complimentary way.

"Perhaps both." Barshion's tone was serious. "You know what I think of Kenar. We can't be certain what his motives are. There's too much at stake–"

"Dr Marlende's life is at stake, and the lives of his crew! This expedition must leave as scheduled. We've already delayed too long." The amusement had gone from Engal's voice, making him sound far more commanding.

Expedition? Emilie wondered. Lives at stake? Fascinated, she edged forward and angled her head to see out the gap.

A man paced into view, slender, with sleek blond hair and the pale skin of Northern Menaen ancestry. He was dressed in a very correct tweed walking suit with a carefully starched neckcloth. He said, "Marlende was... *is*, my friend as well." From his voice this was the one called Barshion. "I want to go to his assistance as badly as you do, but if we have the wrong information, we're risking Marlende's life and the lives of his surviving crew as well as our own."

"I understand your concerns, but we can't wait any longer. Even if Kenar is overstating the urgency, the entire party must be in real danger." Emilie heard a rustle, the click of what might be a pocket watch, then Engal stepped into view. He was big, burly enough to work on the docks, gray-haired, gray-bearded. Like Emilie, and most of the people she had seen in Meneport, his looks were more Southern Menaen, with warm brown skin and dark eyes. "Hickran should be back soon. What's keeping the man?"

"Ricks said he saw the launch returning a moment ago. It should be coming alongside now–"

Sharp cracks sounded from somewhere nearby, and Emilie flinched and knocked her elbow painfully against the cabinet. Startled, Engal said, "What the–"

"Gunshots," Barshion gasped. "The launch–"

The two men ran down the corridor, and Emilie pushed to her feet. Gunshots? she thought, astounded. Maybe the guard of the *Merry Bell* and the other watchmen had been so touchy and suspicious for a good reason. Maybe there really are dock-pirates, Emilie thought. She felt a little like she had stepped into a play.

A door banged open somewhere, men shouted, muffled by distance. Emilie bit her lip. She couldn't stay here. The watchmen would be called, the city constabulary too, probably, and if they searched the ship... Her disastrous plan was getting more disastrous by the moment. Emilie eased to her feet, peeked to make certain the lounge was empty.

She stepped out of the cubby, heard shouts and

running footsteps but couldn't tell the direction. She had to see where the robbers were before she knew which way to flee.

She ducked out of the lounge, heading back to the stairway she had passed on the way in. She hurried up to the next deck, finding a foyer with four closed cabin doors and an entrance to another cross-corridor. She ran back toward the starboard side, passed two open doors that led to a darkened dining area, then found a hatch out onto the unlit glassed-in promenade. She went to the railing, looking down through the windows streaked with damp and saltwater spray. It's robbers all right, she thought grimly.

There was a fight on the deck below, near the gate in the railing, above the ladder to the launch platform. Five or six men in the blue coats common to sailors and several others in dark-colored uniforms. She had no idea which were crewmen and which were the robbers.

A gunshot went off and glass shattered at the far end of the promenade. Emilie jerked back with a muffled yelp. Her throat went dry from fear. If she had stepped into a play, she wished she could step back out of it. She bolted back through the hatch and down the corridor.

It didn't go straight through to the port side, but turned into a confusing maze of service cabins and smaller lounges. Emilie had forgotten how absurdly wide this strange ship was, and blundered into a smoking room and a small pantry before finally tripping over the rim of a hatchway out into another larger corridor.

Before she ran ten steps down it, three men in black livery shot out of an intersecting passage and slammed past her, heading starboard. She gasped and flattened herself against the wall. One threw her a confused glance but they clearly didn't have time to stop and question stray girls, whether there were supposed to be any aboard the ship or not. In the light of the crystal sconces, she clearly looked a lot less like a scout for robbers than she had to the watchman on the dark pier. Those must be crewmen, she thought. The bluecoats are the robbers. That was handy to know.

Figuring she had truly used up every bit of her small store of luck by now, Emilie ran faster.

As she reached a passage that ran parallel to the outer port side, the deck shuddered beneath her and she heard the muffled grumble of the engines. They're casting off? she wondered, heading for the nearest hatch. A quick look through the small porthole told her the deck just in front of the hatch was empty, and that this side of the ship was facing the pier. The hatch was closed and locked and she had to wrench the bolts back before she could yank the heavy door open.

Emilie stepped out into a cool breeze, and heard fighting and shouting from the other side of the ship. The vessel wasn't moving yet, but the throb of the engines was growing louder. There were a few deck lamps lit, but there was no one out here to see her.

The ship was anchored some distance from the pier; Emilie would have to swim for it again. She went to the railing and realized she couldn't jump from here: the deck below was wider than this one. Also, she was much higher up now. She hurried along to an outside stairway, tucked into a sheltered nook in the side. She made her steps quiet, but she was only halfway down when someone stepped out of a hatch on the lower deck.

Emilie froze. It was a man in a greatcoat that was far too heavy for the cool night. He stepped to the railing, stretched to look down, then turned away from Emilie and started away down the deck. She just had time to take a breath in relief when a bluecoat slammed out of the hatch just behind him and swung a cudgel.

"Look out!" Emilie shouted in reflex. The man whipped around and ducked, lightning quick, and the cudgel missed completely. Before the bluecoat could recover, the man seized the cudgel, wrenched it away with a quick twist, and delivered two stunning blows to the bluecoat's chest and head.

Another bluecoat stepped out of the hatch, and Emilie surged forward. She had no idea what she was going to do, just that she had to do something. Then she tripped over a water bucket abandoned at the bottom of the stairs, seized it, and flung it at the bluecoat.

The bluecoat cursed and ducked, giving the man time to whirl around and hit him with the cudgel too. As the bluecoat collapsed, the man caught sight of Emilie and froze for an instant, staring at her. He was standing under a lamp, and the light fell on his face. Emilie yelled in pure shocked reflex.

He wasn't human. The matte black fur, the glitter of reptilian scales, were only an impression, but she clearly saw the gold split-pupil eyes and the pointed teeth.

Another hatch opened further down the deck and half a dozen bluecoats spilled out, brawling with just as many black-liveried sailors. They spread across the deck, shouting and fighting.

Emilie turned to run, but the deck heaved suddenly, rolled under her feet, and knocked her flat. Emilie struggled to her knees, trying to stand. It had to be the engines, an explosion in the boilers. The deck shook again and kept shaking, as if something huge had grabbed the ship's hull from below. The dock lights started to recede, as the ship moved out of the slip and into the harbor. Gunshots sounded nearby, and Emilie looked up to see two sailors with rifles stood on the deck above, aiming down at the bluecoats.

The strange man – creature – man shouted at her, "Stay down!"

That sounded like very good advice, despite the source. Emilie scrambled under the stairs and huddled back against the wall.

The deck shuddered continuously, the water churning below. She heard splashes, saw two bluecoats tumble over the rail. They were losing the fight, or fleeing the potential explosion, or both. The gunshots stopped and the ship's horn blew frantically. You have to get off this ship before it gets any further from shore, Emilie told herself, her heart pounding in her ears.

She crawled forward and peered around the stairway. Several sailors and bluecoats still struggled at the far end of the deck. She saw the strange not-human man toss another bluecoat overboard, then a door crashed open somewhere on the deck above. She looked up to see Lord Engal stood at the rail above her. He shouted, "Get off; jump, you bastards, if you don't want to go with us!" He fired a pistol into the air, emphasizing the order.

That seemed to convince the few remaining bluecoats that retreat was a good idea. Three went over the rail. Two others paused to drag a fallen comrade upright and toss him over, then they jumped after him.

The roar of the engines reached a deafening pitch, and Emilie had to follow them, before the ship broke apart. She pushed to her feet, staggered as the deck rolled violently, then flung herself at the rail.

"No!" someone shouted, and grabbed the back of her jacket, jerking her to a halt. "Too late!"

Barely three steps in front of her a glimmering gold wall sprang up along the rail and arched to form a dome over the ship. "What's that?" Emilie demanded. She looked up, realized it was the not-human man who had grabbed her. She tried to pull away, and he let her go.

He looked toward Lord Engal, who was still on the deck above them, and seemed to be studying the gold barrier with an air of great satisfaction. The man said, "The way home."

"Whose home?" Emilie tried to ask, but the roar of the engines blotted out the words. The deck shook and water rushed up all around them, the brown churning water of the harbor, kept out by the gold wall. No, the water wasn't rushing up – the ship was sinking, sinking fast, as if something was dragging it below the surface.

As Emilie stared upward in baffled horror, the water covered the dome of light overhead as the ship sunk faster and faster, and the brownish water gave way to deep blue.

Two

"I don't understand," Emilie said, too shocked to do anything but stare upward. She thought it was a remarkable understatement considering the circumstances.

The ship was enclosed in a bubble of gold light, traveling underwater. The view was murky, the only illumination coming from the lamps along the deck. But she saw shapes fleeing the ship's lights, a small school of multi-colored umbrella-fish, their jelly-like bodies and drifting tentacles remarkably graceful. Feeling a cold shiver in her midsection, she realized she couldn't see the surface. The air smelled salty, and tinged with seaweed.

Emilie had seen magic before. Mr. Herinbogel, her friend Porcia's father, was a retired sorcerer and occasionally helped the local physician with healing spells. And there had been the occasional traveling conjurer shows at the local fairs. But those had all been very small magics, not like this. This was like something out of a grand gothic novel.

Beside her, the man said, "It's called an aether current. It's carrying us under your sea, to a crack that leads through the bottom of the world." He looked down at her and added, somewhat unnecessarily, "It's magic."

"My sea," Emilie repeated, seizing on that detail. "It's not my sea."

"It's not mine, either." He cocked his head at her. "I'm Kenar."

The Kenar whose word Barshion didn't trust. Kenar who was something-not-human. "I'm Emilie." It seemed beyond rude to say *what are you?* even though it was one of the questions she badly wanted to ask. As if they were meeting in her uncle's parlor, she said instead: "Where are you from?"

He seemed to hear the original question anyway. He said, "I'm Cirathi, from the coast of Oragal."

"I haven't heard of that place. But..." The water was growing even darker. Bubbles streamed by and she realized they were still moving forward, rapidly, away from the harbor. Emilie saw the silvery flicker of a large tail fleeing their lights. The fish was swimming up... No, it was the ship that was still sinking, falling down through the water. "This is all very odd, so maybe that isn't a surprise."

A ship's officer turned to look down the deck, spotted Kenar, and shouted, "You, back to quarters!"

Kenar's hands knotted on the rail, and he ignored the command. Emilie stepped behind him, using his bulk to block her from view, hoping the officer would be too distracted to notice her. It was a little late at this point to be thrown off the boat. She hoped.

The officer strode down the deck and stopped a pace away. He said, "You heard me. Go inside."

Kenar's head tilted to regard him, and with a frustrated edge in his voice, he said, "You could use force, Belden."

The officer's expression tightened, but he didn't give way. He said, "We have to make certain none of the pirates stayed aboard. That will be easier without passengers on the decks and in the corridors."

Kenar was still for a long moment, then stepped away from the railing. This left Emilie in full view of the officer, who stared at her oddly, startled, then motioned for her to follow Kenar.

Emilie had no idea why the man wasn't raising the alarm that a stowaway was aboard this strange ship, but decided to stay with Kenar, if possible. He seemed disposed to be kind to her; human or not, he might be her only ally in this strange situation.

Two sailors conducted them through the hatch and forward down a passage, where another sailor stood guard at a door. He opened it and they were ushered into a large lounge cabin, paneled with thin strips of fine dark wood. The door was closed firmly behind them.

The lounge was as luxurious as the rest of the ship, with upholstered couches built into the walls, lamps with milky ceramic sconces. Then Emilie saw the large crystal port looking out onto the deck.

She stepped up to it, caught again by the impossible wall of water just beyond the deck rail. It was very dark now, but the ship's lights reflected off a school of small copper-colored fish, vanishing into shadow as the ship sped past. Emilie had never been afraid of water, but she was beginning to fear it now. If it rushed in on the ship, how long would it take for her and the others to swim to the surface? It had to be far longer than she could hold her breath.

Knowing that if she kept thinking about it the sense of pressure would just get worse, she deliberately turned away and looked around the cabin. Dr Barshion sat on a couch against the far wall, and from his expression he was almost as sour about being confined here as Kenar. And there was a woman standing beside a drinks cabinet, wearing a tweed jacket and a divided skirt. She was Northern Menaen like Barshion, tall and slender, with her blond hair confined in a bun. She turned to Kenar furiously and demanded, "How did those men get on board?"

He folded his arms, but didn't seem to think her fury was directed at him. "They were on the launch. Hickran and his men must have been attacked while they were picking up the last supplies."

The light here allowed Emilie to see his face better. His straight nose and high cheekbones belonged to a handsome man, though they were coated with tiny black scales instead of skin. His brows were feathery fur, and his hair was dark and plush, almost a mane, that didn't quite conceal the extra folds of reptilian skin at the back of his neck. The greatcoat, the dark brown shirt, trousers, and boots he was wearing concealed most of the rest of him, but his hands had scaly skin too, with mats of dark fur across the back. That, combined with the gold eyes and the pointed teeth, should have made the whole effect horrific. Maybe the shock of the pirate attack and the steamship plunging underwater in a protective bubble of spells had softened the impact, but... He doesn't look monstrous, Emilie thought. He looks like this is how he's supposed to look. And there was something about his voice that was reassuring.

Barshion frowned at Kenar and asked, "How did you get out of your cabin?"

Kenar lifted one shoulder in a shrug. He said, "Someone left the door unlocked."

"He fought the pirates and threw some of them off the boat," Emilie said. She wasn't certain why she was defending him, except that apparently someone had to.

Possibly it was ill considered. The others turned to stare at her in blank surprise. The woman said, "Who are you?"

"I'm Emilie." Emilie had no intention of giving her last name, even if she was on a magic underwater steamship. After everything else, she didn't want news of her exploits getting back to her family, not until she was safe in Silk Harbor. She prompted politely, "And you are...?"

The woman blinked, compelled by courtesy to reply, "Oh, sorry. I'm Vale Marlende."

Marlende. She must be related to the Dr Marlende that Lord Engal had spoken of rescuing. "I'm very pleased to make your acquaintance, Miss Marlende."

Emilie took a deep breath and plunged in, feeling it was better to admit the worst and get it over with. Not that it had ever worked out that way at home. "I'm here because I'm a stowaway. But I didn't mean to stowaway on this ship. I was aiming for the *Merry Bell*. I'm going to Silk Harbor to live with my cousin at her school for girls and I didn't have the money for the passage ticket."

"A stowaway?" Barshion said, astonished. He regarded Kenar with suspicion. "What was she doing with you?"

Kenar was looking at Emilie, his scaled brow quirked in surprise. "I found her on deck. I thought she was one of Engal's daughters."

Barshion said, "Even Engal wouldn't be mad enough to bring his daughters on this voyage."

Hah, Emilie thought. Lord Engal was Southern Menaen too; she thought the resemblance ended there, but no one would have been looking closely at her during a pirate attack. It explained the crew's reaction to her, surprised but not alarmed. It was too bad she hadn't known that while there had still been a chance to get off this ship.

"You swam over from the dock, I suppose, which explains why your clothes are wet." Miss Marlende frowned at her. "Couldn't your cousin have wired you funds for your trip?" she asked.

Emilie set her jaw, sensing an implication that she had somehow failed to think of this sensible alternative. It stung more, since she hadn't thought of it. But she hadn't known she didn't have enough money until she had gotten to the ticket office, and it would have been too late by then to wire and get a reply. And if she had waited a day, Uncle Yeric might have had time to track her down. .

She had no intention of explaining that. Before she could think of a reply, Barshion cleared his throat. "We can discuss that later, Miss Marlende." He looked at Emilie, stern and skeptical. "You really expect us to believe that your arrival, at the same time as the ship is attacked, was a coincidence?"

"It was a coincidence for me," Emilie told him, exasperated. Again, she was being accused of things she hadn't done and being questioned like a criminal. *Maybe it's me*, she thought. *Maybe her face and manner were guilty and suspicious, and she had never noticed before.* Whatever it was, she was damn well sick of it. She planted her hands on her hips. "I'm a sixteen year old girl from the country, of a good family. Do I really look like someone who would be scouting for pirates or dock-robbers or whoever those men were?"

"She has a point," Miss Marlende said to Barshion.

Emilie seized the opportunity to change the subject. She asked Kenar, "Are we really going down through a crack in the bottom of the world under the sea? Is that where you're from?"

Kenar nodded to Miss Marlende. "You explain it better."

Miss Marlende turned to her. "He's from the world inside ours, the inner world. My father, Dr Marlende, is a philosophical sorcerer, an expert in aetheric currents."

She eyed Emilie a little uncertainly. "Your family don't take any of the journals of the various Philosophical societies, do they?"

Miss Marlende didn't seem to think she was capable of understanding the explanation. Emilie would be more angry about that, if she wasn't so afraid that it was true. She had done a great deal of reading, but not of Philosophical Society journals. But there was one thing that she did understand. "I've read about aether-navigators, and how they work," she said. There were aetheric currents in the water and the air. They were what sorcerers used to make magic, and were invisible and intangible to ordinary people. Though there were always rumors that they could make people or animals ill, or that if a house was built in or near one it would suffer hauntings. But recently, philosophical sorcerers had invented a way for ocean-going ships to navigate by known aetheric currents, as an alternative to compasses and celestial navigation. The novel *Lord Rohiro of the Far Seas* had explained it in great detail – in between sea battles and pirates and the wooing of foreign princesses.

Miss Marlende seemed relieved. "Oh, then this won't seem quite so odd. Well, not entirely, anyway." She continued, "My father had been fascinated with the theories that there was another world inside the earth, that the center of the earth was hollow and that it was a nexus of aetheric currents. He began experimenting with aetheric currents in the sea, and below it, as a possible way to contact that world. It all turned out to be far more complicated than the original theory implied, but eventually my father developed an engine that could travel within the aetheric currents, powered by them, and he built a ship to test it on."

Caught up, Emilie said in a rush, "And he took the ship on an expedition to the Hollow World, and something happened and he and the crew were trapped, and Kenar came to tell you where he was and get help." Miss Marlende blinked in surprise, Barshion frowned, and Kenar lifted a brow. Emilie winced at herself. She had to remember, she couldn't trust these people, and they really had no reason to trust her. Pretend you're at home, and you have to watch every word you say, she told herself. But at the moment, there was nothing she could do but explain, "When I was hiding on board, I overheard Dr Barshion and Lord Engal talking about that part. But the rest was new."

"When did you overhear this?" Barshion asked, still watching her skeptically.

"When you were in that lounge with the porcelain stove. I was in the steward's cubby," Emilie said, glad she was able to prove it. She was a runaway, not a liar.

"Oh, yes." Barshion sat back with a sigh. "We did discuss it there. And only someone who was hiding in the steward's cupboard would know that."

Mollified, Emilie felt the tension in her shoulders relax. At least Barshion was willing to admit that she was telling the truth. And she really didn't want to talk about herself anymore. She looked at Kenar, reminded of all the questions she wanted ask him. "Are all the people down in the Hollow World like you?"

"No," Kenar said, absently, looking past Emilie and Miss Marlende, at the port. "The Cirathi are explorers, traders. We travel far, and see many different places and kinds of people. We learn languages with great speed, compared to others; I learned Menaen from Dr Marlende and Jerom and the rest of their crew, before coming here." His voice turning wry, he added, "Lord Engal finds that suspicious."

Miss Marlende said wearily, "Sometimes I think he finds everything suspicious."

She was looking out the port too, and Emilie turned and saw the water beyond the rail was now dark as pitch, impenetrable by the ship's lights. There was nothing out there to betray that they were traveling through water, not even bubbles. A shudder crept up Emilie's spine. They must be very deep underwater, already, and some distance out to sea. *And we're going even deeper.*

Dr Barshion stood, moving to the port. With a trace of concern in his voice, he said, "The bubble seems to be holding."

"Seems?" Miss Marlende lifted her brows. "If it wasn't, I think we'd know by now."

Emilie realized the faint sensation of falling, and of forward motion, had ceased. "It doesn't feel like we're going down," she said. But it was growing colder in the cabin, and moisture trickled down the inside of the port.

"The bubble – the spell protecting the ship and allowing us to breathe – compensates, so we don't feel the weight of the water above us," Barshion told her.

"Or we'd be crushed like an egg," Miss Marlende explained.

Emilie nodded. She hadn't thought about the weight of water before, except when she was trying to carry it in a bucket, but now it seemed obvious that all that water above them must be very heavy. Heavy enough to bend or break metal and glass. "How will we get to the Hollow World, again?"

"There are fissures in the sea floor," Miss Marlende said, her face thoughtful. "Deep ones that lead all the way through, connecting the outer layer of the world with the inner. Passing through them would be impossible, of course, except within the aether currents."

"Most of this, of course," Dr Barshion said dryly, "Is theoretical."

Kenar snorted quietly. Apparently it wasn't theoretical for him. "But Dr Marlende did it, didn't he?" Emilie said.

"My father took a different route," Miss Marlende told her. "He used an airship, and went down through the extinct cauldron of Mount Tovera, on the island of Aerinterre. Kenar took the same route up. The trip has never been made by sea, before."

That wasn't encouraging. Emilie was still having trouble believing she was here. It had all happened so fast. She asked Kenar, "But why did you come here? I mean, I know it was to get help for Dr Marlende, but why...? It must be a long way."

Kenar said, "I owed him a favor." He turned away from the port and said, "So why does a young girl of good family from the country flee her home?"

Emilie thought, Uh oh. The others hadn't bothered to ask, so she had been hoping to avoid the subject entirely. "I wasn't fleeing," she said, to buy time. It was a complete lie, she had been fleeing, but the last thing she wanted to do was explain why.

She was saved from further questioning by Dr Barshion, who said in frustration, "There must be some word by now…"

He went to the door and opened it, and began to interrogate the guard about where everyone was and what was happening. Miss Marlende moved closer to listen, then turned away, muttering to herself in a disgruntled fashion. She said, "It sounds as if we'll be here for a while. They think there might still be some intruders on the ship." She walked back to the drinks cabinet, frowning at it. "I'm desperate for tea."

"The steward's cubby should have a tap and a gas ring," Emilie said, glad to show that she was a little useful. She didn't know much about aetheric magic, but she could do tea. "We can make some, if there's any here."

Miss Marlende went to ransack the cabinets in the cubby, while Dr Barshion argued with the guard, Kenar watched the dark water, and Emilie found some mugs and tried to get over the strangeness of doing something so normal in the oddest place in the world.

❧

Emilie made tea, which everyone drank but Kenar, and waited. Miss Marlende and Dr Barshion talked about aetheric currents in technical detail, with Kenar joining in occasionally. Emilie tried to listen, because some of it was interesting, but it had been a long hard day, and the couch was soft and comfortable. After a time, she drifted off to sleep.

She woke abruptly when the deck shuddered, a vibration that traveled up through the couch and rattled Emilie's bones. She sat up, startled wide awake. "What was that?" The wall clock said she had been asleep almost three hours.

The others were sitting bolt upright, frozen, listening hard. Staring out the port at the bubble, Dr Barshion said, "I don't know. It's not a terribly good sign."

Head cocked to listen, Kenar said, "We hit something?"

"I don't think so." Frowning anxiously, Miss Marlende added, "Perhaps it's just an aberration in the flow–"

The deck shuddered again, more violently, and Emilie's heart dropped to her stomach. She swallowed hard, very aware again of the water pressing in on their fragile bubble. Dr Barshion strode to the door and pulled it open. The sailor-guard was braced against the wall, looking uneasy. Dr Barshion said, "I must be allowed to go to the engine rooms. If there is some sort of interruption to the aether current–"

The sailor was saved from the decision to disobey his orders by a thunderous shout from the other end of the corridor. "Barshion!" Lord Engal demanded, "Where the hell are you?"

"Here!" Dr Barshion stepped out.

"Come along, we've got a problem!"

Barshion hurried away, Miss Marlende and Kenar right behind him. Emilie followed, having no intention of being left behind.

Lord Engal led them down the first stairwell, saying, "Abendle doesn't believe the problem is in the protective spells, but in the motile itself."

Barshion said, "By 'problem' he means…?"

Taking the stairs two at a time, Engal glanced up at him, his face grim. "He thinks it's not getting enough power from the conventional engines."

"What's the motile?" Emilie said, keeping her voice low. Her knowledge of the interior workings of steamers ended at Lord Rohiro's fictional pirate ships.

With an impatient glance at her, Miss Marlende replied, "The motile is the engine that my father invented. It lets us travel in the aether by taking in the aetheric stream and expelling it for locomotive power. The aether helps protect the ship from the pressures and forces outside the current, as we travel through the fissure."

The sound of clanging, banging, and the chug of the engines grew louder until they reached a lower deck with a stained metal floor, low ceilings, and warm damp air. Lord Engal turned down a corridor and led them past several metal hatches. Passing one, Emilie got a glimpse of a room filled with mist and smelling thickly of wet earth and green plants. She stopped, startled, peering inside. All she could see were clusters of white things like balloons, or like stuffed sheep's bladders. An older crewman in a disheveled uniform was poking one with a dubious expression. The others were leaving her behind and she hurried after them, asking Kenar, "What's that room for?"

"It's part of the spell that cleans the air inside the bubble," he said over his shoulder. "I don't know how it works, either."

The air was growing warmer, and, from the clanging and chugging that seemed to be coming from the deck below them, Emilie thought they must be just above the boiler room. Then they came to an open hatch. Dr Barshion and Miss Marlende followed Lord Engal inside, but Emilie stopped on the threshold with Kenar.

The cabin was filled with big pipes and tubing, all connected to a round plinth in the center with a large copper dome atop it. Dials and knobs surrounded the base of the plinth, and two crewmen stood there, tools scattered on the floor around them, pointing to the dials, arguing. They stopped as Engal stepped inside. "Any luck, Abendle?" Engal asked.

"No, My Lord." The man who answered was Southern Menaen also, with grizzled dark hair and deep lines in his face. Both crewmen looked sweaty and exhausted, as if they had been battling something down here for the past hour. "The adjustments didn't help. I don't know–"

His voice tense, Dr Barshion said, "Open the cover, please."

As the younger crewman lifted the copper dome, misty steam filled the room, though Emilie couldn't tell the source. Under the dome was a glass ball, and floating inside it was a bubble of silvery white light. Emilie leaned forward, squinting to see. It wasn't a light, it was a liquid. She could tell from the way it moved. It had an opalescent quality to it, as if it were a liquid drop of pearl. Blue light crackled under the glass, like a miniature lightning strike, and Emilie flinched.

So did everyone else. Miss Marlende said grimly, "That shouldn't be happening."

"What is it?" Emilie whispered to Kenar.

"It's quickaether," he told her softly. "It powers the motile, and the other spells the ship needs to travel the aether currents."

The crackling light inside the glass flickered suddenly. The deck shuddered in response and the ship around them groaned. Emilie swallowed in a suddenly dry throat. That couldn't be good, she thought. The ship sounded as if it was strained nearly past bearing.

Barshion checked all the dials, spoke quietly to the older crewman Abendle, and turned some of the knobs. Then he stepped back from the plinth. His expression wasn't encouraging.

Watching him worriedly, Lord Engal said, "You look blank. I'd like to believe that's a clever ploy to frighten me right before you tell me that of course you know how to fix it."

Barshion shook his head, baffled. "I don't understand what's wrong- All the spell's parameters are correct, but the engine is still failing."

Miss Marlende took a sharp breath. "Then we've got to surface. How close to the boundary are we?"

Engal said, "We've just passed it. We entered the fissure just off the coast and the current's carried us through, just as we theorized."

Kenar didn't seem surprised, but Dr Barshion and Miss Marlende stared at Engal. "You didn't inform us," Barshion said, startled and angry. "If you—"

"I was rather busy; we had three dock-raiders holding out in the forward hold who decided to fight to the death." Engal lifted his brows. "We may be past the boundary, but we're still some distance from your father's last known position. I estimate several more hours of travel, at least. If we leave the current now—"

"But we can surface, that's the important point," Miss Marlende said urgently.

Barshion waved an impatient hand. "I don't think we have a choice. It's either surface intact, now, or surface later as a smashed mass of metal."

Engal nodded sharply. "Then we'll surface now."

Emilie and Kenar stepped hastily out of the way as Lord Engal plunged out of the cabin and back down the corridor. Dr Barshion stayed behind, but Miss Marlende dashed after Lord Engal, her boot heels tapping on the metal floor. Kenar followed her and Emilie hurried after him. Boundary, fissure, surface, she thought. It couldn't mean what it sounded like. Except that it couldn't mean anything else. She asked, "We're not going back up, back to the harbor, are we? We're already there, in the center of the world? That's what the black water meant?"

"Yes." He sounded more relieved than worried, and she remembered they were going toward his home.

"But so fast..." She had thought it would take days.

"The aether currents move through water and air at a pace faster than anything could travel without magic." He threw a quick glance down at her. "But we're here sooner than I expected. It must have something to do with the sea."

She meant to ask him if it had been a long journey for him, flying up through the volcano, but Engal was already pounding back up the stairs and Emilie had no breath to talk.

They hurried after him, forward down a passage, passing a couple of short corridors lined with cabin doors. Everything was as rich as the lounge areas: fine wood, polished brass. They went up a set of stairs to the bridge, to a passage that opened directly into a chartroom. There was a big table in the center, and large cabinets for maps against the walls.

Four crewmen were there, all in the black livery. The oldest man looked up, frowning. It was the officer who had ordered Kenar off the deck and sent him to be confined in the lounge. He said, "Lord Engal, are we–"

"We're going to surface, Captain Belden, prepare the crew," Engal said, moving past the crewmen into the wheelhouse.

The wheelhouse had a curved outer wall, with large ports all along it, now looking out on the black water.

There was also a brass-bound wheel, a speaking tube, and an engine telegraph, for transmitting the captain's commands to the men in the engine rooms. In the center was a waist-high cabinet of polished wood, the top formed out of a heavy glass hexagon. Beneath the glass, something was glowing with a faint silver light. Engal stepped to it and carefully lifted off the top. Emilie edged closer, and saw that there were metal plates inside, rings and wheels, something like an astrolabe. He made a minute adjustment, and Emilie felt a sudden push upward, as if the deck was moving up under her feet. She stumbled, sudden vertigo making her head swim.

Kenar and Miss Marlende went to the railing at the front of the wheelhouse. In the chartroom the captain was frantically giving orders to secure the hatches, batten down this and that.

The water was growing lighter, and Emilie made out the shapes of rock, like a cliff face, a short distance off their bow. She gasped, suddenly realizing just how fast they were moving. Faster than the fastest train, as fast as falling down a cliff, only in reverse. It was the most exhilarating sensation, like how she had imagined flying.

Then the rock fell away and the light was turning blue-green, coloring everything inside the wheelhouse. The ship was moving up through something that looked like an underwater forest, tall stalks of frilly seaweed bending away from their bow and the bubble of magic protecting it. Emilie moved along the port, fascinated, watching the quicksilver flashes as fish raced away from the intrusion.

She could tell the ship was slowing down; bubbles rushed up past the ports as they left the seaweed forest behind. Emilie felt the deck push at her feet again, as if the ship had been lifted on a wave. Her heart pounding, she stepped forward to grab the rail.

A bell rang somewhere in the depths of the ship and Captain Belden took the speaking tube, saying, "All hands, brace for surfacing."

And then the ship rolled over onto its side. Some people staggered, but no one fell. Emilie held onto the rail, gritting her teeth against the urge to scream. Water rushed past outside, the whole ship bobbed upright like a wooden toy in a pond, and Emilie wished she hadn't eaten that sausage roll back at the tap house. But then the motion gentled, and they were floating on fairly low waves. Emilie stared out the port, but couldn't see anything past the golden bubble.

"We did it," Miss Marlende said, awe in her voice.

Kenar let out his breath in a hiss, then leaned on the railing. His shoulders slumped in relief.

Miss Marlende turned to Lord Engal. Sounding a little breathless, she asked, "Should we lower the spell bubble?"

Lord Engal looked down at the device inside the plinth. "From what Barshion said, I don't think we'll have to. It was about to shatter at any–"

Past the port, the golden light of the bubble dissolved, and they were looking out over a sea.

There is a sky, was the first thing Emilie thought. It was a crystal blue, bright and pure, streaked with the white of clouds. And the water under the ship was clear as glass. She could see a school of blue and yellow fish, flickering some distance below the surface.

"What is this place?" someone whispered in astonishment.

Emilie turned to look out the other side of the port, and drew in a breath of pure wonder. They were floating past a flooded city.

She moved to the railing, staring in amazement. It was spread out all across the starboard side, all made of gray-white mottled stone. The tops of square pylons, columned walkways, and towers with odd spiral curves gleamed above the expanse of clear water. Tall feathery trees stood in the sea, waves lapping against their trunks, their soft emerald green foliage vivid against the sky.

Emilie looked up at Lord Engal, standing next to her, and said, "It's beautiful."

He glanced down at her, smiling, then took a second startled look. His brows drawing together, he said, "Who the hell are you?"

THREE

The next several minutes were problematic, at least for Emilie. She had thought Lord Engal looked like a shouter, and he proved her right, railing on about spies and stowaways and wasn't anybody guarding the ship, as Miss Marlende repeated Emilie's story. To her credit, Miss Marlende continued doggedly, despite the noise and interruptions. At the end, Lord Engal turned to Emilie and demanded loudly, "Why shouldn't I throw you overboard?"

Emilie folded her arms, skeptical. After all the shouting and turmoil at home, being threatened with a dire fate wasn't as shocking as it ought to have been. She said, coolly, "I suppose you should throw me overboard, if you don't mind being a murderer. I prefer being shot to being drowned, if I'm given a choice."

Silence fell as Lord Engal was rendered momentarily speechless. Leaning casually against the rail, Kenar said, "You're not killing a child." There was a cold edge to his voice.

"Of course I'm not killing a child!" Lord Engal thundered. "We're not savages," he added, glaring at Kenar.

"I'm glad to hear it," Kenar said, his tone making it clear that as far as he was concerned, the matter was still up for debate. Emilie could have objected that she wasn't a child, but decided against it. Despite Lord Engal's bluster, she thought Kenar was by far the more dangerous individual. It was just lucky that he seemed to have high moral standards.

Lord Engal pressed his lips together, then transferred the glare to Emilie. "You're very confident, if you are what you say you are."

"What else would I be?" Emilie asked. She was discovering how much she had learned about verbal sparring from arguing with Uncle Yeric and her older brother. And Lord Engal had more important things to deal with than Emilie: outside the ports, the flooded city drifted by, small waves from their passage lapping at the white towers and graceful arches. Captain Belden was standing by the wheel and had cleared his throat three times; obviously decisions were called for.

Miss Marlende said impatiently, "Do you really think she's working with Lord Ivers' men? That seems unreasonable to me, and I've been dealing with his machinations much longer than you have."

"Who's Lord Ivers?" Emilie asked.

Everyone ignored the question. Lord Engal said, grimly, "So you'll agree to take responsibility for her, then?"

"Yes," Miss Marlende said. Then she looked a little appalled at what she had just agreed to. Emilie was a little appalled, also. She didn't think Miss Marlende thought much of her except that she was a nosy foolish stowaway. That that assessment was probably accurate just made it worse.

"Then take her below," Lord Engal snapped.

Miss Marlende set her jaw, unmovable. "I will, once I find out where we are and how far we have to go to find my father's airship."

"Ah." Lord Engal rubbed his chin, deflating as he apparently recalled that there were more important concerns at the moment. "Yes, we'd better ascertain that."

Captain Belden looked relieved. He signaled for another officer to take the wheel and stepped into the chart room. "Here, My Lord. I've got the readings from the aether-navigator."

Lord Engal strode after him. "Come along, Kenar, we need your map."

With one brow lifted in ironic comment, Kenar pushed away from the rail and followed.

Miss Marlende took a deep breath, still flushed from the argument. She looked down at Emilie and said, "His bark is worse than his bite, you understand."

Emilie nodded politely, if noncommittally. The expression was appropriate for dogs, who were without personal malice and whose job was, after all, to bark; she didn't think it applied to people.

As they stepped into the chart-room after the others,

Kenar took a folded packet out of his inside coat pocket and spread it on the table, flattening the creases with the blunt dark claws on the tips of his fingers. It was a map drawn in dark ink on thin cloth instead of paper, stained by dirt and grease. There were shapes sketched in, the outline of a coast with a large collection of islands, with notations made in a language with blocky letters that Emilie couldn't read.

"Now, where's... Ah, here we are." Engal took the chart the officer held and put it down next to Kenar's map. Emilie had never been fond of geography, but she recognized Menea's coastline, with Meneport next to the mouth of the Seren River, and Silk Harbor some distance below it, and the other coastal cities scattered here and there. "They're not supposed to match up, are they?" Emilie asked Miss Marlende, keeping her voice low to avoid attracting undue attention. Since Miss Marlende was now in charge of her, maybe she would answer questions.

"No." Miss Marlende shook her head, absently tucking back a frizzy curl of blond hair. "According to the maps Kenar has brought us and his own observations, there's no correlation between land masses."

Emilie nodded toward the port, looking out over the serene sea. Sunlight was glinting off the white facing of a fluted column, the top chipped and worn by weather. "That's not the Sun, is it? It's a sun, but not our sun."

"Kenar calls it 'the warm heart of the earth.' There are other solid bodies in orbit around it that cause periods of darkness. One is called the Dark Wanderer, and the people who live here use it to determine directions. West is darkward, the direction the Dark Wanderer comes from, and east is antidarkward, the direction the Dark Wanderer takes when it leaves the sun." Miss Marlende stared out the port, caught for a moment by the view over the crystal water. "I can't believe we really made it here," she murmured.

Emilie couldn't, either. She supposed it would sink in over time.

Captain Belden was using a triangular plotting instrument to mark a position on the chart, and Kenar had his own system, using the widths of his fingers to measure and a stub of pencil to mark the points.

Lord Engal's brow furrowed as he studied the results. He said, "We left the fissure nearly ten hours early, at this point." He tapped the spot on the chart that Captain Belden had plotted, some distance off the Menaen coast. "We know Marlende's party is here, in the vicinity of the Aerinterre mountain fissure." He tapped another point on the chart, the outline of a large island. Then he looked at the other map, where Kenar had marked the same points. "Hmm."

Emilie craned her neck to see. On the Hollow World map, the space between those points was blank. Kenar drummed his claws on the table and admitted, "Our ship was still charting this area. It was new territory for us."

Captain Belden said slowly, "If our figures are correct, it should be the same approximate distance between the coast of Menea and the island of Aerinterre. That would be about two days' sail, if conditions are good." He gave Kenar a hard stare. "If there's nothing in the way."

"I don't know," Kenar said pointedly. "If I knew, I would have put it on the map."

Lord Engal let out a gusty breath, still frowning. "We've no choice. We can't return to the upper world until the motile is repaired, and if we can't go back, we must go forward. We'll try to reach Marlende's position."

"We might not be able to go back," Captain Belden said, "but we don't have to go forward. We could hold this position and make the repair."

Miss Marlende stepped forward and slammed a hand down on the table. Emilie jumped, startled. Everyone else stared at Miss Marlende. Teeth-gritted, she said to Lord Engal, "The whole purpose of this, the whole reason we contacted you, gave you access to my father's work, was to help him and his crew. If you leave now, when he's within reach, so you can claim the discovery, I will–"

"I have no intention of leaving here without your father and his men," Lord Engal cut her off. "That may not be my sole reason for pursuing this experiment, but it certainly is the most important." He took a deep breath, and added more calmly, "Miss Marlende, you've repeatedly demanded that I trust you and Kenar. I would appreciate it if you would extend a little trust to me in return."

Miss Marlende met his gaze for a long moment, then said, grimly, "Fair enough."

With a pointed glance around, Engal continued, "As

I said, we'll sail toward Marlende's position while Barshion and the engineers try to make the necessary adjustments to the aetheric engine. We'll also try to raise the airship on our wireless, though from Dr Marlende's notes we know that the aether in the air here may interfere with radio waves. If we encounter obstacles, we'll deal with them as necessary. If we can't deal with them, I'll reconsider our course."

Captain Belden didn't look happy, but he didn't object, either. Emilie, as annoyed as she was with Lord Engal, had to admit that this was as fair as possible, and probably what she would have done in his position. Miss Marlende seemed to agree. She said, with a trace of stiffness, "Thank you, Lord Engal. I can't ask for more than that."

Then Lord Engal ruined it by saying, "I should think not."

There was a lot of bustle at that point, everyone putting their heads together over the maps, and Emilie found herself shuffled out of the wheelhouse and into the corridor. Once there, she wasn't sure where to go. Everyone seemed to have temporarily forgotten that Miss Marlende was supposed to be in charge of her, and she didn't want to remind them. And she didn't want to draw too much attention and get herself locked up in a cabin for the duration.

But her stomach was growling, and she felt sure she wasn't the only one; somebody would be feeding the crew breakfast.

She went down the nearest stairs to the main deck, and once there followed the smell of fried bread and sausages down another stairwell to the crew quarters. The corridor opened into a crew lounge fitted up as a galley, with long tables and benches, where an older woman and a boy about Emilie's age were working at a small stove and counter, dispensing food. Several crewmen, some with bandages, black eyes, torn uniforms, and other signs of the fighting, were sitting down to eat or waiting for seconds. Emilie picked up a tin plate and a cup from a clean stack and joined the line.

She noticed most of the crew were Southern Menaen, like Lord Engal, or looked as if they had a mix of both Southern and Northern heritage. They could have all been hired from Meneport, but.they seemed very comfortable with each other, as if they had been together as a crew for a long time. They had fought off the attack on the ship in a very capable fashion; it made her wonder if Lord Engal did this sort of thing a lot.

From the talk she overheard, everyone was unsettled by the fight, tired, and deeply uneasy about their current whereabouts. Emilie thought it was a rational reaction to the whirlwind events of the past few hours.

When it was her turn, the boy who took her cup to fill it at the tea urn just stared at her, but the woman who was dishing out the food blinked in surprise and said, "Now who are you?"

"I'm Emilie." She held out her plate hopefully. "I'm with Miss Marlende." Maybe that would come in handy after all.

"Oh, well then, you should really be eating up in the passenger lounge," the woman told her, but continued scooping sausage slices, fried bread, and potatoes onto her plate. "Verian, the ship's steward, is going to be serving up there."

"But this looks so good," Emilie said, and for once it was the complete truth. The sausage was plump, the bread soaked with butter and sugar, the potatoes nicely browned.

Her sincerity must have been evident, because the woman smiled, ladled more onto the plate, and said, "If you need anything, I'm Mrs. Verian."

Emilie thanked her, took her mug of tea, and retreated. She went back up the stairs to the passenger decks, since she was less likely to be noticed there. Recalling there were tables and chairs on the glass-enclosed promenade, she headed for it.

The hatch was already open. Emilie peeked out cautiously, and saw Miss Marlende seated at a table. Kenar was nearby, perched on a supply locker built against the wall. They were looking out at the view, which was so arresting Emilie had to stop and stare a moment.

The ship was moving slowly, the low throb of the engines the only sound as they sailed along the edge of the flooded city. The clear water sparkled in the sunlight, and their wake lapped at the white towers, the wide pitched roof of a submerged building, a line of artistically twisted columns that marched away to nowhere. Emilie supposed there was no time to stop and explore, not before they had rescued Dr Marlende. But maybe we'll have to come back this way, and have time to stop then, she thought.

Her stomach grumbled again, and she stepped out onto the promenade. She meant to say something polite, but then saw the distant shape in the sky. "What's that?" she demanded, interrupting their conversation.

She couldn't tell how far away it was. It hung in the sky, like a solid band of heavy gray cloud, except something seemed to be stretching up from it, a translucent column that vanished high in the air. Miss Marlende followed her gaze. "Oh, that. It's the other outlet for the Aerinterre aether current, the one that's connected to Mount Tovera in the surface world." She sounded much calmer than she had in the wheelhouse. Perhaps Lord Engal's assertion that he still meant to find her father had reassured her somewhat. "There's so much free aether in the air here that we can actually see it with the naked eye, if the weather conditions are right."

"Oh." Emilie blinked, recalling herself. She stepped toward the table. "I hope I'm not interrupting."

"No, we were wondering where you went- Where did you get that?" Miss Marlende said, as Emilie set her plate down and took a seat.

"The crew galley," Emilie said, and started to eat.

"It's better than what they had in the passenger lounge." Miss Marlende sat back with a sigh. Kenar made a disparaging noise, and she said, "Oh yes, oyster cocktail and salad are fine for you." She explained to

Emilie, "He doesn't eat meat, he thinks our vegetables are odd and our fruit tasteless."

Chewing sausage and potatoes, Emilie glanced back at Kenar. He had shed the greatcoat and changed clothes. Over the trousers and worn leather boots, he wore a sleeveless red shirt studded with gold disks around the hem, and gold chains woven through his mane. It accented his alien appearance, making it easier to see the dark scales on his arms and where they gave way to short dark fur that spread up across his shoulders. He looked much more comfortable and much more at ease. She swallowed and said, "But you have pointed teeth."

He took an apple out of a pocket and said, "You have flat teeth, and look what you're eating."

"True." Emilie polished off a piece of bread, and decided to try to get a few more answers. She asked, "Who is Lord Ivers, and why is everyone worried about him?"

Miss Marlende's brow furrowed, but she explained, "He's a very wealthy man, like Lord Engal, and he studies aetheric currents, like Lord Engal. We believe it's Lord Ivers who was responsible for the dock-raiders who attacked us last night. It wasn't just a coincidence; there were a few earlier attempts."

"He wants the credit for the discovery?" Emilie guessed. She didn't know much about the prominent sorcerers and philosophers of Menea, preferring the more dramatic imaginary versions in popular novels. But in her aunt's society journal, she had seen mentions of awards and royal honors for philosophical achievement, inventions, discovering places and things, all of which seemed fairly minor compared to this. She thought finding a way to visit the Hollow World must be the biggest philosophical achievement of the age. "He's going to steal your father's glory?"

"Well, to put it bluntly, yes." Looking out at the serene sea, Miss Marlende grimaced. "Lord Engal and Lord Ivers and my father were all working – separately, you understand – on mapping the aetheric currents that could be traveled in, the spells needed to protect a vehicle, and perfecting an aetheric engine. My father had an advantage. He's a sorcerer himself, unlike Lord Engal and Lord Ivers, who have to hire sorcerers who are experts in aetheric studies to work with. My father finished his engine first, and rushed to place it on an airship. He took a small crew, and entered the current inside the cauldron of Mount Tovera on Aerinterre. I camped on the island with the ground crew, and waited. He was gone for six weeks. Then Kenar arrived, to tell us the engine had failed and he needed help."

"How did Kenar get back through the current by himself?" From what Emilie had observed, this was impossible, and she couldn't imagine climbing up through a volcano, even a dead one.

"There were several hot air balloons stored aboard the airship for emergencies, and my father fitted one out with the protective spell, so they were able to travel the current in it. Another man came with Kenar, my father's apprentice, Jerom Lindel." Miss Marlende added, bleakly, "He died on the trip."

From behind them, Kenar said, "The journey was... rougher than we expected. Jerom said the spell was meant to protect a large vehicle. It didn't work the way he thought it would, and there was nothing he could do to fix it."

"I'm sorry," Emilie said to both of them, meaning it. The man must have been a friend of Miss Marlende's. Kenar sounded as if the trip had affected him severely, and she didn't think he was someone easily overwhelmed.

Miss Marlende sighed. "Originally, the plan was for Jerom to get the materials needed to repair the airship's aetheric engine, and then he would set the spell on the balloon and he and Kenar would return through the volcano's current. But with Jerom dead, there was no one who could manage the spell."

"I hope it doesn't hurt you to speak of him," Kenar said, watching Miss Marlende.

Emilie said, "Did you have an understanding with him? I mean..." Shut up, Emilie, she thought, realizing belatedly she hadn't been acquainted with Miss Marlende nearly long enough to ask that question.

But Miss Marlende just shook her head, her expression regretful. "He was a good friend, but I wouldn't have married him. I don't intend to marry at all. I'm not sure I ever quite convinced him that I was serious about that." She continued, "But his death also left us with no way to send assistance to my father and the others, so we had to go to someone for help. I chose

Lord Engal to approach." She gave Kenar a dry look. "I hope I made the right choice."

He laughed, a soft huffing noise. "It's too late to change your mind now."

"Well, if I'd chosen Lord Ivers, I'm not sure Lord Engal would have sent men to harass us, shoot at us, and attack the ship before we left." She leaned back, her mouth set in an ironic line. "At least I don't think so."

"I don't think so, either," Emilie offered. "Lord Engal isn't subtle. He seems more the shouting-at-you-in-person type."

Miss Marlende gave her a quizzical expression. "An astute observation."

Emilie wasn't sure if she was being teased. She said, a little stiffly, "I'm used to dealing with people who shout."

"Who shouts at you?" Kenar asked.

"Oh, you know, my uncle." She made what she hoped was an offhand gesture, sorry she had brought it up.

"Is that why you ran away?" Miss Marlende asked, frowning a little.

"Mostly, yes." Emilie made the answer abrupt, hoping they wouldn't ask any more. "And my oldest brother Erin ran away to join the merchant navy and he did very well, so I was just following his example. Without the navy." He had been obsessed with going to sea and exploration, and used to make their other two brothers play his crew. Emilie had always been his second in command. Uncle Yeric had told Erin all his life that he meant him to stay at home and go into business with their cousins who lived in another town, and had never paid much attention to Erin's own aspirations. But in this new world, with all these new people, washed by a cool breeze on the deck of a ship sailing an alien sea, she didn't want to talk about her family. She asked Kenar, "Did our world seem very strange to you?"

"Yes." He smiled, the points of his teeth showing. "The cold weather was rather unpleasant."

"I'm afraid the whole thing was very unpleasant," Miss Marlende said, rubbing her forehead. "Lord Engal didn't trust Kenar's word. I'm not sure why. It's rather a large amount of trouble to go to for an elaborate hoax. And you know, Kenar's not human, and it's rather easy to prove his appearance isn't a sorcerous illusion or trick. We had to be very careful to conceal his appearance when we were in Meneport. You'd think that would have substantiated our story all by itself."

"It did." Kenar snorted amusement. "He thinks I'm luring you down here to kill you and take his engine."

Emilie pointed out, "If you had Dr Marlende down here already, then you'd have his engine. Why would you need Lord Engal's too?"

"There's that," Kenar said dryly. "I don't want any engines."

"Logic didn't seem to enter into it." Miss Marlende sounded as if she was more than fed up with Lord Engal. "Every time I thought we had convinced him, he seemed to change his mind again."

Dr Barshion, Emilie thought. He had been suspicious of Kenar, pressing Lord Engal about it even as the expedition prepared to leave. She debated mentioning it, but she didn't want to be seen as making trouble. And probably they already know Dr Barshion doesn't trust Kenar. Yes, of course they did. Barshion had as much as said so when they were all waiting in the lounge together.

Miss Marlende was saying, "Lord Engal kept having Kenar locked in his cabin, if you'll believe it."

"Thank you for letting me out," Kenar told her.

She shrugged. "It was the least I could do."

After a time, Kenar and Miss Marlende went back inside, but Emilie spent the next couple of hours sitting in a chair on the glassed-in promenade, just watching the flooded city go by. She tried to stay awake, not wanting to miss anything, but found herself napping occasionally, drifting off in the mild sunlight and fresh air.

The towers and columns had been growing fewer, with more distance between them, for the last hour or so. Emilie thought it might be because there were smaller structures in this area, only a single story tall, covered completely by the flood. But even standing on a chair and craning her neck, she hadn't been able to see any sign of it below the clear water. She had caught glimpses of mosaics, blue and green and flecks of other colors, set in plazas between the towers.

Then a shrill whistle from the bow startled her. She heard footsteps pounding along the upper deck, and rushed to follow. She ducked inside, went up to the top

deck, and ran around to the bow, to the open
observation area just below the wheelhouse. A few
crewmen were already there, and Emilie saw
immediately what had caused the lookout to call the
alarm.

Some distance ahead, just visible over the top of a
half-sunken colonnade, was a ship's mast. "What is it?"
Emilie said. From what she understood, they were still
a long distance from where Dr Marlende's airship
waited, and this looked like a sailing vessel. "A Cirathi
ship?" Maybe Kenar's people had come this way
looking for help.

One of the crewmen gave her an odd look. "Don't
know, Miss. It looks like a wreck."

Kenar and Miss Marlende arrived a moment later,
with Lord Engal striding up behind them. Miss
Marlende was asking Kenar, "Is it your ship?"

He went to the rail, staring hard toward the mast. The
crewmen moved away from him a little uneasily. As the
Sovereign drew closer, two more masts were visible, but
the ship seemed to be sitting at an odd angle. He said,
"No, it isn't the *Lathi*. I don't recognize..."

The *Sovereign* was moving past the colonnade that
had blocked their view, and now they could see the hull
of the ship. It was a wreck, lodged half atop one side of
the pitched roof of a half-submerged structure. It was a
long hull, longer than the *Sovereign* or even the *Merry
Bell*, but the steam-driven paddlewheel on its listing port
side was smaller, as was the smoke stack in the stern.
Sails still clung in withered shards to the ruined mast,

planking along the deck had rotted, and the metal hull was scraped and discolored by rust. "It's from our world," Miss Marlende said. "But how–"

"It's the *Scarlet Star*, by God," Lord Engal said, lowering his spyglass. "You can still make out the name on the bow." He turned, waving up at the wheelhouse. He strode away, back toward the hatch that led inside.

"What's the *Scarlet Star*?" Miss Marlende asked, before Emilie could.

One of the older crewmen said, "She was a cargo steamer, heading toward Meneport, when she went missing in a freak storm. This was about ten years ago. There was always something thought funny about it. There was no sighting from the Southern Light, no wreckage washed up anywhere ashore." He looked toward the battered wreck again, brow furrowed. "I guess this explains it."

"How is that possible?" Emilie asked. She hadn't heard the story of the *Scarlet Star* before, but it had happened a long time ago. "It wouldn't have had an aetheric engine, would it?"

Everyone must have been wondering the same thing, because all the men were looking to Miss Marlende for the answer. Frowning, she said, "No, it couldn't have. But there is a theory that violent electrical storms do cause aetheric currents to act in very odd ways."

Kenar said slowly, "Very odd, meaning... snatch a ship from the surface world and bring it through the rift in the ocean floor and deposit it here?"

"But it wouldn't have the spell bubble, like we did,"

one of the crewmen protested. "It would be crushed when it was dragged under, wouldn't it?" It was the young man who had been helping Abendle with the aetheric engine. He looked as if he had been working all night, his curly hair flat with sweat and his uniform rumpled.

"It wasn't crushed, and it got here somehow," Emilie pointed out.

"Yes, but Seaman Ricard is right," Miss Marlende said, leaning on the rail and studying the wreck thoughtfully. "There must have been some protection for it. Perhaps the storm caused a pocket of air to form, and that was what was pulled through the rift, with the ship brought along as part of the pocket."

Ricard looked at the wreck again. "So there could have been survivors?"

Kenar sound grim. "For a time, maybe. There's no help out here, no fresh water, no food."

Emilie saw what he meant. This city must have been empty for decades, perhaps even before it flooded. And there was no land in sight. It would be a rather bleak spot, if you were stuck without a ship or other means of transport.

An officer called from the upper deck, and the crewmen ran to obey. Emilie felt the engines change pitch as the ship began to slow. She said, "We're going to stop and search the wreck." She was torn between excitement at seeing a real ship wreck and feeling sorry for the crew. They must be dead, whatever had happened to them, whether they had drowned when the ship had been dragged into the aetheric current or died of hunger and thirst after being deposited here. She wasn't sure which was a better fate; both sounded painful and frightening.

"We're wasting valuable time." Miss Marlende gripped the rail, sounding as if she was struggling to control her temper.

"No," Kenar said. "It might tell us something about what we're to face in these waters." He added, "And we can use all the help we can get."

But the wreck provided no help at all.

The *Sovereign* slowed to a halt a little distance from it, and the launch was dispatched to investigate. Aboard were Kenar, Captain Belden's first officer Oswin, and six armed crewmen. Emilie and Miss Marlende waited on the deck with Lord Engal and Dr Barshion, who was taking a brief respite from working on the aetheric engine and had come out for some air. They watched tensely, but after a short time of climbing over the wreck, the boarding party returned with little news.

"Nothing there, My Lord," Oswin reported to Lord Engal after they climbed back aboard the *Sovereign*. "I found the cover of the log book but water had washed into the bridge and the pages had rotted away. There was no sign of the crew, alive or dead. I think they must have perished before the ship entered the rift."

"There was no sign of anything," Kenar added. "No supplies at all, in the hold or the cabins, no crates or casks, no blankets on the beds, no clothing, no pots in the cooking area. As if the ship was stripped."

"Yes, but it's been there ten years," Oswin said, before Lord Engal could reply. Emilie felt they had been arguing about this during the entire exploration of the wreck. "Everything that wasn't nailed down would have washed away."

"Not everything," Kenar said stubbornly.

"That aside," Lord Engal put in firmly. "If there's nothing more to learn here, we'll continue. At least we can reveal the solution to the mystery of the *Scarlet Star*'s disappearance when we return."

He went back up the stairs toward the wheelhouse, and the crew dispersed back to their duties. Miss Marlende lifted a brow at Dr Barshion and said, "When we return?"

His mouth set in a grim line, he said, "We're working on it."

FOUR

When night fell, the sun didn't sink toward the horizon; the shape of the Dark Wanderer moved across it, causing an eclipse.

Emilie had seen an eclipse of the moon before, but never the sun. While it was impossible to look directly at even the Hollow World's smaller sun without going blind, they could see the eclipse coming by the line of darkness sweeping slowly across the sea toward the ship.

Once the sun was completely obscured, it was as dark as the most cloud-covered moonless night, with only the ship's running lights to guide them across the water. The *Sovereign* dropped its speed by half, chugging cautiously along, with lookouts in the bow to spot obstacles. Kenar said the darkness should last about eight hours by the ship's clock.

Except for the crewmen on watch, and the group still working on the aetheric engine, most people were going to take the opportunity to sleep. Miss Marlende offered

Emilie the extra bed in her cabin, possibly in order to keep an eye on her. At the moment Emilie didn't care; she hadn't done anything but briefly nap for nearly two days, and was tired enough that she was ready to lie down on the deck to sleep.

The cabin was on the second deck above the hull, an interior one with no portholes. It was nicely appointed with two beds, roomy cabinets, a tap and small ceramic hand basin, mirror, and a door leading to a small private water closet. Emilie was expecting to be given instructions to wash and change and attend to her hair, but Miss Marlende just sat down heavily on her bed to unlace her boots, and waved a vague hand toward the clothes cabinet and the basin. "There's water and things over there. Use whatever you need." Then she lay down on the bed fully clothed and was asleep in moments.

Emilie stared, bemused. It underscored the fact that Miss Marlende was an adventuress; not the romantic kind who got into trouble, but the intrepid kind who explored unknown territories and made discoveries and visited all sorts of strange places. She thought of her friend Porcia, who had been training herself for adventures since Emilie could remember, and had already announced her intention of never marrying, and of traveling the world with several doughty female companions. One of the benefits that she and Porcia hadn't considered was that one could do what one liked and worry about comfort more than appearance. It made a nice change from Emilie's aunt, for whom appearance and what the neighbors thought was everything.

It was nice to be treated as an adult who could make her own decision about whether she should wash or not. Her aunt had never considered her capable of it, seeing her as the same tomboy who had always come in covered with dirt and muck from the garden. Well, that's what you assumed, anyway, she thought. Emilie looked at herself in the mirror, the memory of that last argument with her uncle making her cheeks heat with anger. It seemed obvious now that Aunt Helena had thought Emilie a great deal worse than just a tomboy. All because she had asked to go to cousin Karthea's school.

She realized that the saltwater swim in the harbor hadn't done her hair any favors, and that her clothes were itchy in the most uncomfortable places. She sighed. It would be stupid to forego washing just to spite her aunt, who, since Emilie had run away, was sure to be pretty well spited already. She ended up washing in the hand basin and rinsing out her underthings, taming her hair somewhat, and borrowing a thick cotton nightgown out of the cabinet to sleep in. Leaving one light on near the door, she tucked herself in and fell asleep almost as fast as Miss Marlende had.

She was jolted awake what felt like moments later by the ship's whistle. Miss Marlende sat bolt upright, gasping, "What the hell is that?"

"Ship's alarm!" Emilie realized the ship was slowing down even further, the low thrum of the engines changing in pitch. She struggled out of bed, squinting at the clock. They had been asleep about four hours; from what Kenar had said, the end of the eclipse was still some time away. She heard boots pounding out in the corridor and hurried to dress, scrambling into her still-damp underwear, bloomers, and one of Miss Marlende's shirts. Miss Marlende, older and slower to come to full consciousness, managed to struggle out of bed and get her boots back on. She reached the door only a moment ahead of Emilie.

Not bothering with her own boots, Emilie ran barefoot down the carpeted corridor after Miss Marlende. As they reached the hatch, Miss Marlende flung out an arm to stop her. "Careful," she said, low-voiced. "If there's something out there–"

"Right," Emilie said, making a mental note not to plunge headlong out of hatches at night while in strange worlds.

Miss Marlende peered through the glass window of the hatch, then twisted the handle and pushed it open. She stepped out, still cautious, and Emilie stood on tiptoes to see over her shoulder.

The night was lit only by the lamps along the deck, but someone up by the wheelhouse was shining the ship's spotlight down on the water ahead. "What is that?" Miss Marlende muttered.

"It looks like... seaweed?" Emilie followed her, trying to see in the uncertain light. The water was clotted with some sort of plant. The searchlight picked up vines growing thickly over the surface, with large lumps floating among them. It looked distressingly like a Sargasso Sea, which had featured in frightening detail in one of the Lord Rohiro novels.

Miss Marlende moved to the railing. "Emilie, you should go back to the cabin."

"Why? What is it?" Emilie still couldn't see anything in the searchlight beam but thick weeds. On the main deck below, sailors were moving around with lights, but it was too dark to see what they were doing.

"I don't know what it is," Miss Marlende replied with some annoyance. "That's why I think you should go back to the cabin." She gave Emilie a stern look. "Now go."

Fine, Emilie thought, annoyed herself. "I'm going," she said, with dignity. Moving as slowly as possible away from the rail, she heard voices raised in agitation and caught a glimpse of Kenar standing on the deck below with a lamp. He was talking to someone; she thought it might be the first officer Oswin.

"Kenar!" Miss Marlende called softly. "Do we know what it is?"

Kenar and Oswin turned, looking up, and Oswin said, "It looks like–"

Something flipped up out of the water, a long narrow shape, as if one of the vines had suddenly stood straight up. Emilie pointed and gasped an incoherent warning. Old wood-cut pictures of sea monsters flashed through her head; she thought she was looking at a giant tentacle. It swung toward the ship, slamming into the rail a bare three steps away from Emilie and Miss Marlende. Then something leapt off it, landing on the deck.

Miss Marlende yelled in alarm and Emilie jerked backward. The thing had two arms, two legs, and a slender body – for an instant Emilie thought it was a person, albeit a naked person with green skin. Then she got a better look at its head. It was eyeless, noseless, earless, its face a blank except for a wide slit for the mouth.

Miss Marlende lifted her hands, palm out, saying quickly, "We mean you no harm. If we came near your... your territory, it was an accident, we're only passing by–"

It hissed, opening its mouth to show a shockingly large rictus of fanged teeth. Then it lunged forward and grabbed for Miss Marlende.

Miss Marlende swung at it, hit it in the face with her fist, but it caught her arm and dragged her toward the railing. Emilie shrieked for help at the top of her lungs, then grabbed for Miss Marlende and wrapped her arms around the other woman's waist.

It dragged them inexorably to the rail, far stronger than a human of that size would be. But as they hit the rail Miss Marlende dropped to the deck, throwing the creature off-balance, then used the moment of distraction to wrap her legs around the lower strut of the rail.

Yes! Emilie thought, letting go of Miss Marlende with one arm and wrapping it around the post below the strut. The creature pried at them, hissing, and the metal ground painfully into Emilie's arm. She wrapped a leg around the post and held on with grim determination.

Then a crewman ran up the deck, yelling. He struck at the creature but it let go of Miss Marlende long enough to backhand him. The blow was hard enough to send him flying back across the deck and slam him into the wall. Miss Marlende fell away from the rail, and Emilie sat down hard. The creature reached down and slapped at Emilie, sending her rolling away.

Emilie landed hard on the deck, reeling from the blow, and looked up in time to see the creature drag a fighting Miss Marlende to her feet. Emilie looked desperately around, saw something lying near the fallen crewman – it was a fire ax. She shoved to her feet, snatched it up, and darted forward.

She swung it at the creature and the blade bounced off its head, painfully jolting Emilie's arm. Apparently unhurt, it dropped Miss Marlende and turned to Emilie. She lifted the ax again, for all the good it had done her, but she wasn't going to let it hit her again without a fight.

Then she saw Kenar behind it, climbing up over the railing from the deck blow. Emilie waved her ax, yelling, "Yah! Yah! Yah!" trying to keep the creature's attention on her. It jerked back uncertainly. Then Kenar swung over the railing, grabbed the creature by the throat, and tossed it off the deck.

Emilie lunged to the rail, looking down in time to see creature bounce off the lower deck and fall back into the weed-choked water. But more slim green forms climbed the hull to the lower deck, tendrils of vine waving angrily in the mass of weed. Gunshots rang out as crewmen along the middle deck fired at the creatures. The ship's stack belched as the boilers built up steam for an escape.

Miss Marlende stumbled to her feet, saying hoarsely, "What was that thing? A plant?"

"Yes, it looked like part of the weeds." Kenar turned, reaching out to steady her.

Emilie couldn't tell if the gunfire was driving the creatures off or just startling them. "If they're plants, it can't do much good to shoot them," she said. It might be just as useless as shooting a tree. "Oh, there's Dr Barshion!"

Dr Barshion had stepped out onto the deck just below. He was coatless, his normally sleek hair mussed. He held a small book in one hand, his other hand clenched in a fist. Emilie thought he was reading aloud, but she couldn't catch the words. On the lower deck, a plant-creature swung over the rail, grabbed a crewman, and tried to drag him over the side. But two other men drove it off with blows from their rifle butts. Emilie heard Lord Engal shouting orders. Kenar stepped up onto the rail, meaning to leap back down into the fray, but Miss Marlende caught his arm. "Wait!"

Below them, Dr Barshion raised his voice, crying out something Emilie couldn't understand; then he made a throwing gesture with his free hand. Sparks of red light glittered along the hull; the plant-creatures climbing the rails keened in alarm and fell back away from the ship. A moment later the stacks belched again and the ship angled away from the weeds, and a gap of dark water opened between it and the dark mass.

"He manipulated the remnants of the aether bubble to repel physical objects," Miss Marlende murmured. "Finally. I was beginning to wonder how much good he was as a sorcerer." She swayed a little and Kenar asked, "Are you all right?"

She waved him away, turning back to the deck. "I'm fine. But this man was injured…"

The crewman who had tried to help them was stirring and trying to stand. Kenar went to haul the man to his feet, and in the lamplight Emilie saw it was Ricard, the young assistant engineer.

The young man gasped, "That was… What was…?"

"No one knows," Kenar told him. "But some of that weed was caught on the hull; we can have a closer look at it."

Miss Marlende told him, "Yes, but let's get Ricard inside first so I can check his head." Tugging her jacket back into place and pushing her disordered hair out of her eyes, she turned to Emilie and said formally, "Thank you, Emilie, your assistance was effective and timely."

"You're welcome," Emilie said automatically. She realized she had clasped the ax to her chest. She decided to keep holding it for a while; it was reassuring.

Her heart was still thumping. This had been very different from hitting the robber with the fire bucket. The worst she had thought would happen then was that the man would hit her back, knock her down. She had realized later that that might have been naive; those men were deadly serious and he might have shot her. But even that wasn't as bad as that creature, dragging her and Miss Marlende off the ship to be... Drowned? Eaten? It was possibly better not to know for certain, but her imagination was doing a good job of filling in the details.

They went back inside, and once Ricard stepped into the brighter light of the corridor, they saw he had a bloody gash on his temple. "I thought you were helping Abendle and Dr Barshion with the aetheric engine?" Miss Marlende said, helping Kenar guide Ricard down the first set of stairs.

"It was my turn to take a break, Miss," he explained, wincing. "I was walking around the ship for a bit before I turned in."

"Lucky for us," Emilie put in, following behind them. "You distracted it." And brought me the ax, she thought.

He glanced back, giving her a wan smile. "I think you did a better job of distracting it than me."

Emilie didn't know what to say. She wasn't used to compliments about actual accomplishments, just stupid things, like needlework and decorating hats.

They reached the main lounge, and Miss Marlende caught a steward's assistant and sent him running off to get the ship's medical kit. Kenar left them then to head back out to the main deck, and after a moment of hesitation, Emilie followed him. She had decided that knowing what was out there was better than just imagining terrible things.

Out on the deck, Emilie was glad to see the men with rifles were still keeping watch. The searchlight, sweeping back and forth across the water, showed they were some distance from the vine mat already and moving steadily away. But a small section of it had caught on the ship's hull, and the crew had dropped the launch's platform to get a closer look at it. Lord Engal was down there with a few crewmen carrying lights. Kenar started to climb down, and Emilie realized she would have to relinquish her ax to follow him. Curiosity won out, and Emilie set the ax down on a handy fire equipment box and followed Kenar down the ladder to the launch platform.

The first thing that struck her was the smell; it was more like rotting meat than any kind of plant. The men were poking cautiously at the mass of weeds with boathooks. One of them drew a lump in close to the platform, and another hacked it free of the weeds. "It's a broken cask," he reported. Looking up at Lord Engal, he added, "Could even be from the *Scarlet Star*, My Lord."

"They seemed to try to take anything they could grab," someone said, and Emilie recognized Oswin's voice. "They got two of our life preservers and a coil of rope."

"It explains why the wreck was stripped of everything movable," Kenar added, stepping around Oswin for a closer look.

"At least they didn't get any of us," Lord Engal said. He glanced at Kenar. "Is Miss Marlende all right?"

"Yes. She's tending to the man who tried to help her." Kenar crouched down to get a better view of the weeds. Emilie felt she could see well enough where she was, and

Emilie & the Hollow World

stayed near the ladder.

"Perhaps she'll be more cautious next time," Lord Engal said.

Emilie snorted quietly to herself. Typical and unfair, she thought. With some asperity, Kenar said, "She was cautious. She was two decks above the water. Sometimes caution doesn't help."

Lord Engal didn't reply to that.

"Look at this," another crewman said, holding up a clay sculpture in the shape of bird.

Kenar stood up to examine it. "That's a net weight," he said. "The Lothlin hang them off the rails of their boats."

Lord Engal turned to him. "These plant-creatures are called Lothlin?"

"No, no. The Lothlin are fisherfolk, peaceful. Nothing like those things." Kenar sounded disturbed. "If one of their boats was driven this far from their home territory, trapped in the mat–"

The first crewman said, grimly, "It looks like they didn't make it out."

Emilie stepped forward to look. Prodding at the mass of vines had released dozens of small objects that had been wound up in it. They bobbed free in the water: sticks, odd-shaped knobs, round things like smooth rocks. She tried to see them as wood, the debris of a wrecked ship, but the colors were bleached white, dull yellow, rotted brown... Then a round object floated closer, turned as the crewman poked it with the pole. It had a face, or what was left of one, with empty eye sockets, a hole for the nose, teeth, and the lower jaw broken away.

Emilie pressed back against the ladder, cold shock washing over her. They were bones, all bones, wound up in the vines. Long bones, knobs of bone, fragments, skulls. She swallowed hard as a whole ribcage bobbed up out of the weeds. The sausage from this morning tried to exit her stomach and she took a deep breath, willing it back into place. That's a lot of dead people, she thought. Pieces of dead people. Emilie had seen the dead laid out decorously in coffins, but never anything like this.

Lord Engal stepped back, his grimace of distaste visible in the lamplight. "I think we've seen everything we need to see. Cut this mess free of the ship and draw up the platform."

Emilie realized she was in the way and turned to climb the ladder back up to the deck. She had to grip the ladder extra hard because her hands suddenly felt numb and chilled, as though it was freezing out here rather than only pleasantly cool. Eaten, we definitely would have been eaten, she thought. On reflection, it seemed obvious. Plant-creatures with sharp teeth didn't try to pull people off ships in the middle of the night for a good reason.

She stood near the rail to watch the lights bob as the men hacked and prodded away at the mass. Bits of it broke off and swirled away, caught in the ship's bow wave, then the whole thing finally gave way. Kenar came to stand beside her as the launch platform was hauled up and Lord Engal gave muttered orders to Oswin and the other crewmen.

Dr Barshion came out on the deck a little distance from them, and she heard Lord Engal congratulate him on driving off the creatures. But Barshion said, "Unfortunately, it's not something I can repeat. The aether in the remnants of the protective bubble is completely depleted now. I can't use it to drive off an attack unless I recreate the spell, and I won't be able to do that until we get the motile working again. The two are meant to work together."

That's not good, Emilie thought, hugging herself. It seemed a long time until the night-eclipse would be over; the ship was like a bubble of light traveling through impenetrable darkness. Emilie said, "Do you think we'll run into anything else tonight?" She realized it was a stupid question as soon as the words were out. Kenar had told them over and over again, he had no more idea of what was in these waters than they did.

But he just put a hand on her shoulder and gave her a one-armed hug, saying absently, "I hope not."

Emilie would have thought there was no way she would be able to go back to sleep after everything that had happened. But the shock of seeing the bones had rather crushed the excitement right out of her, and she found herself so heavy with exhaustion that she could barely drag herself back to Miss Marlende's cabin. Without bothering to undress, she lay down on the bed. Her restive stomach found this position much more amenable, and she quickly slid into sleep.

She woke briefly when Miss Marlende came in, drifted off again, then roused herself to see what the clicking noise was. It was Miss Marlende, sitting on her bed, loading a revolver. Miss Marlende saw her watching, and said, "Obviously I should have taken this precaution earlier."

It was a little odd to see a woman with a gun, especially a pistol. But after what had happened, it seemed an excellent idea. Emilie asked, "May I have a pistol too?"

Miss Marlende frowned. "Have you ever used a pistol before?"

"No."

"Then you may not have one."

"Hmm." Emilie subsided, sinking back down onto the pillow to go back to sleep. She recalled accidentally stabbing herself with a penknife while trying to cut reeds for a fishing rod one summer, and decided Miss Marlende was probably right.

Emilie slept through the end of the night eclipse and three hours into daylight. She woke, blearily stared at the clock, and struggled out of bed. After a quick wash, she tied her hair back, laced her boots, and hurried out to see what was happening.

She stepped onto the deck into dim sunlight and a humid breeze. Dark gray clouds filled the sky, heavily bunched in the direction the ship was heading. It completely obscured the cloudy column of the

Aerinterre aether current. They had left the remnants of the flooded city entirely behind, but the sea wasn't empty. The ship was steaming toward a series of small islands. Odd islands, Emilie thought, shading her eyes to see. They all stood high above the water, at least twenty or thirty feet, with trees and clumps of vegetation on top and sharp cliffs dropping down to the waves.

By going to the bow and looking over the rail, she found Miss Marlende and Kenar on the main deck. Miss Marlende was using a spyglass to study the islands. Emilie hurried down the nearest set of stairs to join them. "What's that?" she asked. "Are we nearly there?"

"Possibly," Kenar admitted. "These islands are similar to the ones near where the airship went down. I just hope we can navigate through them."

Miss Marlende lowered the spyglass. "The channels between them seem quite narrow in spots. We're going to have to go very slowly." She tapped her fingers on the rail in frustration.

"And hope nothing tries to grab us," Emilie added, thinking of the Sargasso creatures last night.

"There's that," Miss Marlende added wryly.

There seemed to be nothing more to do at the moment than watch the islands draw closer, and Emilie's stomach was growling. She went back inside, and found her way back down to the crew's galley. Mrs. Verian wasn't there, but her young assistant was scrubbing the tables, and Emilie managed to get him to stop long enough to find her a sausage sandwich, an apple, and a mug of very sweet tea. She was so hungry she ate the sandwich standing up at the serving counter, then put the apple in her pocket and carried the mug of tea out, meaning to head back up to the main deck.

But just down the corridor, at the base of the stairwell, she heard Dr Barshion's voice and stopped to listen. "... I'm sorry, Abendle, I just don't believe that's the right method. We should be adjusting the axis slowly, not trying to reorient it completely."

Abendle. That was the older engineer who was working on the aetheric engine with Dr Barshion and Ricard. Dr Barshion sounds exhausted, Emilie thought. Sounding even worse, Abendle replied, "Yes, Doctor, you know more about it than I do, but I still think these figures don't show what they're supposed to. Maybe if Miss Marlende looked at them–"

"No, Abendle, she's not familiar with her father's work in that detail. I wish she was." Dr Barshion laughed a little wryly. "No, you and I will have to try to puzzle it out."

Steps sounded on the metal stairs above and Emilie hurried away down the corridor, looking for the next stairwell. She made it before the two men reached the corridor, and escaped unseen up to the next deck. She wasn't sure why she had fled, except that Dr Barshion already thought she was an eavesdropper and she didn't want to confirm that reputation by being caught at it again.

∿

Emilie spent the morning out on the promenade deck, with Kenar and Miss Marlende. But Miss Marlende was too impatient to stay in one spot for long, and kept getting up to walk around the ship.

The scenery they were passing was endlessly fascinating. The islands were growing larger and closer together, so sometimes it was difficult to find a course through them. The ship kept having to stop and send out the launch to take soundings, which made Miss Marlende even more frustrated.

The trees were like the palm trees Emilie had seen drawings of, the ones that grew on the coast far to the south. But the fronds were much bigger, stretching out for ten or fifteen feet and then drooping at the ends. There were other trees like none she had ever seen before, squat with thick conical trunks, topped by sprays of feathery fern-like leaves. Beautifully colored birds – blue, yellow, green – flew away from the ship's passage, too quickly for Emilie to get a good look at them.

After the third time Miss Marlende excused herself to go up to the wheelhouse, Emilie said to Kenar, "You're not nervous."

"I'm less nervous." He smiled at her, a quick flash of pointed teeth. "My people are in an area that's foreign to them, but the ship was in good repair when I left, and they had plenty of supplies. And I know they can take care of themselves, and that they will watch over Dr Marlende and his crew. Vale knows that too, but she's waited and worried a long time."

Emilie noted that he had used Miss Marlende's first name, then realized it probably didn't mean the same thing to him. Kenar seemed to have only one name, himself. Though after their shared trouble, he and Miss Marlende did seem to be good friends. And she thought he had been through a lot too, what with the dangerous trip to a strange world, and Lord Engal's suspicion and distrust. "Why did you go with Jerom to get help?" she asked. She had asked him that before, but he hadn't given her a very good answer. "I mean, it was very difficult."

He looked out at the channel again. "Dr Marlende brought his ship and his people into danger to help us. We had anchored near a series of small islands and sandbars, and sent a small boat ashore to replenish our water supply. Rani, my partner, was aboard it."

Just the way he said the name "Rani" caught Emilie's attention. She wondered if "partner" was the correct word or if Kenar was perhaps translating it wrong.

Kenar continued, "The island we chose turned out to be a trap. A giant creature, bigger than this ship, lived on the sea floor beneath it, feeding on the fish and birds that came within range. When Rani, Beinar, and Sanith beached their boat on the sandbar, the creature raised folds of skin out of the water, swallowing the sandbar entirely, trapping them. We couldn't reach them, and we knew if we didn't, they would be eaten alive. But Dr Marlende had seen our ship and been heading toward us already, meaning to try to speak to us. He saw what had happened and took his airship down low over the island, and fired weapons at the creature. When that didn't work, some of his men let themselves down with ropes and hacked at it with axes and burned it with fire. Finally it opened, and he dropped a ladder, and Rani and the others were able to escape with only minor injuries." He let out his breath, as if putting aside the frightening memory, and smiled down at Emilie. "We sailed together for a while, learning about each other, helping each other as we explored this territory. When his engine became damaged later, we felt it was our chance to repay the favor he had done us. And we're explorers. I couldn't let the opportunity to travel to the legendary outer world pass by." He gave her a thoughtful look. "You didn't explain why you left your home."

"Didn't I? Oh." Emilie realized uneasily that she had been asking him a lot of questions, and that he had perhaps noticed that she had been avoiding his inquiries. "I left home because when my mother was only two years older than me, she left home." Kenar frowned, not understanding. Emilie added, "She became an actress. She could have come to a bad end." Kenar still didn't appear to understand. "It was very shocking," she said. "Some people think actresses are, you know..." He probably didn't know, and she found herself extremely reluctant to tell him that some people thought actresses were whores. She was afraid he would ask her what a whore was. Kenar, after all, had learned Menaen from Dr Marlende, and there were probably a lot of words that just hadn't ever come up in conversation. "That they're almost like criminals."

"I'll take your word for it," he assured her gravely. "I still don't see what this has to do with you."

"Because I'm her daughter, my uncle and aunt always felt that I'd do the same. Only perhaps I wouldn't be lucky, and meet a man like my father, who would marry me anyway." Emilie tried to sound matter-of-fact, though it wasn't easy, and she could hear the anger that made her throat tight creep into her voice. She had been told over and over again, for what seemed like years on end, that she was destined to come to a bad end, even before she had had any idea what a bad end was. But deep down, she hadn't really thought that they believed it. Especially when she knew she wasn't really the sort of person inclined to bad ends.

Emilie liked to read, liked to take off her shoes and stockings and wade in the creek, to explore the fields and copses around the village farms. She had only been interested in the local boys while they were all young enough to play at being pirates and highway robbers together; as she had gotten older, it was only the adventurous heroes in books who had caught her attention. She was certain she was the least likely girl in the village to come to a bad end.

But you still could have, she thought. You could have gotten yourself murdered in an alley, crossing through Meneport, no matter how careful you thought you were being. Uncle Yeric's prophecy might have become a self-fulfilling one on Emilie's part.

"Do you want to become an actress?" Kenar said, still puzzled by the whole situation.

"No. It sounds rather difficult, and I can't sing well, and I'm not a good dancer." She tightened her hands on the railing. She had never had any specific ambition, except that she had wanted to travel, wanted to visit places that were just names in books in the lending library or on the maps in the village school's atlas. But that took money, and she had none of her own; she had known she needed a more realistic goal, if she didn't want to be stuck as her aunt's companion for the next twenty years. "I didn't really know what I wanted to do. But my friend Porcia Herinbogel was going off to school, to Shipands Academy."

It was a real school, that taught things like mathematics, history, languages, agriculture, and even mechanics, and it was admitting young ladies for the first time. Porcia had been mad to go; she hadn't inherited her father's magical talent, but she was terribly clever, and wanted to take the courses necessary to be considered for a medical academy in Meneport that allowed women students. Emilie was certain that her uncle would not agree to pay for anything like that, but it had given her an idea.

"I asked my aunt and uncle if I could go to my cousin Karthea's school, in Silk Harbor. She's my father's sister's daughter, and that side of the family isn't as... as my mother's side. I thought I could help with the work, look after the younger girls, maybe, while she took the classes. It's a lot of work, running a school, Karthea talks about it in her letters. I know she needs help." She and Porcia had talked it all over, and her father had offered to bring Emilie along when he took Porcia to Shipands. They would be going through Silk Harbor anyway and could drop Emilie off on their way. It had seemed a modest goal and a perfectly respectable occupation. It had not seemed like much to ask.

Kenar still looked as if he wasn't certain he understood. "You ran away because your uncle and aunt forbade you to go?"

"Yes, partly. It was the way they did it." Porcia, Mr. Herinbogel, and two of her aunt's friends, Mrs. Rymple and Mrs. Fennan, had been invited for tea, and Emilie had chosen that moment to broach the subject. But Uncle Yeric had refused to listen and forbade her to even mention it again. Emilie had lost her temper and shouted. The argument had escalated to the point where her aunt had burst into angry tears and her uncle had accused her of using the school as a ruse to get out from under their watchful eye, where she could become a whore like her mother.

The memory of being shocked senseless with humiliation, sitting on the couch in the familiar parlor while the embarrassed visitors hastily took their leave, still made her cheeks burn. It had gotten worse once they were alone. That was when her uncle had added that he thought she meant to use the trip as a ruse to fix her interest with Mr. Herinbogel, a widower old enough to be Emilie's father.

Thinking about it still filled her with fury, made her pulse pound. She had known then that whatever she did, she would never see her aunt and uncle again, not if she had to run to the ends of the earth. And she really didn't want to tell any of this to Kenar. It was hard enough thinking about it, but she had to finish the story. "They thought I was lying about helping with the school. They thought I wanted to use it as an excuse to get away from home. They said if I persisted, they would send me away to a place to be locked up."

She wasn't certain if Uncle Yeric had meant an asylum, or a prison. She had known that if he told the magistrates that she was a disobedient girl who wanted to run off and become a whore, they would believe him and not her.

Kenar shook his head slowly. Emilie thought he was rather appalled, even at this mild version of the story. "Your mother is not here to... shield you from the rest of her family?"

"No. She and my father died, when I was very young. My oldest brother hasn't come home since he ran away to join the merchant navy, and my other two brothers like my uncle and agree to whatever he says." They had agreed about her, too. She supposed she should have expected it, but it had been just one more shameful blow on top of all the others. She had been close to them once, but when they had been sent off to boarding school, and no longer saw her every day, it was as if the real her had been replaced in their minds by her uncle's version of her. And when their older brother had run away, it had perhaps been worse for them than Emilie. He had confided in Emilie more, so she had been more prepared when he left, though it had still hurt her. To them it had been a bigger shock, and maybe they had turned to her uncle for reassurance, and it made them more susceptible to being swayed by his opinions. It had occurred to her later that she might have been more helpful to them at the time, but she had been so upset and so resentful herself that she hadn't been thinking about anyone else's feelings.

Kenar said, "I see. You could not join your older brother?"

"No. He's on a ship, now." She added, in case Kenar didn't realize, "They don't let women join the navy in Menea."

"That seems an odd thing to forbid. You would make a good sailor."

"Thank you." Emilie felt a huge relief at leaving the subject. She took a deep breath, and felt the breeze cool her flushed face. "If I was a Cirathi, I could be a sailor?"

"Of course. My partner, Rani, is captain of our ship."

Emilie lifted her brows, intrigued. "Really?" She wanted to ask more, but Oswin came to tell Kenar that Lord Engal wanted to speak to him, and he went up to the wheelhouse. She stood on the deck for a long time after that, though, thinking about being the captain of a ship, and mentally rewriting the Lord Rohiro novels with someone like Miss Marlende as the main character.

It was late in the day when the ship's alarm sounded and someone shouted, "There it is!"

Emilie ran out to the rail, where Miss Marlende, Kenar, Lord Engal, and some of the crew were gathered.

They were approaching a sizable island, ringed by cliffs like the others. At the base, anchored next to a narrow stretch of beach, was a large wooden sailing ship. It had three masts, with faded purple sails furled around the lower spars. Cabins with round windows were built all along the main deck, and they were painted various bright colors, now faded by sun and weather. Flowering vines were painted below the railings on the hull. "It's such a lovely ship," Emilie said, before she realized what was wrong, why everyone was so silent.

The sailing ship's deck was empty. There was no sign of life aboard, no one coming out to investigate the chugging sound that signaled the *Sovereign*'s approach. Emilie looked at Kenar, stricken.

His expression was closed, opaque. But she felt it was hiding a good deal of fear.

Miss Marlende said, "Perhaps they had to retreat into the interior of the island for some reason." Emilie looked at the cliffs above the beach, but there was no sign of life or movement there, either.

Miss Marlende lifted the spyglass, studying the trees. "Perhaps they're at the airship, with–"

"We should be able to see your father's airship from here," Kenar interrupted, an edge to his voice. "It's gone."

She turned to stare at him, startled. "Are you certain?"

At her expression, he shook his head, avoiding her eyes. "Maybe they had to move it."

Lord Engal looked from one to the other, frowning. Emilie thought he might say something to make it worse, but instead he just said briskly, "Now then, you can't expect them all to be standing out here waiting for us. They've probably been quite busy in our absence." He turned to Oswin. "Make ready to lower the launch. We'll soon get to the bottom of this."

Kenar and Miss Marlende boarded the launch with Lord Engal, Oswin, and six armed crewmen. Emilie slid into a seat next to Miss Marlende, and no one objected.

Emilie had managed to add herself to the landing party simply by staying close to Miss Marlende and Kenar, who were too distracted to notice her. If they had noticed her, each probably assumed the other had asked her to come along. She was sure Lord Engal, Oswin, and the other sailors noticed her, but they must have assumed that Miss Marlende had given her permission. Emilie thought Lord Engal must be making sure to be more polite to Miss Marlende, after their earlier disagreements, and the fact that...

That they might find her father, his crew, and all of Kenar's crew dead on the island somewhere.

The launch puttered across to the island, its engine sounding very loud in the silence of calm wind and water. The strip of beach was narrow, the rocky bluff above it draped with flowering vines. Two crewmen climbed out to help push the boat up onto the beach, and they all clambered out, splashing in the shallow water. Leaving a crewman to watch the boat, they approached the Cirathi ship cautiously.

Kenar went first, the others following, Emilie bringing

up the rear. The soft sand crumbled underfoot, the scent of green plants and sweet flowers was heavy in the air. It would have been a lovely place, except for the silent ship. Kenar headed for the bow, and the crewmen spread out to search along the bluff. The wooden hull was covered with tar, or whatever the Hollow World equivalent was, and from this angle only the decorative painting made it different from a Menaen ship.

They circled around to the port side, the side facing the island that they hadn't been able to see from the *Sovereign*. A rope ladder hung over the rail there, dangling down to the sand. "Was that here before?" Miss Marlende asked tensely.

"Yes." Kenar started to climb.

"No sign of tracks on this sand, but wind or water may have worn them away," Lord Engal said, mostly to himself.

One of the crewmen called out, "There's a way up the bluff, here, My Lord. Steps cut into the dirt."

"We did that, to get up to the airship," Kenar said, already vanishing over the rail.

Lord Engal turned to follow him, telling the crewmen, "Two of you climb up there, look for signs of the airship. Stay within shouting distance."

Oswin picked out two more men to remain on guard on the beach, then followed Lord Engal up the ladder with the others. Emilie followed them. She looked back to see Miss Marlende hesitating, torn between the ship and joining the search for the airship atop the bluff. Then she turned to follow them up the ladder.

Emilie climbed awkwardly over the solid rail onto the deck. She had been afraid to see the place strewn with bodies, but there was no sign of that. Yet, she thought, a little sick.

Kenar did a quick circuit of the deck, which to Emilie's untutored eye seemed undisturbed. There was nothing broken, no loose lines in the rigging, the casks and barrels of supplies – as gaily painted with vines and flowers as the rest of the ship – were still lashed into place. Kenar opened the door into the long series of cabins along the deck, moving quickly through.

Emilie followed behind Lord Engal and Oswin. The windows were all shuttered, but the slats were tilted to allow in light and air but deflect rain. They moved quickly along, and she got only fast glimpses of bunks and seats built into the walls with brightly-colored cushions, blue and gold pottery jars, a cabinet stacked with scrolls of paper. One scroll had been left unrolled on a stool, and Emilie stopped to look at it. It wasn't a map, as she had thought at first – she remembered the map Kenar had carried had been drawn on a square of fabric – but a long list of notes hand-written in an oddly square script. She wondered if it was a chronicle of the voyage. Maybe someone left a log entry, a note about where they went, what happened to the airship, she thought. And why they didn't take their ship, even though it doesn't look like there's anything wrong with it. She suspected she was being optimistic again.

She hurried to catch up with the others, who were just going down the open hatch into the hold. It was warm down there, and crowded with supplies, mostly casks and more of the pottery containers, so Emilie stayed on deck with Miss Marlende. There was another separate cabin back here, and Emilie stepped inside to see it was a small galley. There was no place to eat inside, but there was a small squat metal stove with a flat cook top, and pots and jars were stored on shelves against the walls, with rope webbing to hold them in place against the ship's motion. The room smelled of herbs and wilted greens. There was a pot beside the stove, still half-full of stale water, a wooden spoon with a carved flower handle standing in it. Emilie took the spoon out, so it wouldn't be ruined by soaking too long in the water, and hung it on an empty wall hook.

Miss Marlende was shielding her eyes, looking toward the bluff. From here there was a better view of the top, and Emilie could see the two crewmen moving through tall grass, in a big clearing half-surrounded by the tall palm trees. They were scuffing at the ground with their boots, poking through the ferny bushes. It didn't look as if they were finding anything. Not anything terrible, anyway. Emilie said, "Maybe they fixed the airship's aetheric engine." It was a stupid thing to say, but she was finding it hard to just stand here silently, as if they were at a funeral. She could hear wood creak as the men below searched through the holds, but she bet they weren't finding anything, either.

Miss Marlende bit her lip. "The Cirathi would leave someone behind to guard their ship. Unless something attacked them and they all had to escape."

The ladder creaked as Lord Engal climbed back up, followed by Kenar, Oswin, and the other crewmen. Kenar moved away immediately to the railing, knotting his fists on it and looking across at the island. Lord Engal cleared his throat. He was sweating in the damp air, and had pulled his shirt collar open. He said, "There's no sign of violence, but there's no sign they took any of the supplies they would need to leave the ship for any length of time." He frowned at the island, the men still searching the top of the bluff. "Hmm. A closer look at the airship's landing site may tell us more." He focused on Miss Marlende and said, "We'll find them. Obviously they had a compelling reason to leave this spot, even if it isn't obvious to us."

Miss Marlende nodded tightly. "We took too long to get here."

Lord Engal's brows lowered, but he kept a hold on his temper. He said, "I apologize for the delay, but I assure you–"

"No, not you." Her voice was thick with the effort to control her emotion. "I should have acted more quickly. As soon as Kenar arrived with the news of what had happened, I should have... had plans already in place, I should have..." She shook her head, and turned away.

Emilie unobtrusively pressed her sleeve to her eyes. It was obviously taking a great deal for Miss Marlende not to give way, and she didn't want to add to the burden by succumbing to sympathetic and completely useless tears herself. She wasn't sure if Miss Marlende wanted to be comforted, or how to go about it, or if the attempt would just make things worse. Kenar, still standing at the rail and lost in his own grim thoughts, clearly wanted to be left alone.

Lord Engal seemed to be facing a similar dilemma. He hesitated, then finally said gruffly, "Not much opportunity to plan for this sort of eventuality, when one had no idea what Dr Marlende was going to discover, if anything. Seems to me we've all been simply doing our best with what little we know." He cleared his throat. "Now let's have a better look at this landing site and see what it tells us."

Miss Marlende pressed a hand to her temple for a moment, then said, in a steadier voice, "Yes, of course."

They went up the dirt-cut steps to the top of the bluff. It was warmer up there than down by the water, and Emilie was glad she was wearing one of Miss Marlende's lighter cotton shirts. The large grassy clearing looked bare of clues at first, but as soon as Kenar and the others began to point things out, Emilie could see the signs that a great many people had been here.

There were footmarks in the dirt, tufts of grass that had been ripped up, divots in the ground and spots of flattened vegetation where large heavy things had rested. Back under the shade of the trees, they found a rock hearth where someone had made a campfire, places where food garbage had been buried, a dropped handkerchief stained with engine oil, a wrench that had been accidentally kicked into a bush. Oswin pointed out that there was only a little rust on it, which it couldn't have been there for more than a few days.

They could see the marks on the nearby palm trees where heavy ropes had been tied, that must have been the anchor lines for the airship. And there was a big square spot in the dirt where Kenar said the main cabin had rested, when Dr Marlende had lowered the craft all the way down to try to repair the aetheric engine. "It looks as if they moved it, at least twice," Oswin said, poking at a tuft with the toe of his boot. He looked at Kenar inquiringly.

Kenar spread a hand, shaking his head. "They may have. When Jerom and I left, Dr Marlende still hadn't given up on the idea that he could fix the engine himself."

"It was only the aetheric engine that was damaged, correct?" Oswin said. "Not the smaller oil-fueled engine that would allow the airship to maneuver."

Kenar nodded, glancing at Miss Marlende. "But Dr Marlende didn't want to move the airship too far without the aetheric engine. He was afraid he would run out of fuel for the other one. That's why we took the balloon to the aetheric air current on the *Lathi*."

"And obviously the ship returned here safely," Lord Engal muttered, walking past them. "We need to search the rest of the island."

But they found nothing, just trees, flowers, and bird nests.

FIVE

When they finally finished the search of the island, it was time for dinner, though there were several hours of daylight left before the next eclipse. Emilie ate with the others in the passenger lounge this time, since she knew they would be discussing what to do next and she didn't want to miss anything.

She sat in the back, eating a potted chicken sandwich, trying to stay unobtrusive. Captain Belden was here, as well as Dr Barshion, Ricard, and Abendle, the engineer. The last three men looked terribly weary; they must have been working almost non-stop on the aetheric engine. Ricard's head was still bandaged from his encounter with the Sargasso creature.

"They could have taken the airship to the aetheric current, to test their repairs," Lord Engal said, thinking aloud. "But why abandon the Cirathi ship?" He turned to Kenar, eyeing him uncertainly. "Your crew weren't eager to travel to our world, were they?"

Kenar rubbed his eyes. With the scales and the fur, it

was hard to see how affected he was, but Emilie thought his shoulders were tense and his usual calm self-possession was gone. Sounding a little exasperated, he said, "Not at all. Until we met Dr Marlende and his crew, we thought your world a legend. We have our own concerns here. They could spare me for a brief visit, to help pay our debt to Marlende, but there is just no reason the others would make the trip."

Captain Belden said, "Dr Marlende could have left with the airship, and something attacked the ship's crew before they could leave the island."

Emilie saw Kenar's jaw tighten at the thought. Miss Marlende sat forward impatiently. "This kind of speculation is useless. Our assumption must be that someone or something attacked the island, and both crews were forced to flee in the airship."

Kenar looked up, his expression thoughtful, and Emilie found herself nodding. If something like the Sargasso creatures, or worse, had attacked, the airship would be the quickest way to escape. "The airship might have run out of fuel then, and be stuck on another island," she said.

Captain Belden frowned at her, as if he didn't think she should be giving her opinion, but Miss Marlende said, "Yes, that could very well be it. The question is, how do we find them?"

"There hasn't been a peep out of the wireless, not that it's supposed to be much use down here," Oswin said, sounding glum. "We can't track them through the air or the water. It's not as if they'll have left tracks."

Abendle cleared his throat. "They might have."

Intrigued, Lord Engal twisted around to stare at him. "Yes? Speak up, man."

Abendle stepped forward, seeming uneasy with all the sudden attention, but he said, "Aetheric engines do leave tracks, My Lord, when they aren't traveling through aetheric currents."

"But the airship's aetheric engine was damaged." Miss Marlende looked uncertainly from Abendle to Dr Barshion. "They shut it down to use the airship's conventional engine."

"If it's even them still running the airship," Oswin said. "If something didn't attack both crews to steal it." Captain Belden nudged his shoulder in silent remonstrance.

Emilie didn't think Oswin was speaking out of turn. There was surely no one on the ship who hadn't considered the possibility that the Cirathi crew, and Dr Marlende and all his men, might be dead or captured by something. It was an awful possibility, but it was still a likely one.

"Aetheric engines can't ever really be shut down, once they're started up," Abendle explained. "The aether that powers them is still active, still producing power, and connecting with the aether in the air, if you see what I mean, even if the motile itself is not being used to draw the vehicle along an aetheric current. It's as if it pulls bits of aether into itself, and leaks bits out as it moves along. Like a normal engine will leak oil. Those bits will be clumped up, so to speak, much thicker than the normal concentrations of aether in the air." He appealed to Dr Barshion. "Isn't that true, sir?"

Everyone turned to Barshion. "Well, yes," he admitted reluctantly. "It's a possibility. But I'm not sure how an aetheric engine would behave here, in this world. Its aetheric composition is different from our own, you know."

Kenar was sitting up straight, listening intently. He looked hopeful for the first time since they had seen the empty Cirathi ship. Miss Marlende said, "We can try, surely."

Emilie eyed Barshion, not sure why he was so reluctant. It's not as if we have a lot of other pressing things to do while we wait for him to fix our aetheric engine, she thought. Everyone else, even Lord Engal, seemed game to go on with the search.

"Yes, how would this be accomplished, Barshion?" Lord Engal said. "There should be some way to detect the traces of aether left behind..." He snapped his fingers. "The aether navigator!" He jumped to his feet, forgetting he still had a sandwich plate in his lap. He caught it agilely before it fell onto anyone's head, and handed it off to Captain Belden. "It should detect the presence of aether, any aether, even a small fragment in the air!"

Lord Engal dashed off down the corridor to the stairwell, apparently intending to test this immediately. Everyone set plates and cups aside as they hurried to follow.

In the wheelhouse, Dr Engal, with Dr Barshion and Captain Belden, poked at the aetheric navigator, making minute adjustments to its silver wheel, and turning it this way and that. Miss Marlende stood nearby, managing to look over the shorter Dr Barshion's shoulder, but Kenar stood back at the port, looking toward the abandoned ship.

Emilie angled around, trying to get a good view without getting in the way or juggling anybody's arm. She finally found a spot where she could look under Lord Engal's elbow.

Emilie had read descriptions of aether navigators in her favorite sea adventures, but never seen one in person. The aether navigator had a flat silver plate, etched around with the symbols and degrees of the compass directions. Two silver rings could be rotated around it, apparently to help figure longitude and latitude, though Emilie couldn't quite follow how. On the plate itself, in a shallow dish, there was a silvery substance that looked like mercury, but was actually drops of clarified, stable aether. It would roll around as the plate was turned and rotated, pointing the way toward aether currents in the air and water.

Then Dr Barshion said quietly, "Wait, wait. I think that's it."

"Yes, it's reacting to a concentration of aether somewhere nearby." Captain Belden carefully marked a spot on the outer ring. "But could it be traces from the airship's earlier movements, when it first arrived at the island?"

Tilting the navigator's wheel slightly, Dr Barshion muttered, "I don't think it would remain that long…

aether outside a current dissipates relatively quickly. And we know they were here for some time, preparing the balloon to make the attempt to get help from the surface..." The base plate tilted, sending the stable aether skittering around its shallow bowl. He stepped back, shaking his head, grimacing. "I'm sorry, I've pushed it out of alignment."

"No, no." Lord Engal frowned, catching the plate, his big hands unexpectedly gentle as he turned and angled it slightly. "Look at this; it's picking up something on the lower strata. Belden, you know more about surface aether navigation, is that what it looks like...?"

Belden leaned forward, reading the marks. "Faint traces in the water. Yes, My Lord. It's definitely there. That's going toward the east..." He glanced up at Miss Marlende. "Could the airship float?"

"Float?" She glanced at Kenar, brows lifted. "I suppose the main cabin might be somewhat buoyant, but I can't imagine that they would try to turn it into a boat. If they had all needed to leave by water, surely they would have taken the Cirathi ship."

Kenar came forward, his scaly brow furrowed. "No, there was no plan for that... Perhaps another ship arrived, placed the airship on board, and carried it away."

"It would have to be a large ship." Miss Marlende paced away, shaking her head as she thought it over. "But it would be possible."

"Did your people encounter anything like that in this area?" Belden asked Kenar, apparently forgetting how much he disliked him under the excitement of the mystery. "A vessel large enough to transport the airship? Or a settlement capable of building one?"

"No. In fact, we thought this area was mostly uninhabited." Kenar pulled the folded square of map out of a pocket inside his shirt and moved over to the chart table to spread it out.

Oswin put in, "That empty city we passed, whoever built that must have had a fleet of ships."

Lord Engal followed Kenar to the chart table. "Yes, of course, but it must have been abandoned for a century or more, long enough for the sea to shift."

"Unless it was built in the sea originally," Emilie said. If there were creatures here as strange as the Sargasso people, she didn't think mermen who lived half underwater and half above it were too far beyond the realm of possibility.

The others hadn't heard, but Miss Marlende stopped and stared at her for a moment. Long enough for Emilie to realize she had possibly said something very stupid. But Miss Marlende just pointed at her and said, "Keep that in mind."

Tracing routes on the map, Kenar was saying, "One of the reasons we wanted to explore in this region is because so little was known about it. We know a great deal about far-flung areas of our world because of traders passing along maps and information. But no maps exist of this place, as far as we know. Except this one, which we were drawing up as we went along."

"You hadn't explored in this direction?" Lord Engal

tapped a spot on the map.

"Due east from this island? Not yet. Dr Marlende hadn't ventured that way either. But we did see signs of ancient occupation, the remnants of very old buildings, similar to the flooded city we surfaced near. That was here, here, and here." Kenar marked the points on the map. "Nothing we saw was anywhere near as large or as extensive as that city. But if these people once spread throughout this area, there may still be remnants of them living now."

Lord Engal nodded thoughtfully. "The question is: why would Dr Marlende accompany these people? Could they have promised him help with the airship? Their old city was nearly right atop an aetheric fissure; they may have had their own knowledge of aetheric engines."

"That might be true," Miss Marlende said. "If the Cirathi weren't missing. There might have been a reason for my father to leave with these hypothetical people, but not the Cirathi."

"Yes." Kenar frowned down at the map, still lost in thought. "My people wouldn't have abandoned their ship. Not unless it was a choice between that and death."

Which really, Emilie thought, is what we all thought as soon as we saw the empty island. She just hoped they were all still alive, wherever they were.

After some discussion, they decided to tow the Cirathi ship behind them. Rigging this up took some time, but the sailing ship was light compared to the *Sovereign*'s bulk, and it didn't seem to slow their pace. Emilie thought it seemed optimistic, too, implying that they were going to find the missing crews. They also topped off the *Sovereign*'s water supply from the freshwater spring on the island, refilled the casks aboard the Cirathi ship, and replenished the food stores with some fruit and wild melons that Kenar said were good to eat.

The *Sovereign* turned east, following the tiny traces of aether. They had to go slowly, to give Captain Belden and Lord Engal time to adjust the navigator.

Steaming down a wide channel between scattered islands, they had come some distance by the time the Dark Wanderer started to move over the sun. These islands were different from the others, flat and low, with wide beaches, green reeds growing thickly out into the water, and shorter brushier trees. Up on the second deck, Miss Marlende lowered her spyglass and said to Kenar and Emilie, "Does this channel look man-made to you?"

Emilie nodded. From up here, she could see how the shape of the islands lining the channel seemed oddly regular. They might have been naturally sculpted by the water to look that way, but still, it was strange. "It does. It looks like a big canal, like someone chopped out whatever was in the middle and left the edges." The light wind moved the reeds, and the air smelled of sun and sand and a little like the jasmine toilet water her aunt had been sent as a gift from relatives in Coress. Except this wasn't cloying, it was clean and fresh.

"I agree." Kenar leaned on the rail. "Which implies that this channel leads somewhere." He seemed outwardly relaxed, but Emilie looked at his hands, so tight on the railing it was stretching the scaly skin over his knuckles.

"We'll find them," Emilie told him impulsively, though she was well aware that she was in no position to make promises. "All of them."

"I know. I won't give up hope until we–" Kenar broke it off, shook his head, and smiled down at her, though the smile was a little wry. "When you get back to your own world, will you really be content to sit meekly in a school after all this?"

Miss Marlende, engrossed with her spyglass again, snorted. "Whatever she does, I doubt she'll do it meekly."

"I don't know," Emilie said, looking out over the sun-drenched islands. Though inwardly she was a little pleased by Miss Marlende's comment, she wasn't sure how she felt about all this yet. As if all her life she had thought her world was one thing: closed-in and solid with carefully defined boundaries; so much so that running away to a relative with a respectable girls' school in Silk Harbor was almost unimaginably daring. Now the boundaries had fallen away, leave a broad vista that was stranger than anything she had read in a gothic novel.

Going back behind the walls would be very hard.

As the eclipse's line of darkness swept across the sea and the sandbars and islands, more crewmen were posted outside on the decks and the ship's lamps were lit. Emilie wanted to see how things were going in the wheelhouse without being labeled a snoop, so she managed to be on the spot when Mrs. Verian needed to send a tray of tea mugs and buns up to the men working there. Emilie hurried to volunteer herself.

She carried it up to the wheelhouse, where a young crewman directed her to set the tray on the chart table. As the other crewmen stationed there helped themselves, she lingered to watch Captain Belden and Lord Engal making minute adjustments to the navigator, and hastily scribbling notes on pads of paper. Sometimes they told the crewman manning the wheel to adjust their course slightly.

It surprised her to see that Lord Engal was so adept at this. She knew he wasn't one of those very rich men who did nothing with his time but hunt and buy horses. Emilie had read about lords who were members of the Philosophers' Society and spent all their time and money hiring philosophers and sorcerers to discover things and form theories and write books, and she knew Lord Engal must be one of them. But she hadn't expected him to be someone who could do some of the work himself.

Captain Belden yawned, quickly covering his mouth with his sleeve. "Excuse me, My Lord."

"You're excused," Lord Engal said absently. "Do you think we should travel through the night, again? We survived our previous experience, but I'd hate to run out of luck."

Belden glanced out of the big window, thinking it over. The line of darkness was nearly upon them, coming at an angle toward the long narrow island on their port side. "I'd rather not run up on whatever it was that took the airship, without some sort of warning. But I'm not sure we can afford to lose a full eight hours."

Lord Engal turned the navigator's wheel and made another note. "I'm not either. Finding Dr Marlende has become less an act of charity and more of a necessity, since we need him to repair our aetheric engine." Captain Belden snorted, startled and amused. Lord Engal cocked an eyebrow at Emilie and added, "You didn't hear me say that, young lady."

"No, sir. My Lord." Emilie was startled, both because she hadn't thought he had noticed she was here, and because she hadn't thought anyone else was worried by the lack of progress in repairing the engine. That was probably silly; they must have all noticed it, all been worried by it, even if they weren't speaking of it. *They aren't speaking of it where you can hear,* she amended. She would bet the crew had some choice words about it. She blurted, "Mr. Abendle thinks Miss Marlende should look at the numbers. Not the numbers, the figures. Something like that, to do with trying to fix the motile."

Lord Engal, caught making a minute adjustment to the ring, didn't look up, but she could tell he was listening. Captain Belden stared at her, frowning slowly. "What's this?"

Emilie took a deep breath. It was a little late to reconsider now. "I overheard Mr. Abendle ask Dr Barshion to show something, some calculations, to Miss

Marlende, to get her opinion, but Dr Barshion didn't want to. He didn't think it would help."

Lord Engal finished the adjustment and cocked his head at her. "When was this?"

"A bit after breakfast, yesterday."

Captain Belden seemed concerned. "Perhaps you should have a look at these calculations, My Lord."

Lord Engal looked thoughtful, tapping his pencil on the pad of paper. "Perhaps I shall."

Captain Belden nodded to Emilie, a clear dismissal, and she walked out of the wheelhouse, taking the stairs back down. She wasn't sure if he was going to listen to her or not. If he does, she realized a little bitterly, it would be a first for me. She just wasn't used to having things she said be taken seriously, especially by men.

But an hour or so later, when the complete darkness of the eclipse surrounded them and the ship had to slow to half-speed a message went around through the ship's speaking tube, calling everyone to the passenger lounge. Emilie wasn't called, but she went anyway.

Miss Marlende, Kenar, and Oswin came to the lounge, and even Dr Barshion and Abendle appeared. Both men looked even more exhausted. Dr Barshion was in his shirtsleeves, his hair mussed, his face lined with lack of sleep.

Lord Engal walked in and said without preamble, "We have a problem. We've lost the trail of aetheric traces."

Kenar looked away, his shoulders slumping. Miss Marlende sank down on the couch, disappointed. "We were too late?" she asked. "The traces have faded?"

Engal shook his head. "No, it's that we're too close to the Aerinterre aether-current. It's so powerful it overshadows any other aetheric traces in the air, and the navigator points only toward it."

"What now?" Kenar asked. Emilie stared at him, struck by a sudden realization: if they didn't find Kenar's crew, he had nowhere to go. Not only had he lost his friends, but he couldn't sail the big Cirathi ship by himself. He would have no way to get back home.

Engal said, "We'll keep our present course. We know the airship at least went in this direction. We can only hope we can see some evidence of it, some sign to point us toward it." He scratched his beard absently, and added, "And in the meantime, Miss Marlende, I'd like you to give your assistance to Dr Barshion and Mr. Abendle. Perhaps your familiarity with your father's work can aid them."

Abendle brightened, and Dr Barshion looked startled. "Oh yes," he said, as if he hadn't heard of the idea before. "Her assistance would be welcome."

Emilie tried to sleep, but managed only a brief nap in Miss Marlende's cabin. She was tired, but whenever she lay down, all she could think about was Kenar, and Dr Marlende, and all the other lost people. And the fact that if Barshion didn't fix the aetheric engine, the *Sovereign* might join them. This place is lovely and strange and exciting, she thought, but I'm not keen to live here forever.

She got up, washed and dressed, and went up on the second deck above the bow, where Kenar was keeping watch. The night was cool, but not uncomfortably so, and the ship's spotlight swept back and forth over the dark water, catching glimpses of the high stands of reeds and the white sand beaches of the nearest island. She saw Kenar standing at the railing with another dark shape. It wasn't until it spoke that she realized it was Oswin. He was saying, "Yes, we've spoken about it, though no one's mentioned it to Lord Engal."

As Emilie approached, Oswin said, "I'd better get back to my duties," and walked back up the deck, giving her a nod as he passed.

She leaned on the railing next to Kenar. He was watching the lights of the launch a hundred yards or so ahead of them. It was taking soundings to make sure the *Sovereign* didn't run aground. She said, "What was that about?" She thought Oswin had left the conversation because he didn't want to frighten her.

Kenar had a better opinion of her nerves. He said, "They're worried about the coal and oil store. This ship carries enough for long ocean voyages, but they were also planning on staying in the aether current for a longer period of time. I pointed out that if they wanted to remain longer, we could find a safe spot to anchor this ship, leave men to guard it, and continue the search with the *Lathi*." He added wryly, "I'd have to teach most of them to sail first, of course."

"That makes sense." Emilie propped her chin on her folded arms. "It would give us more time to search." She thought about asking Kenar what he would do if Lord Engal decided to call off the search and leave. But then we can't leave until they fix the aetheric engine, Emilie thought, so right now we're all in the same boat. Literally. So there was no point in asking painful questions yet.

"What's this?" Kenar said suddenly.

Emilie looked up. She could see the launch's running lights on the bow and stern. It had stopped and turned sideways. That was odd. "Is it coming back?" she said. "Maybe it's too shallow up ahead." If it was too shallow for the *Sovereign* and the *Lathi*, it had surely been too shallow for the vessel which had carried away the airship. I hope we haven't taken a wrong turn already, she thought.

"Perhaps, but…" Suddenly gunshots rang out over the water. "It's under attack!" Kenar pushed away from the rail and ran back toward the stairs to the lower deck.

Emilie leaned forward over the rail, as if that would help her see better. The ship's spotlight swung around, illuminating the water just past the launch, and she gasped. There were suddenly other boats in the water, low flat rafts, as if they had popped up out of nowhere. She caught glimpses of slim figures, tossing ropes at the launch as if trying to catch it and pull it in. And they were throwing things, which reflected silver in the light – Emilie jerked back as a short javelin bounced off the railing just below her. "Uh oh," she gasped, and bolted for the hatch.

She ducked inside and took the first set of stairs down. Coming out on the main deck cross-corridor, she dodged a sailor with a rifle running for the outer starboard hatch. She fell in behind him.

As they neared the hatch Emilie heard yells and a series of thunks. They're boarding us, she thought in alarm. The sailor burst out of the hatch ahead of her, then staggered back, dropping his rifle. He turned toward her, his eyes wide with shock; a narrow metal bolt was sticking out of his shoulder.

Emilie lunged forward and grabbed his other arm, supporting him. He sagged against her, and she stumbled, took a breath to shout for help. Then over his shoulder she saw three silvery forms climbing over the railing.

They looked like people, but their skin was iridescent, glinting in the ship's lamps. And they were carrying short spears. *Oh no.* Panic gave Emilie strength and she pulled the wounded man back through the hatch, half dragging him over the rim.

She couldn't run with him, and there was no one else in the corridor. She shoved him against the nearest wall, and turned back to the hatch. The three men, creatures, whatever they were had seen the open doorway and started toward her. Emilie grabbed the handle and swung it closed, just as they reached it. She slammed the bolt home, feeling a violent tug from the other side that told her she was just in time.

Emilie caught a glimpse of a smooth, silvery face peering through the porthole, and stumbled back. She shook her head, looking down at the wounded sailor. He was slumped against the wall, his face ashy with shock, blood staining his uniform around the bolt. She leaned over him, but he gasped, "The other hatch, check the—"

"Oh hell!" Emilie shoved to her feet and ran down the outer corridor. There was another hatch barely thirty feet down the length of the ship, she could see it standing open, the light from the nearest sconce falling through it out onto the deck. The intruders would surely notice it.

Almost to the door, a silvery form stepped through, spear first. Emilie slid to an abrupt halt. *Oh, oh, no.* It stared at her and she stared at it. Its face was smooth and oddly textured, but more human than the Sargasso creatures, with dark eyes, a small nose, and a thin-lipped mouth. She looked around wildly, but the corridor was horribly bare of potential weapons. There wasn't even a vase to throw.

Then gunshots sounded from the deck, close enough to make Emilie's ears ring, and the intruder jerked back out of the hatch.

Emilie gasped, realizing she had been holding her breath. She went to the hatch, reaching it in time to see Kenar, Miss Marlende, and several sailors running up the deck. The sailors were armed with rifles and Miss Marlende had her pistol.

Kenar flung up a hand, shouting for them to stop. As they halted, Emilie looked down the deck to see there were now perhaps ten of the silvery intruders ranged down near the other hatch. They had the spears, and long tubes that might be projectile weapons. Emilie thought of closing and locking the hatch, but if Kenar and Miss Marlende and the others had to take cover, it was the closest way to reach safety.

Kenar called something to them in a language Emilie didn't understand; whatever it was, it sounded angry. They didn't answer. Miss Marlende said, "Tell them we'll fire unless they get off the ship."

"I don't think they can understand me," Kenar told her. "Try firing over their heads—"

He was interrupted by a strange, loud sound, like someone trying to blow a badly damaged horn, coming from somewhere out in the water. Abruptly, the intruders bolted for the railing, leapt it, and landed with huge splashes below.

"What?" Emilie said aloud. She didn't see any reason for the sudden retreat. Kenar, Miss Marlende, and the sailors cautiously approached the railing, but it didn't appear to be a trick.

Emilie shut the hatch and went back down the corridor, worried about the wounded sailor, but Mrs. Verian and another crewman had already found him. They had stretched him out on the corridor floor, and Mrs. Verian was pressing a towel around the base of the bolt still sticking out of his shoulder. Blood soaked the towel and stained her hands, and the man's eyes were tightly shut, his face taut with pain. Emilie steadied herself on the wall, suddenly light-headed, with an odd heavy darkness trying to creep in around the edges of her vision. She looked away hastily, taking deep breaths. That's right, people faint at blood, she thought. She had never fainted at blood before, but then she had never seen anyone lose what looked like a bucket of it at one time. She couldn't faint; Mrs. Verian certainly didn't have time to deal with her, and the crewmen would think she was a weak ninny. "Will he be all right?" she asked thickly.

"I don't think it hit anything vital, lucky man," Mrs. Verian said, distracted. "Can you find Miss Marlende?"

Relieved to have a reason to escape, Emilie took a quick look out the porthole to make sure the deck was still clear, then opened the hatch. The others were at the railing, looking out into the dark as the spotlight swept the water. The cool air cleared her head, and she called out, "Miss Marlende? There's a wounded man!"

"Is there? Thank you, Emilie." Miss Marlende hurried past her through the hatch.

Emilie went to the railing to stand beside Kenar. The slight breeze smelled of gunpowder. She saw the faint flickers of light as the small skiffs fled. "They all left?" she asked hopefully.

"Something drove them off, and it wasn't us," Kenar said, staring into the darkness. "There's another ship out there, a big one."

"Another ship?" Emilie squinted, but the darkness beyond the ship's lights was impenetrable. *No, wait.* There was something out there, more glowing spots of lamplight, marking a large shape riding low on the water, perhaps a couple of hundred yards away. "I see it. Is there light in the water below it, or is that a reflection?"

Kenar said, "No, it's a smaller boat." A single flicker of light had broken off from the larger shape, and was coming toward them. "They're sending a launch to us." He started along the deck and Emilie hurried after him.

They met Lord Engal and Oswin above the launch platform. There were several crewmen with rifles scattered around the deck and two wounded men were being helped inside. The silver people had obviously tried to board this side of the ship as well. "Do you know who they were?" Lord Engal asked Kenar.

Kenar shook his head, watching tensely as the *Sovereign*'s launch puttered up to the platform. The engine cut and it slowed, and the crewman waiting below tossed a line to the man in the bow.

"What happened, sailor?" Lord Engal called down. "Where did they come from?"

The sailor started up the ladder from the launch platform, saying, "I'm not sure, My Lord. They were in the reeds, waiting for us. Then that larger ship drove them off. It tried to hail us but we couldn't understand them." He stepped onto the deck and hesitated, suddenly sounding self-conscious. "My Lord, after the attack, I thought it was best to return to the ship. I hope–"

"No, no, Feran, you've done right," Engal said, moving forward, looking toward the approaching light. "They seem to have helped us by driving off the attack, but we've got to be very careful here. Any advice, Kenar?"

"Don't shine the big lamp on them," Kenar said immediately. "If the night is their natural time, the light might hurt their eyes. They might think it an attack."

"Good point." Engal waved at Oswin, who bolted for the nearest stairwell, heading for the wheelhouse to pass along the order.

They waited, the air thick with tension. Miss Marlende arrived, a little breathless and with blood stains on her sleeves. "Three wounded," she reported to Lord Engal. "They're all right for the moment, but it would be better if Dr Barshion could take a look at them. A healing spell to prevent infection might make all the difference."

"I'll make certain he does," Lord Engal said, his eyes on the approaching boat.

It was drawing steadily closer and Emilie could make out the shape of it a little better now. A lamp hung on the prow, a few bare inches above the black glassy surface of the water. The boat itself was very broad, made of some kind of light wood, and looked more like a raft with a raised edge. But it moved swiftly and easily for a raft, and the people paddling it so skillfully were balanced on the very edges, one leg in the water.

Closer; and she could tell they weren't human people, either. One of the sailors said, "My Lord, they're the same as the ones who attacked–"

"I know," Lord Engal said. "Steady."

The lamps reflected off iridescent skin, which rippled and changed with every movement and shift of the light. "Look, they have fins," Miss Marlende whispered, sounding fascinated. "I didn't notice that before." She was right; they had long feathery fins along their arms and legs, with a similar crest on their hairless heads. "Kenar, have you ever seen anything like them before?"

He moved along the rail toward them, keeping his voice low. "I've seen water dwellers that looked something like this, but they can't live in the air for more than a few moments. These seem to be made for both."

One of the merpeople lifted a hand, and called out in a language Emilie couldn't understand. The voice was light and soft; it was impossible to tell if it was male or female.

Lord Engal lifted his hand in response. Oswin had returned, and he said, "We've got men posted around the ship, to make sure this isn't a diversion."

Emilie looked around; more crewmen armed with rifles had come out onto the deck. Lord Engal said, "Good. But if anyone fires on this raft without a direct order from me, I'll fling him off this boat. Understood?"

There were muted responses of "Yes, My Lord" from around him.

Dr Barshion stepped out of the hatchway, moving up beside Lord Engal. "My God," he said softly. "Do we know what they are?" Lord Engal shook his head.

With expert paddling, the raft came smoothly to a halt a few yards from the *Sovereign*. There were square openings in the bottom of the raft, presumably so the occupants could slip in and out of the water. A boat for people who are as at home in the water as out of it, Emilie thought, fascinated.

"Half in, half out of the water," Miss Marlende said to herself. She caught Emilie's arm. "You could be right about that abandoned city. If people like this built it – merpeople…"

One of the merpeople waved a hand, speaking again. This close, in the yellow reflected light from the ship's lamps, Emilie was fairly sure it was a woman. Kenar shook his head, tapping his ear to show he didn't understand. He spoke to her in a language that was all breathy growls and clicks; Emilie thought it must be the Cirathi language. But the merpeople didn't appear to understand that, either. Two of them shifted around, taking a box out of a net bag that hung down in the water.

One of the crewmen shifted uneasily, and Lord Engal said, "Steady, men. They seem peaceable and they want to talk, and for all we know they're about to produce a Cirathi phrasebook."

Emilie still had her reservations about Lord Engal, but she had to admit she thought he was handling this well. She leaned on the railing, finding herself barely five feet away from the merpeople as their boat drifted closer. The one nearest was staring curiously at her, and Emilie stared back. She felt certain this one was female too, just from the shape of the slim body. The hands curled around the light wooden paddle were webbed, and the nails were small and neat, not claws. Emilie distinctly remembered the plant-people from the Sargasso as having claws. The merwoman was wearing silvery bangles around one wrist, and little silver beads were woven into the feathery crest on her head. Emilie realized suddenly that the merwoman, indeed all the merpeople on the boat, were naked except for skimpy wraps of metallic cloth around their waists; she felt her cheeks flush with embarrassment. She hadn't noticed before because their iridescent skin seemed almost like clothing, or a protective outer covering. They don't have breasts, she thought, still curious despite the awkwardness of looking at naked people. Maybe that means they lay eggs.

The merwoman who seemed to be the leader took something out of the box, something that looked like an elaborately curving shell, the kind that washed up on beaches at Liscae and the other southern ports. She spoke into it, and projected from it, her soft voice said, "Do you understand me?"

It was one more astonishment on top of everything else. Lord Engal moved up beside Kenar, and said, "Yes, we understand you. How can you speak our language? Have you met our people before?"

The merwoman held the shell to her ear, listening to his voice through it.

"The shell is some sort of translation device," Kenar said softly. "I've heard of such things before, but none that worked this well."

Keeping his voice low, Dr Barshion said, "Yes, it must be a spell. A complicated one."

The merwoman tapped the shell. "This device translates. I am Yesa, I speak for the Queen of the Sealands." She looked from Kenar to Lord Engal. "You are not hurt?"

Lord Engal replied carefully, "We have three men wounded, but other than that, we're quite well, thanks to your intervention. Can you tell us why we were attacked?" Emilie thought he had picked a delicate way to ask that question.

"They were the Darkward Nomads," Yesa said. "They attack all shipping in these seas."

The Darkward Nomads. Emilie remembered Darkward was the Hollow World term for the direction to the west, where the Dark Wanderer came from, so it wasn't quite as intimidating a name as it seemed at first. But still...

Miss Marlende looked at Kenar for information, and he shook his head slightly to show he had never heard the name before. Then Yesa asked, "You are perhaps looking for missing people?"

"Yes, yes, we are!" Miss Marlende called out, then whispered, "Sorry, spoke out of turn," to Lord Engal.

"Quite all right, but try to contain yourself," he said to her. He turned back to the merpeople and said to Yesa, "You have news of them, of people like us?"

"Yes. We have heard of them. You will follow us, speak to our Queen?"

Lord Engal exchanged a guarded look with Kenar, and said, "Yes, but can't you tell us what happened to them? Where they are, if they're well?"

"I don't know if they are well." Yesa hesitated, lifting her elegant webbed hands in a helpless gesture. Emilie got the sudden sense that Yesa didn't know much at all, that she was possibly as nervous about this encounter as they were. If I were her, I'd be nervous too, she thought, sent out in a little boat, to talk to people in a strange big noisy ship, and without the information to answer their questions. Yesa said, "My Queen wants to speak of all this with you herself. If you follow us to our city, all will be explained."

Lord Engal looked at Kenar and Oswin, turning to glance at Dr Barshion, "Gentlemen, I don't think we have a choice."

Six

The *Sovereign*, moving at its slowest speed, followed Yesa's boat through the darkness. Emilie watched from the bow with Kenar and Miss Marlende as the boat led them through the island channels. As the *Sovereign*'s spotlight swept back and forth, they began to catch glimpses of white stone structures on the islands or near them, lapped by the waves from their passage. It was hard to tell in the dark, but they all seemed ruined, or empty, with stones tumbling down or lightless windows.

"The Sealands, she called it," Miss Marlende said thoughtfully. "If their civilization once spread through this entire area, all the way to that ruined city we passed, they must have been very powerful."

"They might still be." Kenar was pacing the deck behind them. He had been restless and uneasy for the past hour, and Emilie wasn't certain it was due to the slow pace of the ship. "I'm wondering how they knew we were out here, in time to intervene during the attack."

Miss Marlende rested her elbows on the railing. "Sentries, perhaps. Hidden on one of these islands. They might have some form of distance communication, like a telegraph."

"Or they might have magic." Kenar didn't sound pleased at the prospect. "That could put us at a great disadvantage, if they carried off our people against their will."

It wasn't an encouraging thought, that the merpeople might be leading them into a trap. Emilie squinted to see the little boat. The larger craft it had come from was just ahead, the spotlight catching occasional glimpses of it. It was big, flat, and barge-like, easily the size of the *Lathi*. But instead of sails it had rows of oars, moving smoothly and steadily against the low sides.

Emilie thought Yesa had been telling the truth. But then maybe the person who sent Yesa didn't tell her it was a trap. Or maybe Emilie was no good at reading the expression and intent of people who weren't human.

She didn't seem to have any trouble reading Kenar's expressions and understanding his intent. But the Cirathi weren't merpeople; from what Emilie could tell, there weren't many differences between Kenar and a human, besides his appearance. Meeting him had been more like meeting someone from a strange distant country than from another species. It was probably why the crew of the *Lathi* had gotten on so well with Dr Marlende's crew. And as explorers and traders, they had more in common with Menaens than not. Just be careful, she reminded herself. She didn't like judging other people, having had more than her fill of being judged herself. But she didn't want herself or any of the others to be hurt or killed.

"We've got Dr Barshion," Miss Marlende was saying. "He does seem to be quite a decent sorcerer, even if he's not as expert with aetheric engines as he thought."

"Has there been any progress?" Emilie asked her. "Did you look at the figures Abendle wanted you to see?"

"Yes, and Abendle's right; the problem isn't in the way the motile is calibrated." Miss Marlende didn't quite sound defeated, but she didn't sound enthused by their prospects, either. "It should be working. I suggested they try to dismantle the aether navigator and make certain there's nothing wrong with it. If one of the rings had been jostled during our descent, that might cause the engine instability."

"The navigator?" Emilie had thought it was working fine, from what she had seen in the wheelhouse. "The one we were using to follow the aether traces?"

"No, that's the standard ship's navigator, used for surface vessels. The motile has a separate aether navigator built inside it, which allows it to stay within the boundaries of the aether currents."

"Oh, I see." Emilie wasn't sure she did see, but at least now Dr Barshion and Abendle would know what was specifically wrong with the motile.

They traveled for the rest of the night, and finally reached their destination as the eclipse ended, the wall of light moving slowly across the islands and the sea. As it advanced, it revealed the city spread out before them.

It was made of white stone and stretched for miles. Bridges and open air plazas and pillared walkways marched across the low-lying islands, to towers and large buildings with pitched roofs standing in the broad channels between. For such a vast city, the buildings weren't very tall, not even the towers standing more than a few stories above the water. But then, they're resting on the bottom, so they're taller than they look, Emilie thought, fascinated. Borrowing Miss Marlende's spyglass, she could see people out on the walkways, the sun glinting off their iridescent skin, casting back rippling reflections of blue and green. They wore jewelry of silver chains and pieces of polished shell, and very few clothes, mostly just kilts or drapes around their waists. It still wasn't as disturbing as it should be. Perhaps because it was natural for them, and they were all doing it. As she watched, she saw a merperson leading a merchild down a set of steps into the water, vanishing under the surface. Another walked up the steps, shaking his head to get the water out of his feathery head fins. There were more merpeople on the islands to either side of the channel, some in boats and some in the water, fishing in the reeds with nets and small spears. They stopped to stare at the *Sovereign* and the *Lathi*, pointing at them, clearly amazed by the two ships' appearance.

"They've never seen anything like this vessel before," Kenar said under his breath. "It doesn't mean they haven't seen the airship."

"I'm hoping they have seen it," Miss Marlende murmured, her eyes on the city ahead.

Yesa's boat was leading them into a harbor of sorts at the edge of the city, where the channel broadened into a large lagoon. A long building with two stories of pillared galleries stood at its edge, with piers stretching out across the water. The piers stood only inches above the surface, so they were constantly awash, which didn't seem to bother the merpeople at all. Dozens of boats were tied up along them, of all sizes. Their large escort ship broke away to head toward the other end of the harbor, where several larger barges of a similar design were anchored, some bigger than the *Lathi* and even the *Sovereign*. From what Miss Marlende and Kenar had said, one of them should be more than large enough to carry the airship. But it's not here, Emilie thought, studying the further docks. At least not where we can see it.

The *Sovereign* slowed to a crawl, then dropped anchor near the end of one of the piers. Yesa's small boat came around to speak to them again, and Emilie followed Miss Marlende and Kenar back to the port side.

Lord Engal, Captain Belden, and Oswin were already waiting there. The boat drew up next to the *Sovereign*'s launch platform, and Yesa took out her talking shell to say, "You will come in your small boat and speak to our Queen now?"

Everyone looked at Lord Engal. He let out his breath, and said, "Give us a moment to ready ourselves, please."

Yesa nodded and lowered the shell. The other

merpeople were taking the chance to get a better look at the *Sovereign* and her crew in the daylight, pointing and talking among themselves.

They moved back from the railing. Lord Engal scratched his chin and said thoughtfully, "We'll have to go. It would be the height of rudeness to ask her to come out here to speak to us."

Captain Belden said, "You shouldn't go, My Lord."

"I'll go," Kenar said. "I've met with stranger people than this, believe it or not."

"And I," Miss Marlende added. "Kenar and I have the most at stake, after all. We should take the risk. If there is any."

With some asperity, Captain Belden said, "I appreciate your confidence, Miss Marlende, but all we know about these people is that they might have made off with an airship and kidnapped a number of people, and then lied about it. If you–"

"That's enough," Lord Engal said. He told Belden, "Of course I'm going, it's a foreign monarch, I can't risk insulting her. If Menea develops any sort of trade and diplomatic relations with this world, we'll have to deal with these people as they're the closest to the aetheric current outlets and they clearly claim this territory. I'm not going down in history as the man who started off on the wrong foot."

Captain Belden pressed his lips together, clearly unhappy. "I'm not keen on going down in history as the man who stood by while Lord Engal was killed, My Lord."

"Well, that's just a chance you'll have to take." Lord

Engal added, "I'll take Kenar with me, and Oswin, and two sailors. Sidearms, but no rifles. If we don't reappear or send a message within…" He checked his pocket watch. "Two hours, leave the harbor, and do what is necessary to get the ship back to the surface world."

"The Queen sent a woman as her emissary," Miss Marlende said pointedly. "It would only be sensible to send a woman to speak with her–"

Lord Engal cut her off. "Sensible, but not absolutely necessary, and I'm not risking anyone else on a whim." He stepped to the railing and told Yesa, "We'll be ready to leave in a moment."

Yesa waved an acknowledgment, and signaled her boat to withdraw, taking it toward the nearest dock to speak to some merpeople waiting there. Oswin called for sailors to lower the launch, and everyone scrambled to get ready. Emilie stood aside with Miss Marlende, who fumed silently, her jaw set. Emilie sympathized. There hadn't been a hope in hell of getting herself included in the party, but she had thought Miss Marlende would surely have a chance to go. She said, "At least he didn't say it was because you were a woman."

Miss Marlende folded her arms and muttered something grim about stiff-necked blowhards.

But when the launch was lowered into the water, and the landing party started to climb aboard, Yesa's boat returned to hail them again. Using the shell, she said, "I apologize, I should have told you, our Queen will wish to meet your female leaders, also. This is our custom."

Lord Engal, one foot in the launch, stopped and said, "Oh, is it?" He was clearly scrambling for a polite way to decline. "Ah, our custom is not quite so–"

Yesa pointed up at Miss Marlende and Emilie, standing at the rail. "Perhaps they would accompany you?"

Miss Marlende said immediately, "I would be happy to go, but Emilie is rather young–"

Lord Engal stared up at them, disconcerted. "Miss Marlende, yes, I suppose, but I don't think the girl can possibly want–"

Emilie bit her lip, trying to control herself. Jumping up and down like a little girl and begging *Please! I want to see the Queen of the merpeople too!* was hardly likely to engender confidence. She knew it could be dangerous, that they had been attacked once already, that human people could be violent for no sensible reason at all and there was nothing to say that these merpeople weren't the same. But that didn't matter. She said, a little too loudly, "I'll go. I don't mind. I mean, I'd love to."

Miss Marlende frowned at her. She had one hand on the ladder, clearly torn between establishing herself in the launch before anybody raised more objections and a need to dissuade Emilie. Keeping her voice low, she said, "Emilie, I don't think it's wise. It is a risk; after the past few days you have to realize how big a risk it might be."

From the platform, Lord Engal said, "Yes, I'd better ask Mrs. Verian to accompany you instead." He waved to one of the sailors up on deck. "Send someone to find her."

Seeing her chance slip away, Emilie hastily whispered to Miss Marlende, "It's pretty risky to be on this ship at all, with a sorcerer who can't make his aetheric engine work. We might have to live here."

"Emilie!" Miss Marlende glanced around to make certain no one had heard. "I thought the crew was gloomy, but you're the biggest pessimist on this ship."

Emilie didn't think it was pessimism, just the result of having her expectations continually stamped on while growing up. She said, "Are you really going to let him ask Mrs. Verian to go? She won't want to at all, and Mr. Verian won't want her to go either, but they'll think they don't have any choice, since they work for Lord Engal. I've got a choice, I'm a volunteer."

From Miss Marlende's expression, the point about Mrs. Verian must have hit home. She said, reluctantly, "You're right. If we drag the poor woman along against her will... But if... when we get back home, don't let any word of this get back to your uncle. I don't want him trying to have me taken in charge, or dragged into court for God knows what."

Just in time, Emilie reminded herself not to jump up and down. "Thank you," she breathed.

Miss Marlende called to Lord Engal, "It's not necessary to send for Mrs. Verian. Emilie can accompany us." She started down the ladder, Emilie right behind her.

Lord Engal frowned at Emilie, but he glanced at Yesa,

still waiting in her boat well within earshot, her translator shell held up to listen. He appeared to swallow a more forceful objection and only asked Miss Marlende, "Is this wise?"

"I think so," Miss Marlende said. Kenar gave her a hand to steady her as she stepped into the launch. "If it's safe enough for you, it's safe enough for her."

"I hope you're right," Lord Engal said, and helped Emilie into the boat himself.

The sailors cast off from the platform, and started the launch's small engine. Yesa waved for them to follow, her boat leading them between the piers toward the big open structure fronting the harbor. Merpeople in other boats and working along the piers stopped to stare at them; Emilie resisted the urge to wave, feeling it might not be entirely appropriate. Miss Marlende, leaning out to look down over the side, tapped her arm. Emilie looked too, and saw slender iridescent shapes flickering in the water below them: merpeople swimming along the harbor's shallow sandy floor.

The big structure was made of white stone, and stood three tall stories above the harbor. Broad pillared galleries along the front were open to the sea breezes. It looked like part of the second level might be a market, where goods were piled up for sale. From the clay jars and bundles stacked in the lower level, it could be for storing or selling cargos. Emilie noticed the place didn't smell like a harbor; it smelled fresh and clean, with no stench of dead fish or tar. *They live in the water at least some of the time, so they have a much bigger stake in* keeping it clean, she thought.

Yesa was leading them toward a tall archway where a water channel cut through the lower floor of the building. Her boat turned down the channel, passing inside.

At the tiller, Oswin asked Lord Engal, "My Lord, do we follow?"

Lord Engal didn't hesitate. "Go on."

Kenar said, low-voiced, "It would have been better if they met with us on the docks. But I can see why they want a demonstration of trust."

"On our part and theirs," Miss Marlende said.

The launch turned down the channel, passing under the arch and between the high stone walls, the putter of its motor suddenly much louder. The walls were carved with tall figures of merpeople, fighting with some large tentacled creature. Very large, perhaps big enough to wrap around the *Sovereign* and pull it under. Emilie leaned forward to ask Kenar: "Is that like the creature that Dr Marlende fought off?"

He turned his head to tell her. "Very similar, but it seemed much bigger at the time."

Emilie sat back, impressed.

They passed out from under the archway into the open again, the channel leading through a plaza surrounded by towers with balconies. A bridge arched above them, and they passed pillars with water pouring down the sides. Looking up at the bridge, Emilie caught sight of startled iridescent faces looking down at them.

Then they were moving into another building, small

but with a vaulted ceiling and an elaborate waterfall grotto to one side. Merpeople were gathered waiting, but they wore more jewelry than the people working in the harbor, polished shells and more silver chains woven through their head fins, and drapes of metallic fabric that caught the light in different colors. There was a short dock extending into the channel and Yesa was guiding her boat toward it.

"I think we're in a palace," Miss Marlende muttered to Emilie. "It certainly looks like the right spot to meet with a Queen."

The launch bumped the dock and Yesa's crew moved hurriedly to help the sailors tie it up. Stepping out of the launch down onto a stone surface level with the water was awkward for Emilie, mostly because she had shorter legs than the others. She found herself having to cling to Kenar's arm to manage it without falling. Miss Marlende and Lord Engal were more graceful.

"This way, please," Yesa said through the shell, leading them toward the grotto. Emilie walked beside Kenar, following Lord Engal and Miss Marlende, with Oswin and the two sailors bringing up the rear. The merpeople were all staring, murmuring to each other, and Emilie felt her face heat. The startled stares from the harbor people and those on the bridge hadn't bothered her; the curiosity had been mutual. But at close range, it was harder to ignore.

As they got closer to the grotto, Emilie saw the rocks had been shaped by the water into formations like giant swaths of lace. The floor they were walking across was set with medallions that looked like mother-of-pearl. At the foot of the grotto, a woman was sitting in a carved stone chair, the water lapping at her feet. She wore a headdress of polished shell and pearl, more pearls draping her body, wound around a dark blue stole shot with metallic streaks.

The Queen, Emilie thought, her heart pumping. It was hard to tell how old she was; unlike Yesa, there was a faint darkening of the smooth skin at the corners of her eyes and mouth. Other merpeople, men and women, sat in the water at her feet or stood behind her.

Yesa said, "This is my lady, Queen Tath-Alare." She bowed her head.

One of the Queen's attendants lifted another translation shell, holding it up for the Queen. She said, "You are from the upper world." Her voice was deeper than Yesa's, but still soft.

Lord Engal gave her a formal half-bow. "Yes, Your Majesty. All but our friend Kenar, who is of the Cirathi, and has graciously agreed to guide us through your waters."

The Queen inclined her head. Emilie got the impression that she was pleased with Lord Engal's manner. It was probably handy to have someone with them who was used to speaking to royalty. Though speaking to the king of Menea must be vastly different from greeting the Queen of the Sealands. The Queen said, "Your world is a legend to us. I had never thought before that it might be real."

Lord Engal said, "This is what we thought of your

own world, Your Majesty." Emilie hadn't heard any of those legends; she suspected he was just being polite. "I am Lord Engal, and this is Miss Vale Marlende." As he introduced the others, Emilie watched the Queen's face. Had she reacted to the name "Marlende?" It was hard to tell. He continued, "We came here to search for missing companions. Your emissary, Yesa, said that you wish to speak to us of this."

The Queen nodded, her eyes thoughtful. "I did. Your lost companions came in a ship that flew through the air. We have seen it."

"Where?" Lord Engal managed to look as though he was only politely interested in this information.

"The ship was seen being carried on a barge, belonging to the Darkward Nomads, who also attacked your ship. They live in the outskirts of our empire, in the cities and other parts of the Sealands that have fallen to time and been abandoned."

Brow furrowed, Lord Engal said, "Why would they have taken the airship? And attacked us, without provocation?"

"They take things," the Queen said simply. "Small boats, cargos, fisherfolk who live on isolated shallows, ships, if they can get them."

Oh, that doesn't sound good, Emilie thought. Lord Engal said, "For what purpose?"

The Queen made an open-handed gesture, as if the answer was obvious. "This is how they make their living, rather than fishing or farming. Perhaps they take the people as slaves, or perhaps there is a darker reason.

We do not know."

There was an uneasy stirring from the assembled courtiers. Emilie felt uneasy herself. "A darker reason" suggested all sorts of terrible things.

Miss Marlende cleared her throat, and said, "Your Majesty, has no one ever escaped the Nomads, to explain why they were taken?"

"No, never... that we have heard of," the Queen replied. She said to Engal, "You wish to secure the return of your people and property?"

"Yes, Your Majesty." He was watching her carefully. "You have a suggestion?"

"We are planning a raid, to drive the nomads away from our borders, to protect the fisherfolk who ply those waters." The Queen tilted her head. "You could join us, add your might to ours, and we would help you search for your people."

Emilie was standing a little behind Kenar, so she saw the reptilian folds of skin at the back of his neck twitch. He exchanged a look with Miss Marlende, whose expression was close to horrified. The Queen just asked us to go to war with her, against people of her own country, Emilie thought, feeling a wary sickness in the pit of her stomach. It happened all the time in books about explorers venturing in far countries. And it never ends well.

Lord Engal gave the Queen a polite half-bow. "If we could have a moment to speak of this in private, Your Majesty?"

ও

The room they were taken to was above the grotto, with one wall open to the outside. A balcony extended out from it, looking down on a little submerged courtyard filled with richly flowering water plants. Lord Engal had sent one of the sailors back to check in with Captain Belden and tell him that all was well so far.

"We're not here to fight a war," Miss Marlende said, as soon as they had privacy.

With some impatience, Lord Engal said, "I agree completely, but that may be our only way to free our people."

Miss Marlende lowered her voice. "If we believe her." She looked at Kenar. "What do you think?"

He folded his arms, and Emilie thought he looked deeply troubled. "I don't know. It isn't…" He shook his head, frustrated. "It's possible, but our appearance here seems very convenient for the Queen."

"You believe the woman has constructed some sort of plot to deceive us?" Lord Engal sounded almost amused.

Looking down into the courtyard, Emilie recognized the superior tone in his voice and rolled her eyes.

"You don't think it's possible?" Miss Marlende challenged. "Because she's too naive and simple, perhaps?" She waved a hand toward the city. "Look at this place! It's the capital for a fallen empire that must be hundreds of years old; their monarchy must go back for generations. If there's anyone who could engage in intrigue and deception, it's her."

Emilie watched them worriedly, thinking of the

decadent nation of Simyahi from the Lord Rohiro novels. She suspected Miss Marlende was right. There was no reason to discount the merpeople's intelligence or their desire to pursue their own motives. We haven't helped them, saved lives, like Dr Marlende did for the Cirathi. We haven't become their friends, she thought. The merpeople had no reason to be kindly disposed toward them.

"I will take it under advisement," Lord Engal said, which caused Miss Marlende to flush with fury, "but I don't see that they have any reason to lie to us–"

"Unless they want to use us as cannon fodder against these nomads–" Miss Marlende supplied.

"Do you have any other suggestion as to how we're to find your father and the others?" Lord Engal said. "Because I'd like to hear it."

That gave Miss Marlende pause. She pushed her hair back in frustration. "No. I wish I did."

"These marshy islands seem to go on forever," Kenar pointed out. He didn't look happy, either. "Unless we have some idea of where these nomads camp, we'll have no way to find them."

Miss Marlende said wearily, "Yes, I see the problem. I just wish there was another solution."

Lord Engal eyed her, apparently unsatisfied with that admission. "I'd like you to stay here while I continue our conference with the Queen."

Miss Marlende frowned at him. "So I don't interrupt you with valid objections? Yesa did request my presence."

"Exactly. And if she asks for you to return, I'll send for you." He set his jaw. "Or would you prefer to wait on the ship?"

Miss Marlende smiled thinly. "I'll wait here."

Lord Engal walked out, collecting Oswin and the sailor on the way. Kenar touched Miss Marlende's shoulder and said, resigned, "At least he knows that this might be a trap."

As Kenar followed the others, she muttered, "Does he? I'm not so sure."

"He's awfully stubborn, and he likes to be right," Emilie said. Everybody liked to be right, of course, but some people were so invested in it that it blinded them to common sense. Though she was mostly thinking of Uncle Yeric and her brothers; she didn't think Lord Engal was quite as bad as they were.

Miss Marlende jumped, as if she had forgotten Emilie was there. She sighed and came to stand beside her. "If it was just his ego at stake..."

Emilie frowned, considering. "Do you think it would help if we took a look around? Maybe, if it was these merpeople who took the airship and the Cirathi, and not the nomads, we could see some sign of it." She didn't really think they would be that lucky, or the merpeople so careless, but maybe they could see something that would help make their decision easier.

Miss Marlende stared at her. "Surely the merpeople would object... They wouldn't want us to wander their city unescorted."

"Yes, but we could be ignorant people who don't

know any better," Emilie said. Even her vigilant aunt had fallen for that one a time or two. It was how Emilie had gotten to see the Explorer's Society exhibit at Starling Hall in Meneport one year, by wandering off from a shopping trip in apparent innocence. Of course, it had probably just been more fodder for her aunt's belief that Emilie was actively looking for opportunities to disgrace herself in some disgusting way, but she hadn't known that at the time. "No one said specifically that we had to stay here. I mean, Lord Engal did, but really, he meant you weren't to come with him–"

Miss Marlende was already heading for the door. She stopped just inside, looking out to the gallery that overhung the grotto room. She came back to Emilie. "I don't know that we can slip out that way. There are some merpeople standing by the stairs."

Emilie stepped out to the balcony. There was no railing, just a low curb around the edge, barely a foot high. The drop wasn't far, and they could jump down into the water filling the court below, but that was bound to be noticed. And the water was thick with reeds and flowering plants, and the big blue-green pads of something similar to water lilies; it would be hard to explain how they had thought jumping off the balcony into a garden was a sensible thing to do.

But the wall of the palace had heavy carving; wide ridges of it, curved out like a narrow steep stairway. It led down the wall to a little platform even with the surface of the water.

Emilie braced a hand on the wall to steady herself and

leaned out. She thought it was a stairway, but meant for people who normally went barefoot, with no large clunky shoes or boots. The platform below it had bigger stairs leading down into the water, but it also led to a colonnaded walkway, stretching along the side of the building. "If we go down this way, we can get to that walkway. It has to go somewhere."

Miss Marlende stepped past Emilie, craning her neck to see down. She said, "Yes, that waterfall inside the audience room was against this wall, so there aren't any windows down there where they could see us." She gripped a piece of the carving, and carefully stepped out onto the first narrow step.

Emilie followed her carefully, one hand on the gritty stone wall to steady herself. She reached the platform, which was a colonnade running along the side of the building. Miss Marlende led the way down it. The paving was set with shells, and vines growing up out of the water twined around the columns, and small brilliantly-colored fish darted among the floating pads.

They came to the corner of the court, and Emilie was relieved to see an arch leading through a small passageway, with a smooth stone stairway. They climbed up to a roof terrace, the upper galleries of the palace looking down on it. The terrace faced toward the city, with a beautiful view of the bridges, tiled rooftops, and towers surrounding a big open plaza. But the terrace wasn't unoccupied. There was a big square pool in the center, with several merwomen seated in it talking. They had seen Emilie and Miss Marlende and were staring curiously.

"Uh oh," Emilie said under her breath. She knew they would be spotted, but she didn't think they would be spotted so soon. Someone was bound to ask about them and carry the word back to the audience room. "Sorry," she told Miss Marlende. "I thought it would work better than this."

"It's all right," Miss Marlende told her. She walked to the edge of the terrace, where it looked out over the city. Emilie followed her, standing at the low balustrade. The plaza below was filled with water, but there was a blue and green mosaic set into it, and merpeople swimming past. Miss Marlende added, "It was a long shot, at best."

The sun sparkled off the clear water and the breeze was cool and fresh. Merpeople moved along the bridge at the far side of the plaza, and small boats plied the waters of the canals beyond. "I'm glad we did it, anyway," Emilie said. She wouldn't have missed this view for anything.

Miss Marlende turned back to face the palace, muttering, "This place is larger than I thought. They could have the airship anywhere, even outside the city. If they have it at all. What we need is a small portable aether-navigator."

"Do those exist?" Emilie asked. All the aether-navigators she had read about were fairly large and cumbersome.

"Unfortunately not." Miss Marlende turned and started for the far side of the terrace. "Let's try to see as much as we can before we're stopped."

They made it almost to the steps leading up to a short

bridge, before Yesa came hurrying out of the lower gallery. Obviously startled to see them, she fumbled for the shell around her neck to ask, "What are you doing here?"

Miss Marlende smiled as if she had been hoping to see Yesa all along. "We wanted to see more of your beautiful city. I hope that's all right."

Yesa hesitated, taken aback. Emilie kept the smile on her face, imitating Miss Marlende, but she felt all the weight of her presumption. Being rude to possibly innocent strangers was much worse than being rude to relatives. Yesa said, "Oh, I see. I will come with you."

"We would be honored," Miss Marlende said. As Yesa turned to lead the way, Miss Marlende gave Emilie a frustrated look. Emilie agreed. Yesa was hardly likely to lead them on a tour of the city's secrets. And they had to hope that whoever had alerted Yesa to their excursion hadn't passed word along to the Queen and Lord Engal.

Yesa looked out over the terrace thoughtfully, deciding where to take them. Then she turned toward the steps, leading them up toward the bridge. Emilie felt depressed; if Yesa was willing to take them there, then there couldn't be anything that shocking to see.

The bridge led them over more courts filled with flowers, to a gallery that provided another view of the city. Miss Marlende let Yesa give them the tourist's tour for a time, making polite interested comments as Yesa pointed out views, public buildings, the major waterways. Emilie didn't have to pretend to polite interest; everything was new, strange, and fascinating.

Then, as they were walking over a bridge, Miss Marlende said thoughtfully, "The Queen told us about the problems with the nomads. How long has that been going on?"

"As long as I can remember," Yesa said. "We are told that they were from one of the outer kingdoms, to the darkward side of the Empire. That when the old wars started and the Empire fell, the central Sealands lost touch with many of the far flung territories. When embassies were sent many years later, they found only empty cities, abandoned."

Miss Marlende said, "We saw one of those, to the... antidarkward, where we entered this world."

Yesa nodded. "Just so. We think the nomads are the survivors of those cities, forced to leave to find better fishing grounds."

"Did they find them?" Emilie asked, shading her eyes to look out over the view. There was a plaza just visible that seemed to be a market, with all the goods displayed in the vendors' boats.

"Yes. It was only fishing grounds around the cities that had begun to fail, which is one of the things that caused the wars. There were plenty of others among the archipelagos, and islands to farm."

"So why do they steal, then?" Emilie turned back to Yesa. "If they like moving around, they should have more food than they know what to do with."

"I don't know," Yesa said. It was hard to tell through the translation, but she sounded a little troubled. "It is one of the frightening things about them, that we don't know why they do such things."

Miss Marlende was frowning in thought. "Have you ever known anyone who was kidnapped – stolen – by them? Or seen a farm or a fishing area that was raided?"

"I've seen places that were raided, within the past season. It has been getting worse. I don't know anyone who was stolen…" Yesa made a little throwing away gesture, which Emilie thought might be something to avert bad luck, like knocking on wood. "But I have seen the empty settlements in the darkward shallows and the archipelago." She looked at Miss Marlende, her delicate brows arched. "Did you doubt that the stories about the nomads were true?"

"I'm sorry, but yes," Miss Marlende admitted. "We're strangers here, and we know nothing about this situation."

"I understand. I will say: I do not like this plan of going to fight the nomads." Yesa turned back, heading out of the bright sunlight into the shaded gallery behind them. "I will take you back through this part of the palace."

They passed inside, into a wide passage, and Emilie blinked, temporarily blinded by the transition from sunlight to interior shadow. Yesa turned left abruptly, through a small grotto room with an elaborate stone waterfall, surrounded by deep-blue flowering plants. Emilie stopped, waiting for her eyes to adjust, wanting a better look at it.

Miss Marlende and Yesa passed into the next room.

Suddenly Miss Marlende shouted a warning. Startled, Emilie stared. There were three men in the next room, human men, two Northern Menaen and one Southern. For an instant she tried to recognize them as crew members from the *Sovereign*. Then she saw the blue uniforms, that these men were rougher, unshaven. Like the men who had attacked the *Sovereign* when it was docked at Meneport. Lord Ivers' men. Emilie moved forward, her first impulse to help Miss Marlende. But one of the men grabbed Miss Marlende's arm and yanked her out of sight, and the other two started forward. Get help, Emilie thought wildly, and whirled around and bolted.

Right into the two men coming out of the passage behind her. She bounced off one's chest and he grabbed her arms. Emilie struggled furiously, kicked him, bit at his hands, but the other one forced a sack over her head. Then the first one flipped her upside down, trapping her arms in the sack and making her head swim.

Distantly, muffled by the heavy coarse material, she heard Yesa say, "I don't like the plan. But I have no choice but to participate."

SEVEN

Trapped in the sack, Emilie fought in a panic, struggling furiously, until her lungs ached from lack of air. She sagged limply and tried to breathe through the rough material.

"She's out," one of them said, his voice muffled by the blood pounding in her ears, and the other grunted an acknowledgment.

They thought she had fainted. That... isn't a bad idea, Emilie thought. She would rather like to faint and not experience this, but as a long term solution it was impractical at best. Solution, think of a solution. They hadn't strangled her or drowned her immediately, and they seemed to be taking her somewhere in a very purposeful way. She could try to question them about where they were going, or keep pretending to be unconscious. The pretend-unconsciousness seemed to offer the best chance of escape; if they put her down to rest, she might be able to wriggle away before they noticed. She admitted that that was probably not likely, but at least it gave her something to think about besides being strangled or drowned or shot.

They carried Emilie for some distance, hauling her like a sack of potatoes. She concentrated on breathing and trying to listen for any indication of where they were going. She heard water lapping and the occasional distant voices of merpeople. Sometimes the men spoke to each other: gruff instructions to turn right or left or go that way; it didn't tell her anything except that there were at least two of them. And she couldn't hear any hint that Miss Marlende was anywhere nearby. Though I bet they meant to capture her all along, Emilie realized suddenly. That's why Yesa came back and asked for us to come with the others to speak to the Queen. Someone had perhaps passed along a description of Miss Marlende, but what was obvious to another Menaen wasn't obvious to Yesa, and she had asked for both of them as the only two women in view.

Sometimes they walked outside and sometimes through buildings; she could tell by the light working its way through the sackcloth and the feel of the sun on her legs. It seemed to take a long time, but the sack was hot and her arms ached from where the men had grabbed her, and she suspected discomfort was making the trip seem much longer.

Finally they went into a cool shadow that meant they were inside a building, and started to go upstairs, up a lot of stairs. Emilie tensed, her heart pounding again, knowing they must be nearly at their destination. Whatever that was. Maybe she would find herself facing

Lord Ivers himself. An evil nobleman, she thought. It was just like something out of one of her favorite adventure novels. Only very real, very uncomfortable, and very frightening.

The men reached a landing and started down a corridor. Ahead she heard keys rattle and what sounded like a heavy metal door creak open. There was some shuffling around, a gruff voice said, "Don't move, or I'll blow your head off."

Emilie caught her breath, wondering if he was talking to her. Then she was dumped on a cool stone floor. She lay like an unstrung puppet, keeping her breathing even, listening to footsteps walk away, and the metal door shutting. They hadn't deposited a second person, so Miss Marlende wasn't with her. She waited a moment, and then was glad she had; there was something else alive in the room. She could hear breathing, a scrape against the floor as something moved.

"You can get up now, I know you're awake. Though don't misunderstand me; it's very convincing."

The voice had a thick accent Emilie thought she recognized. She dragged the sack off her head, taking a deep breath of the cool damp air. She was in a small bare stone room, light coming in from a little round window high in the wall. The only furnishing was a couple of wooden buckets, and a blanket. The door was made out of silver metal, showing streaks of rust in the damp. She sat up, twisting around to stare at the other person.

He – she – sat back in the corner, watching Emilie with a quizzical smile. It was a Cirathi.

Her face was fuller than Kenar's, though it was coated with the same tiny black scales instead of soft skin. Her dark eyes were wide-set under brows of feathery fur, her lips full. Her dark hair was braided with strings of beads, hanging down over the folds of reptilian skin at the back of her neck. She wore dark leather trousers tucked into low boots, armbands and bracelets and rings of gold metal, and a stretchy blue camisole that made it easy to see she was female. Emilie didn't know whether to be shocked or admiring; on her the skimpy clothing was somehow more obvious than on the merpeople, maybe because the Cirathi seemed so much closer to human. "Who are you?" Emilie demanded.

She smiled. "I asked you first."

"You did not," Emilie pointed out. "But I think I know who you are. Are you from the ship *Lathi*?"

"Yes." She cocked her head, still smiling, but with a trace of skepticism. "But you would know that."

"If I was one of Lord Ivers' crew?" Emilie saw the difficulty: the woman thought she was a spy. "But does Lord Ivers know Kenar, and how he and Jerom went into the aether-current to bring help for Dr Marlende's airship?" Of course, if the Cirathi woman was a spy, Emilie was giving the game away, but she thought that was so unlikely as to be worth the risk.

The woman eyed her sharply, all the teasing forgotten. "You know of Kenar?"

"Yes. Do you know Rani? She's his... friend." Emilie wasn't quite sure what to call their relationship and didn't want to make a hideous social gaffe.

"I am Rani." She sat bolt upright, new delighted energy in her face, her voice. "Kenar brought you here? He's alive?"

"Yes, he is! He's here in the city, with Lord Engal, who brought us here in his ship, with Miss Marlende, Dr Marlende's daughter. But then they caught us – Lord Ivers' men, Miss Marlende and I – so I don't know if the others are still free or not." It sounded very confusing put that way, but the Cirathi woman seemed to be following it. "I'm Emilie."

"I am very happy to see you, Emilie." Rani pushed to her feet, reaching to give Emilie a hand. Emilie took it, finding the blunt claws and the calloused palm of Rani's hand a strange contrast with the softness of the fur on her knuckles. Rani pulled Emilie to her feet, so energetically that Emilie bounced. "I haven't been able to reach that window by myself, but if you stand on my shoulders I think you might."

"Yes, I think so," Emilie said, and sat down to quickly take off her boots and stockings. Facing the wall with the window, Rani crouched down and Emilie clambered onto her shoulders, being familiar with this process from rampaging around the village with the neighboring children.

Rani straightened up slowly, and Emilie held her clawed hands to help her balance as she put first one foot, and then the other, on Rani's strong shoulders. Emilie pushed herself upright, let go of Rani's hands to lean against the wall and guide herself the rest of the way up. They did it as smoothly as a pair of acrobats at a fete, and Emilie was rather proud of them. She gripped the smooth edge of the window to steady herself, though there wasn't much purchase. By stretching and craning her neck, she could just see out.

The view was of a huge open court surrounded by sizable buildings. Floating in it was the curve of a large dull gray-white object, almost filling the big space. There was some sort of netting over it, perhaps to hold it down... "It's an airship!" Emilie said, startled. "Is it Dr Marlende's?"

"No, that one isn't here. At least I hope not. That belongs to our meddlesome Lord Ivers." Rani lifted her a little higher. "Can you see anything else?"

"No, it's a bad angle." Emilie peered down at her. She thought Rani was quite strong, as strong as a real acrobat. "Can I stand on your hands?"

Emilie almost fell once, but after a moment they managed it, and Rani was able to lift her so Emilie's head was level with the top of the window.

Now she could see the rest of the airship, and more of the court. They were about four stories up. The balloon wasn't round, as she had been half-expecting, but long and bullet-shaped, coming to nearly a point in the front, stretched over a rigid framework. Below the huge swell of it and running nearly half the length, there was a long cabin with curving wooden walls and big round windows. It looked large enough to have at least two decks, which surprised Emilie. She had thought it would be smaller, more like the hot air balloons that sometimes came to holiday fairs. The buildings lining the court had the open galleries that were usual for the city, but she didn't see any sign of life on them. And the walls and pillars looked dingy compared to the buildings around the palace, as if these structures weren't much occupied or cared for. She said, "These buildings look empty. I wonder how many merpeople know Lord Ivers is here. Is Dr Marlende's airship that large?"

A little breathless, Rani said, "Less sight-seeing, more cogent information."

"Sorry!" Emilie reached through the window and grabbed the outer edge, chinning herself on it. Now she could see the platform dock just below the airship's cabin. The airship itself was floating over the water filling the court, but it was tethered to the stone pillars of the lowest level with thick cables. A gangplank had been stretched over the water, between the open cabin hatch and the dock. She saw three men dressed in dark blue uniforms carrying supplies aboard, small metal casks, boxes. "They're loading it. They might be getting ready to leave. I don't see anyone who might be Lord Ivers."

"Oof, all right, come down." Rani lowered her part way, until Emilie could jump down.

They faced each other. "What happened?" Emilie asked. "We found the island where you were supposed to be, and your ship."

"These people, the same sort of sea people who live in this city, arrived one night, slipped past our watchmen, and captured us. Then they threatened us, and forced Marlende and his men to surrender." Rani made an elegant gesture. "It was not our finest moment as a crew of intrepid explorers."

"Were these the nomads? The Queen of the merpeople told us you and Dr Marlende's crew had been captured by nomads," Emilie said, and had a moment to wonder at what an odd turn her life had taken that it made sense for her to say something like that.

"Yes, they took the airship, and accused Marlende of being in league with this Queen to destroy them. He was trying to persuade them otherwise, but without much luck. We still hoped help would come to the island, so on the third night of our journey, the others contrived a distraction, and I slipped over the side of the nomads' ship. Then I returned to the island, hoping Kenar and Jerom would show up soon."

Emilie nodded. "How did you get back? Did you steal a boat?"

Rani said, "I swam, from island to island." Emilie stared, and Rani added, "I didn't say it was easy." She continued, "But I had only been there a day or so, when another airship arrived."

Emilie suddenly saw what had happened in disheartening detail. "Oh. Lord Ivers. But you thought it was us."

"Yes, another of those not-finest-moments," Rani said, her voice dry. "Marlende had not made clear that he had enemies who would follow him here."

"I don't think he knew. Miss Marlende knew he had

rivals, but I think it was a surprise to everyone just how…" Emilie waved her hands. "…Big a rivalry it was. Lord Ivers' men boarded our ship and shot at us while we were leaving the port, but I don't think Lord Engal knew that Lord Ivers had already come down here."

"I see." Frustrated, Rani turned to pace the cell, like a big cat in a cage. She tugged on the door handle, apparently just to see if their captors had forgotten to lock it, but it didn't budge. "Now which one is Lord Engal?"

"He's the one Miss Marlende asked to come down here to help her father. Well, not asked, but bribed him with her father's work. He's here with his ship, but he and the others don't know Lord Ivers is here too. The Queen told them the nomads had captured you, but she didn't say anything about the rest. Do you know what Lord Ivers is planning?"

"He has not been forthcoming on that point," Rani said with considerable irony. "But I think it is the Queen who has the plan. The nomads were convinced she meant to destroy them with the help of some foreign weapon."

"Lord Ivers' airship," Emilie said, feeling a sinking sensation. But Lord Ivers shouldn't want to get into a war, particularly a war in the Hollow World. He was an explorer, a scientist like Lord Engal, if more violent and ruthless. If he helped the Queen fight the nomads, he would just waste time… Oh, that has to be it, she realised. "It was a trade!"

Rani stopped, startled. "What was a trade?"

"Lord Ivers wants to get back home before Dr Marlende and Lord Engal, so he can take the credit for the discovery. He must have got mixed up with the Queen somehow, and promised her he would help her fight the nomads. Somehow the nomads learned about it, maybe they have spies in the city, and that's why they went after Dr Marlende's airship. But Lord Ivers doesn't want to keep his promise, so he's gotten the Queen to get Lord Engal to take his place." Emilie turned to look up at the window, frowning. "I bet they are leaving. They're getting ready to go back up the aether-current to home."

Rani stared, appalled. "That is what this is all about? Who claims credit?"

"Yes." Emilie admitted, "It's stupid."

"That is one word for it." Rani shook her head, her beaded braids flying. "I don't want my crew mixed up in a war. No good can come of it."

She was right about that. "Lord Engal will know something is wrong. He'll want to know what happened to Miss Marlende and me."

"The Queen can hold you hostage, force him to do as she says." Rani looked down at Emilie, her brow furrowed in consternation. "Would he do that?"

"I think he might." Emilie looked up at the round window again. It looked small from this angle, but when she had pulled herself up into it, it had been an inch or so wider than her shoulders. "I can climb out that window."

Rani looked from Emilie to the window. "And then what, fly?"

"I can climb down. Then I could warn Lord Engal." Emilie felt the need to swallow in a suddenly very dry throat. This was much higher than the balcony over the water garden. But she had to be the one to do it. Rani, who was at least as big and strong as Kenar, would never fit through the narrow space, let alone the fact that Emilie could never lift her high enough to reach it. "I saw on the opposite wall, there's an open gallery on the level just below this one. If this side matches it–"

"That's a lot to place on an 'if.'" Rani eyed her worriedly. "Are you sure?"

"Yes." Emilie made her voice firm. Rani lifted a skeptical brow and Emilie amended, "Mostly. We've got to try something."

"That we do." Rani looked at the window and winced. "But I hate to throw you out a window on such short acquaintance." She crouched down for Emilie to climb on her back again.

It wasn't any easier than it looked. Once Emilie got up to the window, she made sure there was still no sign of anyone on the galleries opposite, and that the men below, loading supplies onto the airship, didn't seem inclined to look up. Then she pulled herself halfway through the little opening, with Rani hanging onto her ankles to keep her from falling. That way, Emilie was able to lean out and look straight down the wall.

Dangling, the cool breeze in her hair, she could see the low balustrade of a gallery on the floor just below this one. The wall was rough and ridged, but instead of water below, there was a stone platform with a pretty shell pattern, extending out from the lowest level. So if Emilie fell, there would be no chance of survival. Or not pleasant survival, anyway. "All right, I think I can do this," Emilie muttered.

"Be certain," Rani said from below.

"I'm certain." Emilie gritted her teeth. I am certain, she told herself. I can do this. She edged around until she was braced across the windowsill on her back. Gripping the ridge just above the opening, she wriggled forward out over empty space.

The moment when Rani had to let go of her ankles was not an easy one, and Emilie had to take a deep breath. She hadn't known how reassuring the feeling of having someone very strong hold onto you was until it had suddenly gone. Rani whispered, "Careful, little one. Go straight to your Lord Engal."

"I will." Emilie eased one leg out, straddling the window and finding purchase on the ridge below it, then did the same with the other leg. Still gripping the window opening, she took one glance down to make sure Lord Ivers' men hadn't looked up. It made her dizzy, and she decided that all the dramatic adventure stories she had read were right: it was better not to look down.

Feeling for hand and toe-holds in the ridges, she started to climb down. It went well enough, until her right foot reached for a toe-hold in empty space. Her stomach lurched, her head swam, and she nearly lost her grip. Deep breaths, deep breaths, Emilie chanted to herself, fighting down the fear. She lifted her foot again, found purchase, and started to edge sideways. After about a foot, she gingerly tried again. Still nothing. Keep going, she thought.

On the fourth try she found purchase, the rough surface of a column. A little fumbling and her foot found a decorative finial on it. Carefully, she eased herself down, one ridge at a time.

Finally she could wrap her legs around the column and edge down it, until she could swing over onto the gallery floor. As soon as her feet touched the firm stone surface, her legs gave out and she sank down into a huddle. Shaking in relief, she realized: If I'd known it was going to be that hard, I'd never have tried. Her hands and feet were scraped, her fingers sore, her arms trembling from the effort. So it was a good thing I didn't know, she thought. She couldn't believe she had actually done it. The idea of getting caught after that effort was horrific.

If you can do that, a voice in her head whispered, *you can do anything*. Anything she had to do to get herself and Rani and Miss Marlende out of here. Huddled trembling on the stone, she suddenly felt a hundred times stronger.

Now get on with it, Emilie told herself, and eased forward to take a careful peek between the balusters. The men had stopped loading the airship, and were standing on the platform, talking to a man dressed in ordinary clothes rather than a uniform. He was in his shirtsleeves, no coat. Lord Ivers, maybe, or someone else of high rank in the crew. He was tall and slim, with the blond hair and light skin of someone of Northern Menaen descent. That would be a good clue, if she had ever heard a description or seen a photograph of Lord Ivers, which she hadn't. She couldn't hear what they were saying either, just snatches of words carried on the breeze.

She crawled back from the edge and stood, padding barefoot toward the nearest door, the tiles cool under her feet. It was an open arch, leading in to a big empty room with a blue and green mosaic floor. It had a lonely air of long disuse, and there was even a patch of mold on one wall. She slipped through it and two other similar empty chambers, and found an open door out to a corridor. It was empty and shadowy too, no lamps in the niches, the figures of merpeople painted on the walls faded and blotched. She couldn't hear any voices or movement. As Emilie stepped out into it, she spotted a large curving stair at the end.

She knew what she should do; she should run immediately back toward the harbor and swim out to the *Sovereign*. The problem was, she had no idea where she was or how to get to the harbor from here. She didn't know the language or have a translator shell to ask for directions, and she had no way to tell which merpeople were involved in the plot or which were innocent bystanders, so she couldn't risk approaching anyone for help. And if she did somehow make it to the *Sovereign*, the Queen could still hold Miss Marlende and Rani hostage against Lord Engal's cooperation. If he and Kenar aren't hostages now, too, to force Captain

Belden to attack the nomads, she thought.

The obvious conclusion was to rescue Miss Marlende and Rani before proceeding. Rani first, since Emilie knew where she was.

Emilie started toward the stairs. Just as she reached the stairwell, she heard voices echoing up from below, and she froze like a startled rabbit. It was Miss Marlende, and a male voice with a Menaen accent, that she didn't recognize.

Miss Marlende was saying, "I think you must be mad."

The man laughed, not sounding offended. "No more mad than your father or Engal."

Lord Ivers, Emilie thought. Funny, he didn't sound evil.

Fury in her voice, Miss Marlende said, "My father and Lord Engal aren't causing a war simply for their own gain!"

"I'm not causing this war, young lady. The Queen would still be fighting the nomads even if none of us had found our way down to this world. She's considerably more cunning and more determined than she looks, believe me." With a laugh, he added, "Those were her men who attacked the *Sovereign* during the last eclipse, not the nomads. Didn't you think the arrival of Yesa and her warship was excessively fortuitous?"

Miss Marlende said, startled, "She didn't–" After a moment, sounding more thoughtful, she said, "Of course, I see."

Emilie shook her head, but it did make sense. She

remembered what Miss Marlende had said about the size and age of the city, as a relic of a disintegrating empire, and what the rulers of such a place must be like. Miss Marlende must have remembered it too. Sounding less certain, she said, "Why is she so determined to fight the nomads, then?"

"Because they are the future," Lord Ivers said, as if he was giving a lecture. "If what she and the others have told me is true, the Sealands have been changing for generations. The weather has grown warmer, and it's affecting the water depth, the way the fish run, how the plants grow, the way the islands form. These shallow seas can no longer sustain cities this size, the way they could in the Empire's golden age. Now the fishers and gleaners and growers have to go further and further afield to bring in enough food for the rest of the population."

Lord Ivers' voice warmed with his enthusiasm for the subject, and Emilie leaned on the stone banister, listening intently. The footsteps she could hear sounded as if they were made by more than two people, so Lord Ivers must have one or more of his men with him.

"The nomads' ancestors saw the writing on the wall a long time ago, and changed their way of living and their way of governing themselves. They left the cities, broke up into smaller groups, and now travel to different fishing and farming grounds throughout the year, giving the sea and the land time to replenish itself. They've succeeded marvelously. So marvelously, the outlying farmers and fishers of this city, the greatest and possibly last outpost of the old Empire, often desert their posts to join them."

Ah, Emilie thought. The merpeople aren't being stolen away. They're deserting to the other side. No wonder the Queen was angry.

Miss Marlende must have come to the same conclusion. In a different tone, she said, "I see."

"Of course you do. There's nothing I could do to stop this," Lord Ivers concluded. "There's no place for the Queen or her nobles or their way of life in this new style of living. If the Queen was a forward thinker, she would form her people into their own tribes of nomads and send them off to look for new fishing grounds. She isn't, and she won't. She's determined to preserve her control over this dying city for the rest of her generation."

"But you're using her for your own purposes–" Miss Marlende protested loudly. Then Emilie realized her voice wasn't getting louder, it was getting closer – Lord Ivers and Miss Marlende were coming up the stairs to this floor.

Oh, hell. Emilie bolted up the stairs, trying to keep her steps quiet. She reached the upper floor, where the stairwell foyer had two arched doorways opening into corridors, one to the left and one to the right. The room Emilie and Rani had been locked into should be on the right, facing out into the court. And Emilie didn't think it would be unguarded. Mindful that Lord Ivers would be here in a moment, she stepped silently to the righthand archway and took a cautious peek.

The hall was lined with doorways, all with heavy

metal doors, and midway down it there was a man in a blue uniform, sitting on a camp stool. The door nearest him had a big padlock through the metal handles. Emilie drew back, thinking: damn, I was afraid of that. She had no idea how she was going to get Rani out of there.

Movement and voices moving up the stairs made her dart across the foyer and through the archway on the left. Fortunately, that corridor was empty, leading out to a long room of open galleries. She crouched behind a pillar, trying to make herself small, and hoped they went the other way.

She heard them reach the landing and turn down the righthand corridor. There was a scrape and shuffle as the guard got hastily to his feet and greeted Lord Ivers respectfully. Then Lord Ivers said, "Open the door, Cavin."

Uh oh, Emilie thought. She heard the jingle of keys, clicks as the man fumbled with the padlock, then the door creaking open. Rani said, "Finally. I was wondering if you had planned to settle here permanently, perhaps take up reed farming or some other useful occupation."

There was a moment of fraught silence, then Lord Ivers demanded, "Where is the girl?"

"What girl?" Rani said, sounding completely unperturbed. Emilie wondered where Rani had hidden her boots and the sack, the only evidence that she had really been in the cell.

Lord Ivers must have looked at Cavin for confirmation, because the man said, a little desperately, "Semeuls, Rail, and I put her in there, My Lord. They can vouch for it."

Rani said, complacently, "He is lying. You should hire better henchmen."

"Perhaps you're right." Lord Ivers' voice was tight with fury. "Let's go."

More footsteps. Emilie risked a peek around the pillar and caught a glimpse of Miss Marlende, Rani, Lord Ivers, and three uniformed men with rifles, two of whom must have come up the stairs with Lord Ivers and one the unfortunate Cavin.

"And where are we going?" Miss Marlende asked.

"Back to the surface." Lord Ivers' voice sounded more distant as he started down the stairs. "I've persuaded the Queen to accept Lord Engal's help instead of mine, and I have no reason now to linger."

"Ah, you will be dropping me off on the way, then?" Rani said, still sounding as calm as if she was having this conversation at a garden party, or the Cirathi equivalent.

"No, you'll be coming with me," Lord Ivers said. "You'll provide incontrovertible evidence of my achievement."

Emilie gasped in outrage. Rani's reply was drowned out by Miss Marlende's angry protests as the group continued down the stairs. I can't let them get on the airship, she thought. Emilie stood and ran to the archway, then to the top of the stairs. The group was about two floors down. She needed a weapon. She didn't even have anything to throw.

She went to the archway to the other corridor and

looked down it just to see if there was anything helpful left behind. The metal camp stool still sat beside the wall. It was better than nothing. Emilie hurriedly retrieved it, then started down the stairs, her bare feet noiseless on the smooth steps.

She reached the third floor landing, and looked over the open banister to see Lord Ivers and the others on the second, just turning down the stairs. The bottom level of the structure was an open area two floors high, with no floor, just narrow walkways level with the water and big pillars supporting the upper structure. One more stairway down and they would be out on the platform next to the airship, with the rest of Lord Ivers' men. Miss Marlende was still protesting loudly with occasional profanities, and one of the men had her arm, dragging her along. Rani's shoulders looked tense, and the other two guards watched her warily.

Emilie went to the top of the stairs, aimed at the man on Rani's right, and slung the camp stool at the back of his head. "Rani! Run!" she yelled.

The stool hit the man right between the shoulders and sent him jolting forward to tumble down the last set of stairs. It was poor Cavin, Emilie noted. Lord Ivers was knocked into the banister, and Miss Marlende shoved against the man who held her, knocking him off balance. Rani moved like lightning. She grabbed the rifle of the man on her left, slammed the barrel into his face, twisted it away and vaulted the railing to land with a splash in the water below.

Struggling with her guard, Miss Marlende yelled

frantically, "Run, Emilie, run!" and Emilie realized she really should be running. Lord Ivers turned toward her and Miss Marlende's guard tried to get his arms free to shoot at her. She turned and bolted back along the corridor, hoping there was another way down. It's a big building, she told herself, panting more from fear than exertion, surely there's more than one stair!

There wasn't, at least not off this corridor. The guards shouted behind her and a bullet rang off the stone wall. Emilie yelped and ducked into the room at the far end, praying that there would be a window. There was – a big one, which looked out over an open waterway at the far end of the building. She scrambled up onto the sill, glanced back to see a guard just behind her, and as he lunged for her she jumped.

By pure luck she missed the stone dock platform and plunged into the water. She floundered to the surface, coughing and gasping, heard someone yelling about shooting at her, and flailed away, swimming frantically.

She managed to get headed down the waterway, away from the window, but another gunshot rang out behind her. Then something grabbed her ankle and jerked her under water.

Emilie struggled wildly, until she realized whatever had a hold of her was both furry and scaly. It had to be Rani. She hoped very hard that it was Rani. They passed through a dark section of water and she thought they were going under a solid object. Right at the point where Emilie thought her lungs would burst, they surfaced abruptly.

Emilie coughed and spat out water as Rani pulled her up onto wet stone. Emilie sputtered and managed to get a full breath. "You all right?" Rani asked.

Emilie nodded weakly. They were inside a building, perhaps next door to the one the airship was docked in. The ceiling was low and arched, cracked and stained with mold. There was more floor space between the pools of water.

"I had to stuff your boots and the sack they brought you in into the slop bucket," Rani said. "Sorry. I saved these." She pulled Emilie's dripping stockings out of the front of her shirt.

"That's all right." Emilie took the stockings, though she wasn't sure what good they would do her at the moment. "I don't think Miss Marlende got away." She coughed again.

"No, but she was very helpful, your friend. I would not have gotten away without her. And you," Rani added, giving Emilie a friendly nudge to the shoulder that almost pushed her over. "You are one brave little person."

"Thank you." Emilie was too worried to be flustered by the compliment. "We have to rescue Miss Marlende."

"That we do." Rani got to her feet, giving Emilie a hand up. "This way."

They made their way through the long building. It was quiet except for the water lapping in the pools, and Emilie saw cracks in the pillars and more splotches of mold; it had clearly been abandoned for some time. She wondered how many empty structures there were in this section of the city. Probably many, since the Queen had chosen this area to dock Lord Ivers' airship. This city was not as prosperous as it had looked at first, more evidence that what Lord Ivers had said was the truth.

They came to a doorway on the far end, opening out to a narrow canal, with steps and platforms for merpeople to enter the water. It was lined with three- and four-story buildings, with large windows and balcony platforms. There was no sign of life or movement. Rani turned back toward the airship building, and Emilie kept close to the wall. Being shot at was not an experience she wanted to repeat. We need to steal a gun, she thought. The rifle Rani had jerked out of the guard's hands had fallen into the water, and Emilie wondered if they could retrieve it, if it would still work. She rather thought it wouldn't.

They reached a doorway leading into the airship building, and Rani stopped abruptly, holding up a hand. Emilie froze, and realized she could hear a low metallic buzz. "You hear that?" Rani whispered, then she said something in Cirathi that was probably a very bad word, adding: "The engine!"

Rani ducked through the doorway and Emilie hurried after her. They went through a wide shadowy passage with a shallow stream of water running down the center, toward an archway that opened into daylight. That must be the courtyard, she thought. Emilie's heart was pounding. If they had already started the airship's engine...

Rani stopped at the edge of the archway, taking a cautious peek through it. She cursed again and said, "We are too late, Emilie."

Emilie looked, in time to see the cabin of the airship clearing the top floor of the building, the enormous balloon throwing a huge shadow over the water court. *Damn it, no!* Desperate for it not to be true, she said, "Maybe they left her behind."

Rani ruffled Emilie's hair sympathetically, but said, "We'll search."

Cautiously, they looked through the lower floor, then worked their way back up, all the way to the cell level. There was no sign of Miss Marlende, but they could see the place had been occupied. In one room they found fruit rinds and crumbs, and bits of food trash that had clearly come from Menea: a couple of brown bottles that had probably held beer, and a wrapper for a cracker packet. There were some bits of crumpled paper and a blue uniform cap someone had dropped.

Emilie rescued her boots from the slop bucket in their cell, and admitted bleakly, "They didn't leave her behind."

Rani turned back toward the stairs, asking, "Do you know what they will do with her?"

"I don't know." Emilie hadn't thought Lord Ivers had seemed like the type to murder people, until his men started shooting at her. "If he just takes her back to the surface, to Menea... If he doesn't hurt her, when Lord Engal gets back he can tell the magistrates what happened. They'll arrest Lord Ivers if he doesn't let her go." Lord Engal must have just as much influence as Lord Ivers, and the magistrates would have to believe him and take action. If Lord Engal can get back to Menea, she thought. If we can all get back. "What do we do now? Try to get to the harbor and find Lord Engal and the others?" If he wasn't a hostage too.

"Yes, I think it must be your Lord Engal, for now," Rani said, thinking it over. "If he has no solutions, we'll have to think of one for ourselves. And I wish to retrieve Kenar as soon as possible." She paused on the landing to confide to Emilie, "Men are not good left on their own, you know. They pine."

Emilie had never heard that before and the thought kept her occupied all the way down the stairs.

Getting to the harbor was just as difficult as Emilie had suspected it might be, even with Rani's help.

Rani knew what direction they had to go in, but when they came to the edge of the empty area, there were too many merpeople between them and the waters of the harbor. Merpeople swimming in the waterways, towing little rafts piled with bundled goods, merpeople walking along the bridges and the galleries. The light was starting to get that edged quality that meant the Dark Wanderer was bringing the night eclipse, and Emilie thought this might be the rush to get home before dark, or to get the last things done for the end of the working day.

She was glad she had decided to try to rescue Rani and Miss Marlende, and hadn't fled alone toward the harbor for help; not only would Lord Ivers have been able to leave with both of them in his airship, but Emilie would have become hopelessly lost and recaptured by the merpeople.

Rani left Emilie to hide in an enclosed passage in the last empty building, and made several forays to check on different possible routes. Emilie sat on the cool smooth floor, washed her boots off in a little pool, and worried. Her stomach was also starting to growl; it had been a long time since breakfast. She had also had time to feel her bruises from being manhandled into the sack; her arms looked like she had put them into a vice.

Rani returned finally, surfacing in the pool suddenly and giving Emilie a start. "It's not good news," Rani reported, and slung herself out of the water to sit on the platform. "The harbor area must be the most crowded part of the city. I think we must wait until dark before we try to make it to the docks."

"That's not long, though, is it?" Emilie asked, trying not to sound as weary and anxious as she actually was. "Maybe another hour?"

"Not long." Rani absently wrung out her long braids. "Your Lord Engal's ship would not travel at night, would it?"

"Um, yes. It has spotlights. We've been traveling at night all along, because we wanted to find Dr Marlende and you all as quickly as possible." Emilie bit her lip. "You think the Queen might have made them leave already?"

"Ah." Rani frowned, preoccupied, but she said reassuringly, "We'll see. Perhaps we'll be lucky."

Emilie thought Rani was probably an optimist.

About an hour later, the complete darkness of the eclipse settled in, and they crept out of hiding. Lamps, burning oil that smelled vaguely fishy, had been lit along some of the waterways and bridges, but most of the byways were dark. Rani moved silently over the walkways, giving wide berth to the lighted areas, leading them toward the docks.

Emilie was relieved to be moving. The wait for darkness had worn on her nerves, though at least the anxiety had kept her awake. It had been a long time since her last good night's sleep, as well as a long time since breakfast. At one point Rani had demanded, "What is that noise? Is that you?"

"It's my stomach," Emilie had replied defensively. She had noticed that Rani didn't speak Menaen as readily as Kenar; she thought that was because Kenar had been with Miss Marlende, probably talking himself hoarse to help her convince Lord Engal of what had to be done to come to Dr Marlende's rescue, while Rani had been locked up with not much of anyone to speak with. "Doesn't your stomach grumble when you're hungry?"

"Yes, but not that loud. No one's stomach is that loud."

Now Emilie was almost willing to believe she was right, and hoped her stomach didn't alert any merpeople swimming through the dark water below them. She had kept her boots off in case they had to swim, tying them together and looping them around her neck, and the smooth stone was cool underfoot.

They came down a narrow walkway above a deep canal, and out onto the docks, under the shelter of the lower level of the big gallery. It was quiet except for the breeze on the water, and this part of the gallery smelled of the bundles of wet reeds stacked and piled everywhere. There were more lamps lit here, illuminating the piers that ran out into the water. Rani drew Emilie forward, using the reed bundles as cover, to where they could look out over the ships.

Emilie's heart sank immediately, but she still squinted, studying the piers, the place she was sure the *Sovereign* had been anchored. But the *Sovereign* would have been the most obvious thing in the crowded harbor, with all its running lights lit. "Not there?" Rani asked quietly.

Emilie shook her head, unexpectedly and stupidly feeling tears well up. They had known this was a possibility. She swallowed hard and managed to say, "No, it's gone."

"Hmm. Then we go with the other plan. Wait here." Rani ghosted away down the gallery before Emilie could say, "What other plan?"

Emilie crouched on the cool stone, waiting. She heard merpeople talking somewhere nearby and flinched, but after a moment it was obvious they were on the gallery a level or two above, and walking away. She realized she was trying not to bite her nails, recalled that her aunt was not here to remonstrate with her about it, and that she could bite them as much as she liked. It was a relief to her abused nerves.

Rani finally returned with a net bag slung over her shoulder. "This way," she whispered, and they went the other way down the gallery, away from the lighted piers. Emilie wanted to ask where they were going, but was afraid their voices might carry over the water. If one of the merpeople in the gallery heard a conversation of more than a few words, they might realize they were hearing a strange language and give the alarm.

They left the shelter of the gallery and were heading toward the far side of the harbor. It was so dark, Emilie couldn't make out much, but when she tripped over a coil of rope and stumbled on a ramp, she realized they were passing the taller piers where the big barges had been docked. *Had been docked.* Now that she looked, she could see the empty water glinting faintly between the dark shapes of the piers. She tapped Rani on the back, and whispered as softly as possible, "The barges are gone."

Rani stopped, leaned back to cup her hand around Emilie's ear and say softly, "They've gone with your ship, after the nomads."

Oh, no, Emilie thought. They must have left when the *Sovereign* was forced to go, sometime this afternoon. When Rani started to pull away, she caught her arm and whispered, "Where are we going?"

"After them," Rani replied.

Oh. Startled, Emilie followed Rani through the dark.
Good, she thought.

EIGHT

Past the big barge piers, Rani turned and stepped down onto a platform at the water level. From the dim glow of the lights on the gallery, Emilie could just make out the shapes of small boats, no bigger than the rowboats that plied the village pond at home, tied up along it. Rani selected one, motioned for Emilie to climb in, and began to untie it.

Emilie managed to clamber in and sit down on the narrow seat running down the center without flipping the boat over, though it was a near thing. The hull was made of something as light as straw; it must be dried reeds. Rani cast off, and stepped in to push away from the pier. She took a seat in the back, dumping her net bag in the bottom of the boat. Something poked Emilie in the back, and she twisted around to take the paddle Rani was handing her.

They paddled as quietly as possible, Rani guiding them out of the harbor, away from the city. The dark was so complete they had to navigate by brushing against the stands of reeds that bordered the outlying islands. After a time Emilie made out isolated lights that must be burning in the windows of the occasional outlying settlements; she hoped that Rani knew where they were going, because Emilie was completely lost.

Finally, when the lights of the city were a good distance behind them, Rani said, "We must stop for a moment."

Relieved, Emilie pulled her paddle in, and stretched her neck and back. She turned around, listening to Rani rummage in the net bag. Then Rani handed her a heavy soft object. It felt like a big peach. Emilie said hopefully, "Fruit?"

"Yes. You can eat the peel." She crunched into one herself, and Emilie hastily followed suit. It was sweet, with the texture of an apple, but the inside was thicker and more filling. She hoped the sack was full to bursting.

Rani rummaged in the bag again, and Emilie heard a faint clank of metal. Then a small flame sparked and she saw Rani was lighting a lamp with a big matchstick. Or it looked like a matchstick, except that it sparked blue and didn't smell of sulfur. "There, that will make our journey a little easier." She handed Emilie the lamp.

Emilie took it and stretched forward to hang it on the hook above the bow. Swallowing the last bite of fruit, she asked, "How do we know where the nomads are?" She remembered that Rani had escaped before the nomads had reached their final destination.

"This." Rani pulled off one of her necklaces, and handed it to Emilie. She couldn't see detail in the dark, but it felt like a piece of soft round stone. Rani said, "Spit on it and rub your thumb over it."

Emilie followed instructions. After a moment, light gleamed inside the stone, forming an arrow. It swung around like a compass, pointing toward Emilie's right. She looked up, smiling, and handed it back. "A magic compass?"

Rani looped it around her neck again. "Dr Marlende made it, and gave it to me in case our ships became separated. It shows the way to find him, wherever he is." She leaned over to feel along the side of the boat, where a long reed wrapped in cloth was clipped to the hull. She lifted it up, and Emilie realized it was a sail. "The Queen's ships will have to search around for the nomads, even if her spies know roughly where they have taken our friends. With the compass, we can beat them there." She added more quietly, "I hope."

Emilie shifted around on the seat to help her hold the pole steady while Rani got it fixed into the base mounted to the bottom of the boat. She had almost forgotten that Dr Marlende was a sorcerer, like Dr Barshion. Except better, apparently. "I wish he'd given one to Kenar. At least then we could have dealt with the nomads and skipped the Queen."

Rani tossed Emilie another piece of fruit. "He didn't have to. Jerom had the magic of his own, to find us." She hesitated. "Jerom is not with your ship?"

Emilie hesitated. She hadn't told Rani that part yet. "No, he died, I'm sorry. It was more dangerous than they thought it would be. But Kenar got through it all right."

"I see." Rani sounded pensive. She was silent for a time, finishing her second piece of fruit and tossing the rind into the water. She said finally, "I think your people are a little more delicate than us. And perhaps the ease of their journey down here made Marlende and Jerom incautious."

Emilie thought that was very likely. "Our journey was easy up to the point where the engine stopped working and we would have been crushed to death if we hadn't been so close to the Hollow World already."

Rani snorted with wry amusement. "That sounds typical. Now..." She stretched out the light fabric of the sail, fixing it to the lower reed. "If we can get this to work the way it's supposed to, we can make better time."

With Emilie to hold things and help tie the light seaweed-braided ropes, Rani got the sail rigged. It caught the breeze and they began to move, skimming lightly over the water.

They sailed through the night, sometimes having to stop and use the paddles to get the boat through a narrow island channel, or through stands of tall reeds. Emilie knew she was lucky the boat was light and easy to paddle, and that there seemed to be no strong current to fight. The wind was light but steady, full of the scent of the sea, and the jasmine-like fragrance of the reeds. When Emilie's stomach started to growl again, Rani passed out more food from her bag, including some pieces of dried fish that tasted salty-sweet. It wasn't entirely pleasant, but it gave Emilie the energy to carry on.

For a while, at least. They had been passing through an empty stretch of water for some time, with no islands or obstructions that required them to use the paddles. Emilie caught herself slumping forward. The second time, her forehead banged her knees before she woke up. Behind her, Rani said, "Sleep, before you fall out of the boat."

Groggy, Emilie rubbed her eyes. "What about you?"

Rani chuckled. "After too many days as Lord Ivers' prisoner, with nothing to do but sit or sleep, I could go on forever."

Emilie was sure even Rani couldn't go on forever, but she appreciated the chance to sleep. She shifted around in the bow, easing down to the bottom of the boat, and put her head down on the seat. She was asleep instantly.

It took them a day and a night of sailing, just Emilie and Rani, out on the sea. When daylight returned, they stopped at a small island with a spring, so Rani could refill the clay water jug in the bottom of the boat. Rani gave Emilie a small knife she had managed to find along the dock, and Emilie used it to cut some dried reeds. Once they were underway again, she wove sunhats for them both.

The hats made the glare off the water bearable, though at least the wind was cool and the sun down here in the Hollow World didn't seem as bright or as hot as the one above the surface. Emilie would never have thought that weaving sunhats, a skill gained during long summer afternoons at her aunt's sedate garden parties, would come in this handy.

They passed islands with strange spiny trees, which rustled with all sorts of animal life, and long-legged bright blue water birds standing amid the reeds in the shallows. They saw crumbling towers and halls and other remnants of the old Sealands Empire. And sometimes there were waterspouts in the distance, which Rani said might be caused by some sort of large sea life.

At one point, after they had to use the paddles to guide the boat through a maze of sandbars, Rani said thoughtfully, "You know, I think this thing is even better than I thought."

Emilie twisted around to see her examining the compass. She lifted her hat to wipe the sweat off her forehead. "Why?"

"I noticed it was taking us on a route through the islands that was too quick to be luck. Then it led us on the best path through these sandbars; if I had used my own judgment, we'd have run aground and had to go all the way around the other end of the island to get here." Rani slipped the thong around her neck again. "I think it shows the way, the best turns and twists, to get to Dr Marlende, and not just the direction toward him."

It made sense. "It's the aether," Emilie said. "Aether's in everything: air, land, water. I bet that's a bit like an aether-navigator, only it's using the aether currents to find Dr Marlende."

Rani lifted her brows. "You study this stuff too?"

"No, not really. I just read about it; in the Lord

Rohiro novels."

"Now which one is Lord Rohiro?"

So Emilie told her about Lord Rohiro's adventures, which occupied the next few hours.

Emilie learned a lot about Rani's past adventures, too. They had been traveling for a long time, and had been crew together on Rani's mother's ship before Rani had grown up and acquired the *Lathi*. They had gone to some exceedingly strange places, and the stories about the sinking islands and the people who lived inside giant, dead-sea creatures would have sounded made-up, if Emilie hadn't known better.

Rani also taught Emilie how to hold the tiller and the sail to keep them on course, so they could keep going while Rani slept. Emilie would never have thought she would do something like this, sailing a small boat, let alone voyaging over an otherworldly sea, guiding it with a sorcerer's compass. Being so close to the water, dependent only on herself and Rani, mostly Rani, for safety, was very different from being aboard the *Sovereign*.

In all, she was enjoying the trip immensely, except for the fact that all their friends were in danger. Emilie knew she should feel guilty about that. But she had never done anything like this before, and the sea and sky and the islands were endlessly diverting, providing a constant distraction from their predicament.

They were both awake by the time the next eclipse passed on, and Emilie, squinting at the horizon in the gradually brightening light, was the first to say, "Land!"

"I see," Rani said thoughtfully. "I think we are there, Emilie."

Emilie hoped so. The island ahead stretched for some distance, and was higher than the others in this region. From this vantage point, it looked like the shore was lined with rocky cliffs, topped with tall dark green vegetation. If this wasn't their destination, Emilie didn't know how they were going to get their little boat around it. "How do you know?"

Rani, her hands occupied with the sail and the tiller, jerked her chin toward the starboard side. "Because I think that is one of the Queen's barges, over there. We did not beat them here, after all."

Emilie looked, staring hard, knowing by now that Rani's eyes were sharper than hers. After a moment, she made out the dim gray-blue shapes, long and low, in the water toward the far end of the island. She could barely see them, but the good thing was, she didn't think anyone aboard would be able to spot their tiny boat. She thought she saw the sun glinting off something metallic, and said, "Can you see the *Sovereign*?"

"I see something big and coppery; I think that must be it." Rani grimaced, tipping her straw hat back. "But it is surrounded by the barges, so that's one of our plans in the crap hole."

Rani's language was also a bit more earthy than Kenar's, something else Emilie liked about her. They had talked about possibly sneaking aboard the *Sovereign*, once they located it, and joining forces with Lord Engal and Kenar and the others. They could warn them about

Lord Ivers, and tell them that Miss Marlende was aboard his airship, heading toward the surface, and not a hostage to the Queen. "You don't think we could sneak aboard it?"

"No, we would have to swim underwater, amid a small fleet of people who live underwater part of the time; I think we would be as obvious as if we painted our boat red and beat a drum as we sailed right up to them."

She was probably right. "So we're going to try the island?" The other plan was to locate Dr Marlende and the Cirathi, and try to rescue them. It was a broad, vague plan, at best. "And hope the Queen hasn't attacked the nomads yet?"

"We try the island," Rani agreed, as their little boat sped toward it. "And hope."

Several hours later, they dragged their boat up onto the narrow strip of beach below the short sandy cliff. Emilie stumbled a little and had to stop and stretch. They had been stopping briefly on the low islands, sometimes to look for springs, sometimes just to answer calls of nature and stretch their legs. Last night was the longest interval they had gone without stopping. She helped Rani take down the sail and clip the poles to the side again, and they pulled the boat up behind some rocks to hide it if any Sealands' or nomads' ships patrolled past this shore. The sand was soft, and their feet and the boat kept sinking into it. Emilie fell down a few times, but they managed it.

They left their straw hats in the boat, but Rani took

the bag with their dwindling supply of food and filled a waterskin from the clay jar in the boat. She also had a knife to tuck into her sash, a long one made from bone that she had picked up along the city's dock with the rest of their supplies. It was a good weapon, though Emilie still wished they had been able to get one of the rifles.

Getting up the cliff was easier. It was about twenty-five feet high, with tall trees that had large palm leaves below crowns of red spiny clumps, and tall grassy bushes. Rani found a spot with lots of rocks and weeds, and told Emilie to climb onto her back. Then she dug her hard claw-like nails into the clumps of weed and scaled the cliff.

Emilie had brought her boots, tied together and slung over one shoulder. When they reached the top, she sat down to hastily put them on as Rani scouted around. As Emilie was tying the laces, she noticed the ground was unexpectedly hard. It was sandy, with clumps of green-yellow grass between the thick ropy tree roots. She scraped at a bare patch, and, after only a half inch or so, encountered stone. It was flat and smooth, and there was a straight groove through it, too straight to be natural.

She looked at the nearest tree, feeling the roots, and saw they had burrowed down right through the stone. Like weeds, she thought. Very big weeds. As if sand from the other islands had washed up here over the years, the seeds for the grass and trees carried with it or blown here by strong winds.

Rani returned, saying, "No one around here, at least. What are you looking at?"

Emilie pushed to her feet, dusting her hands off on her shirt. "I think we're on top of a wall, or a roof, or a plaza or something. Part of one of the old Sealands cities."

A thoughtful "Hmm," was Rani's only comment.

They made their way forward through the trees and tall bushes. There were birdcalls, the hum of insects, the rush of waves and the wind, but no sound of voices. Keeping her own voice low, Emilie said, "If the Queen's ships came straight here, they would have started fighting already, wouldn't they? Maybe they've already defeated the nomads."

"Maybe. If not, I wonder what they are waiting for." Rani was distracted, listening. "Do you hear that water?"

Emilie had heard it, but she had thought it was the sea. Now that she thought about it, the waves hadn't been that loud down on the beach itself. "A waterfall?" But she had trouble imagining a big waterfall on this island. She couldn't see any sign of rocky cliffs or hills above the trees.

With a frustrated grimace, Rani shook her head. "This place gets odder and odder."

They pushed forward for a time, and Emilie began to see more light through the trees ahead, as if they were coming to an open area. Or the other side of the island, she thought. The sound of rushing, falling water grew steadily louder as they walked.

Rani was just ahead of her, pushing through the last stand of bushes, when she made a soft exclamation of surprise and stopped abruptly. Emilie bounced with impatience, then Rani reached back and drew her forward.

They were standing not far from the edge of a cliff, looking out over a giant canyon. It was at least two hundred feet deep, and surely more than a mile across. Past the drifts of mist that laced the air, Emilie saw the far side had the waterfall, running the entire length of the cliff. It didn't come from a river, but from a slot in the cliff rock itself, about twenty feet below the top, which was lined with a forest similar to the one they were standing in. "That's not possible," Emilie said, baffled. She had to raise her voice to be heard over the din. "It's deeper than the island is tall."

"I know." Rani pulled her down and they crawled toward the edge. Peering over, Emilie saw the waterfall ran down this side too, and the air was heavy with its spray. It fell down the rock wall to a canal far below, running all along the base of the cliff. The canyon was a huge oval, and must take up the whole center of the island. The mist obscured much of the view below, but what Emilie could see was a green forest, more lush than the one up here, dotted with streams and ponds.

Rani scraped at the dirt and grass on the edge, sending it crumbling down into the rush of water. "You were right, Emilie." She tapped the hard gray-white surface under the dirt. "This place was built, ages ago."

"The water is coming from the sea?" Emilie

wondered. "If we fell off the boat in the water around the island, would we be sucked under into this waterfall?"

Rani gave her a dry look. "You have a very interesting imagination, but this water is fresh. Maybe it comes from underground."

"Or the surface? My surface, I mean." She imagined a subterranean river, wending its way down through the earth, until it was tapped by the ancient builders of the Sealands.

"At the moment anything is a possibility..." Rani sat up a little, saying with satisfaction, "Aha, there's our airship!"

Emilie craned her neck, trying to see. "Where?" Rani pointed. A drift of mist was shifting with the wind, and as it cleared, the gray bullet shape of an airship's balloon was visible above the trees. The shape and color was just different enough from Lord Ivers' balloon to make this one distinct. There might be some buildings near it, obscured by leaves and branches. It certainly wasn't a city, unless it was buried underground, which seemed very unlike the merpeople. She bet the nomads used this place as a temporary refuge, or meeting place. "This is why the Nomads were so suspicious of the airship, so afraid the Queen would use it. If this is their fortress, it would be a perfect way to attack it."

"So perfect, I wonder why she let Lord Ivers go," Rani said, with wry emphasis.

Emilie blinked, thinking it over. It was an excellent point. "You think it was a trick, that she stopped him somehow, after he left the city?"

"It's a possibility, though I'm not sure how she would do it. At least we haven't seen him around here yet." Rani crawled back from the cliff edge, withdrawing into the stands of grass, and Emilie followed her.

They sat in the shelter of the brush, and Emilie said, "There has to be a way down there, beside airships. Maybe stairs under the waterfalls, or a ladder- Ooh, that's a good idea."

Rani was holding Dr Marlende's compass, rubbing her thumb over the smooth surface. "Yes, I hope it works the way we think it does."

Meaning it would lead them to the way to find Dr Marlende, not just point directly toward the airship. Emilie held her breath.

The arrow pointed not toward the canyon, but parallel to it, in the antidarkward direction. "Ha," Rani muttered in satisfaction, pushing to her feet.

They followed the arrow through the spiny palm forest, having to stop frequently and rub spit on the stone again, then adjust their course. Emilie had been expecting to find something right away, but after about an hour of walking on the hard sandy ground, finding their way among the tall curving trunks and the clinging grass-bushes, the excitement started to pall.

They stopped briefly to eat the last of the fruit, and a little dried fish, and drink some water. As they started again, Rani admitted, "I hope this thing isn't confused, and is not just telling us to circumnavigate this island."

Emilie hoped not, too. If it was, she didn't know what

they were going to do next, except perhaps try to get past the merpeople to the *Sovereign*. Somehow.

But after another long time of walking, the compass suddenly pointed away from the canyon wall, back toward the beach. They exchanged a look, and Rani cautioned, "Don't get too excited. It could be telling us to go jump in the sea and stop bothering it."

Emilie couldn't take that advice. Forgetting all about her sore feet, she hurried after Rani.

They had just passed a big mound of grass-bushes when the compass abruptly started to point back the other way. "It means in here!" Emilie plunged into the bushes, stopping just as abruptly when Rani grabbed her belt and hauled her back.

"Me first," Rani said. "And remember, we're looking for a way down, so watch the ground and don't fall down any holes."

"Oh, good point," Emilie muttered, and went more carefully, testing the ground first with each step, the way Rani did.

A moment later Rani started to take a step, and jolted forward, flailing an arm for balance. Emilie grabbed her arm to steady her. Looking down, she saw Rani's foot had broken through a crust of dirt over a perfectly round hole. "I meant that to happen," Rani said breathlessly, freed her foot, then crouched down to knock away the rest of the dirt. Emilie hurried to help, beating at the hardened dirt until it fell away.

Her scaly brow furrowed, Rani said, "This is clearly not the way the nomads use to get down there. That worries me."

She was right, this wasn't a disguised entrance. The dirt plug had been formed by time and weather. "But the compass did point to it," Emilie said.

"I wonder at the compass' judgment," Rani said wryly.

Soon they had the hole clear. It plunged straight down through the earth, a dark stone-lined pipe. Steps had been cut into it, like the rungs of a ladder, a good indication that it led somewhere. And cool air flowed up from it, a sign that the bottom, wherever it was, wasn't blocked up. It smelled of dirt and damp stone.

Rani muttered a Cirathi curse. "I should have brought the boat lamp."

"It was bright daylight and we certainly didn't know there'd be any caves or tunnels," Emilie said. It would be too long a walk back to get it. "But you've got the matches?"

"Yes, that will have to do." Rani checked her bag, making sure they were still there. "Here, take some in case we are separated."

Emilie took the matches, tucking them into the pocket of her bloomers. Though the idea of being separated from Rani down in that underground space was frankly terrifying.

Rani leaned down, running her hand around the inside of the pipe. "Emilie, can your little claws manage this? I think you must stay here."

"No, I can manage it." The ladder looked sturdy and she could get her hands all the way around the rungs, which would make it easier to climb. It was the dark she was rather more worried about. The open dark of a moonless night, or the Hollow World's eclipse, didn't bother her. This enclosed darkness was different.

Rani leaned down, trying to get a better view of Emilie's expression. "Are you sure?"

Emilie made her chin firm and nodded. "Yes."

Rani sighed. "I wonder about both of us." She eased down, got a foot on a lower rung, then started to climb down. Emilie gathered her courage and followed.

The rungs were roughened slightly, in a way Emilie thought was deliberate, to help keep your hands from slipping off. As they climbed further and further down, she was very glad of the light from the opening overhead. Below them the pipe was utterly black. At least she could still look up at the sky and know it was there.

The circle of light that marked the opening was much smaller when Rani said suddenly, "Oof! I think we're there."

Emilie stopped, wiping sweat off her face onto her sleeve. "What?"

"There's a floor here." Rani's hand patted her ankle. "Come on down."

Emilie climbed down, and even though she was prepared for it, it was still a bit of a jolt when her foot hit the solid stone floor. She leaned against the ladder in relief, taking a deep breath. Now that she had stopped, her shoulders were shaking, her hands ached, and her stomach felt loopy. It was from pure nerves, and from gripping the ladder rungs too tightly, but knowing that didn't help.

The darkness was nearly absolute, but she could hear Rani running her claws over the walls. "Doorway here," Rani reported. "A passage. Here is where it gets interesting."

"Actually I haven't been at all bored up to now." Emilie stepped over to her, hands out, and bumped into Rani, who steered her to the wall. She felt the slightly rough stone walls, finding it was a good-sized doorway, stretching up above her head and about three feet wide.

Rani said, "Here, Emilie, keep your hand on my back so we stay together. I don't want to use the matches unless it gets worse."

Emilie wondered how the intrepid Rani was going to define "worse." After some fumbling, she took a firm grip on the strap of the supply bag. "Ready."

They made their way along, stumbling a little, leaving the faint light from the opening at the top of the pipe behind. Emilie forced herself not to think about walls closing in. The air was still flowing down the passage, heavily scented with earth and water, and she tried to imagine they were passing down a wide open road over a dark plateau. It almost worked.

But then Emilie began to hear the rush of the waterfall, vibrating through the stone, and the sense that they were close to their goal made the enclosed darkness easier to bear. We're so close, she thought. She just hoped the way wasn't blocked somewhere. She hoped the compass knew the difference between a tiny gap that aether could pass through and an opening big enough for people.

Not long later, Rani stopped suddenly. As Emilie bumped into her, she said, "Light ahead."

"Oh, good," Emilie breathed.

As they moved on, Emilie started to see it too, a faint lightening at the end of the passage. It grew gradually lighter, and she was able to let go of Rani and walk beside her. The rush of the waterfall grew louder, until she could almost taste the spray in the air.

They reached the opening, a narrow slot about two feet wide, lined with flat smooth stones. Past it they could see a curtain of falling water. Cautiously poking their heads out, they saw the doorway opened onto a narrow stone walkway that ran along the base of the cliff, behind the waterfall. The water itself was falling into a stone channel, far too regular to be natural.

Emilie followed Rani out onto the walkway. The din was too loud to hear anything, including each other's attempts to talk, and the walkway seemed empty as far as they could see. The curtain of falling water extended as far as they could see as well. Emilie couldn't make out much of what lay past it, except for glimpses of rich green vegetation.

Rani checked the compass again. Emilie stood on tiptoes to see it; it was pointing straight through the water. Rani looked up and down the walkway, her expression vexed. Emilie thought she understood: the nomads must not know about this way down, or the top of the pipe wouldn't have been blocked with dirt. But they had to know about this walkway, and if the Queen's forces hadn't found a way down here yet, they would surely be patrolling it. Rani made her decision and motioned for Emilie to follow her.

They climbed down to the flat stone edge of the channel, and Rani paced along it a short distance. She stopped at a spot where the water seemed to be falling less heavily; at least, Emilie could see a bit more of what was on the other side: the opposite edge of the channel, and another walkway. Rani, with waving gestures and pointing, managed to communicate that they were going to swim under it, and that Emilie should hold onto her very tightly. Emilie nodded, and sat down to pull her boots off.

Rani took off her own boots, tucked them and Emilie's into the bag and tied up the neck of it tightly, took off the thong holding the compass and tied it tightly to her wrist. Then she mouthed, "Ready?"

Emilie wrapped her arms around Rani's waist, and took a deep breath. They jumped, and Rani pulled them under, swimming strongly.

Emilie helped her kick against the rough current, thinking it would be easy because Rani was so strong. Then they hit the water under the fall, and suddenly they were in a pounding, churning void. She tightened her hold on Rani, knowing she was holding on for her life. The force of it was like blows raining down, Emilie lost her last breath and inhaled water, choked, and thought they would both die.

They surfaced, Emilie choking and gasping. Then she

realized Rani was limp, barely moving, starting to slip under again. Panicked, Emilie kicked out, letting go with one arm so she could paddle, dragging her toward the edge, saying, "Rani, Rani, wake up!"

Fortunately the water came right up to the flat rim of the channel, spilling over it, so Emilie was able to heave Rani and herself partially up onto the edge. She pounded Rani on the back, until Rani choked, pushed her off and spat out water. Rani collapsed over the edge, but she was breathing, and groggily conscious.

Emilie sank against the stone for a moment, relieved and too exhausted to move. But they were out in the open, there was a wide area of low moss-like grass between the channel and the forest. A white stone path ran through it, and anyone coming along it could see them for a long distance. "Rani, we have to get into the forest." The trees were tall and slender, with green trunks and darker green leaves sprouting out in big fan shapes. Tall ferns grew between them. It would provide good cover, if they could just get there.

Rani managed a nod, and started to push herself up. Emilie got a toehold in the side of the channel wall, and dragged herself up all the way onto the rim. Once there, she took Rani's arm, helping to pull her the rest of the way out. Some of the water dripping onto the stone was tinged with red. "Are you all right?" Emilie asked Rani, peering at her in new alarm. "I think you're bleeding."

"I think I'm not as waterproof as I thought," Rani admitted. She probed at her forehead, just at her hairline, and her fingers came away bloody. "And possibly hit my head on the bottom."

"We were that far down?" Appalled, Emilie glanced back at the water. She couldn't see the bottom.

"Yes." Rani staggered upright with Emilie's help, leaning on her. "This was perhaps not the best idea."

"I don't know what else we could have done." Emilie stumbled a little on the grass as they headed for the concealment of the trees. "The merpeople must be–"

She meant to say the merpeople must be guarding every entrance they knew about. But she caught movement out of the corner of her eye. She turned her head, and gasped, "They're here!"

Some distance down the open pathway, several silvery gray shapes were emerging from the forest – merpeople.

Rani looked, and snarled a curse. She pulled away from Emilie, stumbling, and ripped the thong with the compass off her wrist. She pressed it into Emilie's hand, and said, "Run."

Emilie darted a look at the merpeople. They pelted toward them over the mossy grass, carrying the short fishing spears they used as weapons. Rani gave her a push, her eyes on the merpeople, and shouted, "Run, I'll catch up with you!"

Emilie choked back a sob, and ran.

NINE

Emilie bolted through the forest, crashing through ferns, dodging past the slender green trunks. Instinct told her to run in a diagonal and not a straight line. Half-forgotten memories of hide-and-seek games with her brothers, back when they had been young enough to still want to play, came back to aid her. She stopped crashing through the brush, running more slowly but taking care not to make noise and leave obvious signs of her passage.

She made herself stop and listen, holding her breath and trying to hear past her pounding heart. Bodies smashed through the vegetation not far away, and she knew Rani would never have made that much noise. Grimacing, Emilie fled off to the right and ducked between the bushes. She had left her boots back in their supply bag, but the ground was covered with a spongy moss that was soft on her feet and made no sound when she stepped on it.

The forest was cloaked in deep green shadows, the air damp and thick with earthy scents. The soft birdcalls and the occasional darting insect seemed different from the dryer forest up on the island. This place is below the sea level, Emilie remembered. Maybe it was different, an artifact of the old Sealands Empire, like the flooded cities.

She stopped three more times, and the third time she couldn't hear any sound of pursuit. Breathing hard, she kept moving but slowed her pace to a walk. They must have captured Rani, she thought, sick. Because I abandoned her. They would have both been caught if she hadn't, but it still felt like cowardice. Smart cowardice, but still cowardice.

Emilie was sick of being compelled to abandon people. First Miss Marlende, then Rani. And your aunt and uncle, your brothers, and the rest of your family, a traitor voice whispered. That was different, she told herself desperately. That was a daring bid for freedom. But her family wouldn't see it that way, and now she might be trapped here and never able to send word to anyone. Her aunt and uncle would probably assume she had gone off to become a prostitute, but there were others – her oldest brother, Porcia and Mr. Herinbogel, Karthea, other friends – who would worry, who would think something terrible had happened to her.

And they might be right.

Emilie stopped, crouched down behind a tree, and gave way to tears. Once the first hard sobs were out, it was a relief, and she felt as if she could think more clearly. Still dripping tears, she licked her thumb and rubbed the surface of the compass. The arrow formed, pointing the way through the forest toward Dr Marlende. If he was dead, would this still work, she wondered suddenly. Surely aether-navigators still worked, if the sorcerer who had made them died, otherwise they wouldn't be very practical. But maybe spells like this were different. She hoped so, because if the Nomads hadn't hurt any of their prisoners, maybe they wouldn't hurt Rani.

Emilie wiped her face on her sleeve, looped the compass' cord over her head, and took quick stock of her resources. The matches and the knife Rani had given her were still in her pockets, though the matches would have to dry out before she could use them. Other than that, she had nothing. Just herself. You can do this, she thought, still sniffling. Whatever you have to do, you can do it. You aren't Emilie, runaway girl from the country. You're Emilie, the adventuress. Now get on your feet and find Dr Marlende. She stood up and followed the compass through the shadowy forest.

Emilie made her way through the trees and brush for perhaps two hours, though it was hard to judge the time. Water wasn't a problem – she had crossed three shallow clear streams cutting through the mossy floor – but she knew she was going to be pretty hungry by the time of the next eclipse. The texture of the moss kept her bare feet from getting too sore, but she was collecting an impressive array of bruises and scratches. She stopped at one point to climb a tree, finding handholds and footholds in the hard ridges that circled the trunk. It was a dauntingly tall tree, but she climbed just high enough to catch a glimpse of the airship's balloon through the heavy screen of palm leaves.

Her first indication that she was nearing her destination was when she stubbed her toes on a rock. Hopping and muttering curses she had heard the *Sovereign*'s sailors use, she realized it was a line of paving stones, half-buried in the moss. I bet I'm close, she thought, stepping over the paving and moving more carefully. There must be an old Sealands city or fort or something down here, which the Nomads had taken over.

After a short time, the ground started to slope up, and she could see the trees and ferns thinned out ahead. She ducked down to creep close to the ground, and pressed on. As she got closer to the edge of the forest, she saw the ground dropped away into a bowl-shaped depression, and above it rose the silver-gray curve of the airship's balloon. Near it was a collection of conical white stone roofs. Emilie flattened herself down in the moss in the shadows under the last clump of ferns, and crept as close as she dared.

Now she had a better view. Down in the shallow valley was a small city, much bigger than it had looked from the top of the waterfall cliffs when it had been concealed by the trees and mist. There were round towers, each a few stories tall, and between them short squat single-story buildings of smooth white stone. Unlike those in the Queen's city, they were round with bulbous curving sides. The floor of the little valley was dotted with large pools, all perfectly circular. She could see the airship where it was anchored near this end of the valley, the cabin hanging level with the roof of the nearest round bulgy tower.

She could also see merpeople. Several moved purposefully out of one tower and toward another. There were three standing in front of the doorway of the tower nearest the airship, clearly on guard. All were armed with the short fishing spears. As she watched, another two merpeople surfaced in one of the pools, walking up the steps and out onto the mossy ground. The pools must be connected, to each other and maybe to the buildings. And maybe to the channel that circles the canyon? Emilie wasn't sure that would help her, if it was true. But there had to be a hidden harbor somewhere, where the Nomads kept their boats, and it would make sense if it was reached via underwater tunnels. She thought this place must be used as a fortress, rather than a permanent settlement; she didn't see any children, just adults.

She looked harder at the airship, trying to see if anyone was aboard it. Like Lord Ivers' ship, the cabin was tucked up below the oblong balloon, and ran more than half the length of it. Unlike his, the cabin looked like it was made of some light coppery metal, and had a narrow walkway with a single railing running all the way around. She didn't think it was large enough to have two decks. The oblong windows were larger, but she couldn't see anyone moving around inside. The compass pointed toward the airship, or at least toward that end of the compound.

A plank bridge ran from the flat roof of the tower up to the closed door of the airship. The prisoners could be inside there, Emilie thought.

There were no windows in the top of the tower, but there were big trees along the ridge of the valley; and the bottom of the cabin, and the metal catwalk, were just above their heavy branches. It looked like a possibility to Emilie. Maybe the only possibility. The plank bridge suggested that there must be a trap door in the roof to allow access to the airship. But surely that door would be guarded too. Maybe not, if the prisoners are locked up in rooms inside the tower, she thought.

Emilie settled back into the ferns to think about it, knowing this was no time to act rashly. And that she had a few hours left until the next eclipse, so she might as well spend it resting, spying, and trying to think of a less mad plan.

But by the time the eclipse fell, she was fairly certain a mad plan was the best way to go.

Sometime after darkness fell, Emilie crouched on the edge of the valley, in the stand of big trees that overhung the airship, impatiently waiting for someone to notice her distraction.

The Nomads had lit their encampment with lamps made from big curving shells, burning fish oil. The lamps lit the paths between the buildings and the pools, but the light didn't quite reach the airship, which was now just a big shape in the dark. While that would prove helpful, Emilie was afraid it was too dark to see her distraction.

Maybe I should just go ahead, she thought. She chewed her lower lip, considering it. The problem was, she wasn't sure she could do this at all, let alone do it in complete silence. But you can't just sit here, she thought in frustration. She couldn't come this close and stop.

Then below, a merperson came running from the opposite end of the compound, calling out to the others, pointing back over his shoulder. Emilie sat up, relieved. *Finally.*

Earlier, as the eclipse had been about to descend, she had crept around to the opposite end of the valley from the airship, and heaped up a big pile of dead brush and fallen palm fronds. The wood was green and damp, so setting it on fire had taken most of the Cirathi matches that Emilie had tucked into her pocket. But it had finally started to smolder and then burn.

She still couldn't see the smoke, but a moment later the breeze brought her the scent of it, which must have alerted the merpeople. Many of them ran toward that end of the compound, calling out to each other. Several dived into one of the pools, disappearing under the surface, presumably to carry the word or get reinforcements. The three men who were guarding the door of the tower moved away from the open doorway, facing down the valley, trying to see what was happening.

Emilie took a sharp breath; she had hoped they would leave, but had known that was a little much to expect.

All right, here goes, she thought, and stood and turned to the tree she had picked out.

She started to climb, gritting her teeth as the ridges around the trunk dug into her fingers and toes. This tree was older and pointier than the one she had climbed earlier, but the trunk was also bigger around, giving her more room to climb. It was so dark she couldn't see her hands on the trunk, and the merpeople were all still occupied trying to decide if the fire meant an attack by the Queen's forces. But it was still a relief when she reached the shelter of the screen of drooping palm leaves.

Emilie was sweating by the time she reached the gentle bend where the trunk broke up into individual branches, extending in curves out toward the airship. She shook the sweat out of her eyes and peered ahead. So far, so good. The balloon and the cabin now blocked her view of the tower and the guards, but also their potential view of her.

She gripped the trunk with her legs and scooted awkwardly forward, out onto the highest branch. She climbed along it, closer and closer to the dark bulk of the airship. The branch was getting more slender, and Emilie winced when it creaked under her. She tried to tell herself it wasn't as bad as climbing out the prison window, but she wasn't so sure. Those ledges seemed quite wide and safe compared to this tree. She couldn't think what was worse, falling and dying or falling and breaking a leg or an arm or both, and being at the Nomads' mercy. Neither, she thought, please let it be neither.

She edged further and further forward, until finally the airship's catwalk was just above her. About five feet above her. Hell, it didn't look that far from across the valley. Emilie tried to ease up slowly, felt herself start to slip, and dropped back to grip the branch tightly. She held back a sob of terror. This won't work, she thought, feeling the branch sway beneath her. It had to work. She couldn't go back.

She looked up again. She couldn't do it slowly, so she would have to do it fast. She pushed herself up into a crouch without letting go with her hands. Then she braced herself, and shoved upright in one quick motion, making a wild grab.

Her right hand brushed metal, she gripped the slim post of a railing, just as her feet slipped off the branch. She hung for a moment, her arm straining, then found the edge of the catwalk with her other hand. She hauled herself up as far as she could, her heart pounding with the effort, then managed to pull a leg up and hook her foot onto a supporting strut for the catwalk. Pushing from there let her drag her weight up onto the metal walkway. She huddled for a moment, breathing hard, astonished to be still alive. That was a lot harder than I thought it was going to be, Emilie thought, and scrubbed sweat off her forehead.

She eased to her feet, gripping the railing because her legs were still shaking. She felt the airship move slightly under her, pushed by the wind. She realized belatedly that it might have moved when she had been hanging off the railing, but it was far too big to tip or shudder with her weight. If the Nomads had noticed anything, they would think it was just the wind.

Emilie crept around the catwalk, stopping to peer into the darkened windows, but she couldn't make out anything inside. As she came around the bow of the cabin, she had a good view of the compound, while still being in the shadows above the reach of their lamps. There was still activity at the far end, toward where she had set the fire. She bet the darkness in the woods was helping her; the fire had been slowly smoldering rather than burning brightly. The Nomads were probably having trouble locating it. The three door guards were still looking off that way, and there weren't any other merpeople around, at least that she could see.

Keeping her steps as quiet as possible, Emilie moved along the catwalk down the airship's side, to the narrow plank bridge that led from it down to the round roof of the tower. *Ha, I was right.* There was a round opening in the roof, dimly illuminated by a light somewhere inside. It would have been disappointing, to say the least, to discover that there was no way inside the tower from here and that they had reached the airship with ladders up the outside or some other unusable method.

Emilie reached the catwalk and started across, moving slowly to keep the light wood from creaking. It was too dark to see the ground below her, and the bulk of the tower blocked her view of the guards.

She stepped down onto the smooth material of the roof, reflecting that the good thing about this stone was that it didn't creak. No one below would hear her moving around up here. She went to the opening and cautiously peered down.

All she could see at first was a white stone stairway with shallow steps, spiraling down the center of the tower. Emilie crouched on the edge and listened, but couldn't hear any movement or voices inside. She circled the opening, angling for a better view; she could see some bare floor in the room below, but that was all.

Nervously, Emilie leaned down far enough to get a good look, ready to dart away if the room was occupied. But it was just an empty room, at least from this angle. She stepped cautiously down the stairs, until she could see the rest of the room. It was empty, except for an old pile of ropes and nets in the corner. There was only one big room, too, no doorways.

She kept going down, and repeated this process at the next opening in the floor, which led down into the room below. It was empty except for a few clay storage jars, and a bowl-shaped lamp hanging from a ceiling hook, providing the wan light. All right, this isn't good, Emilie thought, moving quietly down the stairs. This place wasn't big to start with and she was running out of room to discover prisoners. What if those men outside are just guarding the airship, she thought. What if the prisoners are all locked up in another building nearby? She suppressed a groan, and checked the compass quickly.

The arrow now formed a circle. Emilie's brow furrowed. It wasn't doing that earlier. It looked like it meant for her to go down. All right, then.

Emilie went down to the next opening, the one that looked down into the ground level. She lay flat on the floor, angling her head so she could see toward the open doorway that looked out into the compound. She couldn't see the guards from here... No, wait, there's one, Emilie thought. She could just see his leg and part of his back, as he was facing away from the door. She leaned down a little further for a peek at the room, and grimaced in disappointment. It was empty, too, bare of anything except a round medallion on the floor, a few steps from the end of the stairway, on the furthest side from the outer door. Emilie blinked. A medallion with a handle, and a bolt. That had to be it. *There's an underground room. And it's locked from the outside.*

Emilie threw another look at what was visible of the guard, then ghosted silently down the stairs. At the bottom she stepped quickly to the trapdoor; the solid stairs blocked a little of the view from the doorway, but if anyone walked past... She knelt, slid the bolt back, and carefully pulled at the door. It lifted on slightly rusty metal hinges; it was heavy, and didn't creak.

Below was a stairwell with steps spiraling down, and a flickering lamp set into a niche. There was a door at the bottom, about twelve feet down, with light shining through it. Emilie swallowed in a dry throat, hesitating. There could be more guards down there, she could be trapping herself, this might be the stupidest thing she had done yet- Then she heard voices from somewhere outside, coming closer; she slipped down through the opening, carefully pulling the door down into place above her.

Emilie sank back against the cool wall, letting her breath out in a silent sigh. There wasn't anything to do now but go forward.

She went down the stairs to the doorway, and cautiously peeked around the edge. Yes! she thought. I was right!

It was a big lamplit room, much larger than the tower rooms above her. Stretched across a portion of it was a wall of metal bars, forming a jail cell, and on the other side, sleeping on worn blankets, were five Menaen men. They were all disheveled, dressed not in uniforms but in sturdy jackets and trousers meant for rough outdoor work. The cell was bare of necessities except for the blankets and a couple of covered jars that must serve as the water closet; it smelled like they had been imprisoned here for a while.

There was no guard, just another door on the far side of the room, and a pool of water across from the cell. Emilie tiptoed to the pool first, looking down into it to make sure there weren't any merpeople lurking there. The water was clear enough to tell the pool was empty, but there was a dark shape low on one side: an opening to some sort of water-filled underground passage. I bet this is connected to the pools in the compound, she thought, moving back to the cell. Which meant merpeople might appear in it any moment.

She went to the bars and, keeping her voice low, said, "Hey! Wake up! You're being rescued!"

One of the men flinched awake, then sat up and stared at her. He had dark weathered skin and dark hair peppered with gray. He demanded, "Are you a dream?"

"No, I'm Emilie." She realized she must look somewhat disheveled herself, covered with scratches, her hair wild and probably ornamented with twigs and leaves, barefoot with stains and tears on her bloomers and shirt. Not very much like a rescuer, probably, but they would just have to settle for her. Impatiently, she added, "Miss Marlende sent me." While not strictly true, it was close enough.

And it did the trick. The man scrambled to his feet, stooped to shake the others awake. "Come on, boys, we're getting out of here."

Emilie hoped they were getting out of here; she had just realized that the cell didn't seem to have a door. She tried to shake the bars, but they didn't budge. "How does this thing open?"

The older man pointed across the room behind her. "There. That lever. It cranks the whole thing down into the floor."

It was on the far side of the room, a metal lever sticking out of a slot in the wall. Emilie hurried over and grabbed it, and tried to push it down. "Oof." It was stiff, and she leaned on it with her full weight. The lever moved slowly, all the way down, but when she glanced at the bars, she saw they had only lowered a few inches. Oh, come on, she thought in exasperation.

"Let it come back up and then push it down again, like a pump," the older man told her. To the others, he said, "Here, grab onto the bars and put your weight on them when she pushes the lever down."

"Right." Emilie let the lever come up to its original position, then forced it down again. With the men adding their weight to the bars, it was much easier, and got them nearly a foot of clearance. "You're not Dr Marlende, are you?" she asked the older man. There wasn't any resemblance between him and Miss Marlende, and despite his gray hair, she didn't think he was quite old enough. The other four men were all too young. Three were Southern Menaen, one Northern, all very scruffy. Though now that she had a chance to look at them, they all seemed more the scholarly type, once you saw past the dirt, lack of shaving, and rough clothing.

The older man said, "No, I'm Charter, his engineer. We haven't seen Dr Marlende for two days." He nodded to the other men. "That's Daniel, Seth, Cobbier, and Mikel."

"It's nice to meet you," Emilie said, gritting her teeth as she forced the bar down again. "Do you know where the Cirathi are?"

"We haven't seen them since we got here," Daniel said, hauling down on the bars again. He was clearly the youngest Southern Menaen, maybe only a few years older than Emilie. He had handsome features, rather unkempt curly hair, and cracked spectacles. "We think they're locked up down here somewhere, though. We keep asking about them, but the Nomads won't tell us anything."

That was going to be a problem. "Have you seen Rani? She was with me, she gave me Dr Marlende's compass, but she was captured when we got here yesterday."

There were startled exclamations from the men. "We didn't know she was alive," Charter said. "We haven't seen her since she escaped from the ship. She's here?"

Damn it! Emilie thought, and threw her weight down on the lever again. "Yes, I think so, but I don't know where." Hopefully the merpeople were keeping her with the other Cirathi.

With the next effort they managed to get the bars down far enough that the men could fit through the gap between the ceiling and the top rail. As they were climbing over the bars, Emilie checked the compass again. It pointed toward the far wall, where the door was. She hurried over to it. "The compass says Dr Marlende is this way." Hopefully he was with Rani and the rest of the Cirathi crew. She cautiously tugged on the metal loop that functioned as a door handle. The door didn't budge, and the lock appeared to be a hole under the handle that clearly needed some sort of key. Emilie poked at the little opening. "Do you know where the key is for this?"

Charter reached her side. "Where are the others? Who else is with you?"

Emilie set her jaw, prepared for an argument. "There aren't any others. There's just me."

Charter and Daniel exchanged a baffled look. The other men looked dubious. Cobbier said, "What do you mean, 'no others'?"

"Isn't this a rescue mission?" Daniel added.

Impatiently, Emilie explained, "We came on Lord Engal's ship, me and Miss Marlende and Kenar. But we ran into the Queen of the Sealands and she's forcing Lord Engal and everyone to help her attack these Nomads. Miss Marlende was captured by Lord Ivers, and is aboard his airship somewhere. Rani and I were coming to free you, but she was captured this morning."

Everyone stared. "Lord Ivers is here and has Miss Marlende? We didn't even know he had a working aetheric engine," Seth said, astonished.

"Yes, he does." Emilie finished, "So you'd better stop worrying about my qualifications as a rescuer and get on with finding the others before we all get captured again."

Daniel looked mulish, but Charter held up a placating hand, stepping forward to examine the door. He said, "I take your point, Emilie. We can't go out the way you got in?"

Mollified, but still wary, Emilie said, "Not easily. I set a fire as a distraction, so I could get past the guards at the outside doorway, but it might be out by now."

"But is our airship still out there, moored to the top of this tower?" Daniel asked. "Can we get to it?"

"Yes." It belatedly occurred to Emilie that securing the airship might be a good idea. She had been so fixed on the goal of finding Rani and Dr Marlende, she hadn't even thought about it. "If you're very, very quiet. The guards were maybe a few steps from the outside doorway."

"We can get past them." Charter nodded grimly. "I'll go after Marlende and the others, the rest of you get aboard that airship. Lay low for now, but don't let the ship be recaptured."

"Cobbier can get the others past the guards. I'll go with you," Daniel said, looking mulish again.

"And me," Emilie added. "I have to find Rani."

"You should go back to the ship," Daniel told her, his tone bearing an unfortunate resemblance to the way Emilie's brothers spoke to her.

Seth and Cobbier and Mikel were all protesting to Charter that they should stay together, and Emilie knew there wasn't time to argue. She said to Daniel, "You mistake me for someone you have the right to order around."

He looked taken aback, and Charter cut off all the argument with a sharp gesture, saying, "There's no time for this. Now go!"

Reluctantly, the other men went toward the doorway to the stairs, and Charter knelt to peer into the lock, ignoring the fact that Emilie and Daniel had both remained behind. Charter asked, "Have you got a pocket knife?"

"Yes, here." Emilie fished in her pocket and handed over the little knife Rani had given her.

As Charter used the blade to probe the inside of the locking mechanism, Daniel said, "It had been so long, we thought Jerom and Kenar didn't make it back to the surface."

Emilie groaned inwardly. Being the one to have to

deliver the bad news was not pleasant, and this was the second time she had had to do it. "Jerom didn't make it. Kenar said the trip was much worse than they thought it was going to be. I'm sorry."

Daniel took a sharp breath. "Oh." He shook his head. "I knew I should have gone."

Still occupied with the lock, Charter said, "Jerom was a stronger sorcerer. He had to be the one to go."

"Are you a sorcerer?" Emilie asked Daniel.

He frowned at her, as if the question was too personal. "I'm studying to be one."

Though she should be feeling sorry for him, something about his attitude made Emilie say, not quite innocently, "But you couldn't do anything like get the cell door open?"

Charter snorted, and Daniel frowned even more. "It's not quite that simple–"

"Quiet," Charter muttered, still working the lock. "I'm about to open it."

They went quiet. Emilie held her breath, hoping this wasn't the end of their escape. If there were guards in the next room, there was little they could do without weapons. The other men must have gotten up to the trapdoor by this point, and she didn't hear any sounds of fighting or alarm, so that was encouraging.

The door made a dull clunk as the lock snapped open, and Charter winced. So much for stealth, Emilie thought. Charter eased the door open a crack and peered through, then pushed it open and got to his feet.

Daniel stepped forward into Emilie's way, but she

managed to stretch to see around him. The door opened into a shadowy corridor, with a curving roof and walls of rough light-colored rock, the air dank and cool. There were no merpeople, but it couldn't be entirely deserted: a flickering lamp hung from a peg on the wall.

Charter stepped through into the corridor, Daniel managing to get in ahead of Emilie. She tugged the door closed behind them; it might slow pursuit, but only for a few moments. The merpeople had to know their captives couldn't escape through the pool's underwater passage. "What is this place?" Emilie asked as they went down the corridor. "The Nomads don't live here, surely?"

"No, they use it as a stronghold," Daniel said. "It was some sort of sacred place for the old Sealands Empire. It's so old, I don't think they're sure what it was for anymore."

The corridor opened into a foyer with another pool of water. Three more shadowy corridors led away from it. The whole area under the compound must be honeycombed with tunnels, with a system of water passages below it, and one above, connecting the surface pools. Emilie quickly checked the compass again.

The arrow pointed to the corridor to the left. Emilie nodded to it, whispering, "That one."

Charter took a step toward it. Just then a merman surfaced in the pool, heaving himself half out onto the stone floor. For an instant they all froze, and he looked just as startled as they were. Then he started to push back from the edge. Charter lunged forward, punching him in the head. The merman fell backward but two more surfaced, and Charter yelled, "Run!"

Emilie ran, taking the corridor the compass had indicated before considering whether it was a good idea or not. It was a long corridor, with several guttering lamps hanging on the wall. She heard Daniel shouting behind her and slowed, looking back. Then he and Charter came pounding after her and she hurried on.

They caught up to her as she reached another open foyer, but this one had only one other way out, a narrow spiral stair up to a silvery metal trapdoor in the ceiling. The merpeople had to be right behind them and it was the only way out. Emilie started toward it, but Charter grabbed her arm and whispered, "Wait, don't move!"

Daniel stood at the open passageway, holding up a hand as if pressing against an invisible door. He was whispering quietly to himself. Emilie stared, and then realized: he's doing a spell. She hoped he was more useful as a sorcerer than previous circumstances would seem to indicate.

Daniel took a sharp breath and stepped back from the doorway. A moment later four mermen arrived, sliding to an abrupt halt. Daniel was frozen in place, and Charter squeezed Emilie's arm, reminding her to be still.

The mermen stared through the doorway, obviously puzzled. As they looked around, their eyes seemed to slide past Daniel, Charter, and Emilie without focusing on them. They see an empty room, she thought, holding her breath. And it hadn't seemed to occur to them to step past the doorway and investigate further.

Tension stretched Emilie's nerves almost to the point where she felt compelled to make a sound, but finally the mermen turned away. They started back down the passage, talking agitatedly among themselves. As their voices faded, Daniel's shoulders slumped in relief, and Charter relaxed a little. Emilie let herself breathe again, feeling her pulse pounding in her ears. "It's a charm," Charter explained, keeping his voice low. "It makes people think they can't see you. But they can still hear you, and feel you."

"You couldn't use it from inside the cell?" Emilie asked. "To make them think you escaped?" Though that wouldn't do much good, unless the merpeople were incautious enough to lower the bars.

Daniel wiped sweat off his forehead. "It doesn't work if they know you're there. That's why we had to get to another room – we had to be just far enough ahead of them that they would be able to tell themselves that they'd mistaken the passage we took."

Emilie made a mental note that Daniel was a little more useful than he had seemed at first. And that explained why they had been so certain that Cobbier could get the other three crewmembers past the guards outside the tower; he must be an apprentice sorcerer too. She checked the compass again, and was momentarily puzzled when the arrow made a circle. "Oh." She looked up at the ceiling. "I think we're close."

Charter stepped past her and started up the stairs. Emilie and Daniel waited below as he cautiously pushed the trapdoor open just enough to get a view of the next room. After a moment, he opened it all the way and motioned for them to follow him.

Emilie hurried up the stairs. The room was bigger than the foyer below, and better lit, with a larger stairwell spiraling up to the next floor, and a closed door. "I think we're on the surface," Emilie whispered. The air in this room was fresher, laced with the green scent of the forest. She checked the compass again. "It's still pointing up."

Daniel went to the door and listened at it. He shook his head. "Can't hear anything."

Charter grimaced, looking up the stairwell. He muttered, "This place is too quiet." But he added to Daniel, "You stay here, we'll go up."

Daniel nodded, and Charter and Emilie started up the stairs. She knew what Charter meant; the merpeople had seen them now and there should be more commotion outside as they searched for them. They reached the next floor, where a wide foyer held a single closed door.

Emilie hurried over to listen at it. She heard voices, and thought: *Uh oh*. But they didn't sound like merpeople; the voices were too deep. Wait, there is something familiar about... "I think it's the Cirathi!" she whispered to Charter.

He tugged cautiously on the handle. The door didn't budge, and he crouched to peer into the opening for the lock, taking out Emilie's knife. "We don't know if they're alone in there," he said, keeping his voice low. "There might be guards inside."

"We could knock and ask," Emilie murmured. Then it occurred to her he might think she was silly enough to be serious.

But Charter just gave her an ironic smile and started to tinker with the lock. Then a bang and a muffled yell from the room below made Emilie flinch. Charter shoved to his feet, cursing, but half a dozen merpeople were charging up the stairwell. Emilie ducked back against the wall with a yelp, suddenly confronted with a forest of sharp spear points.

TEN

One of the merpeople shouted an order, and the others drew back a little. A few of them were female, but they all wore belts of some kind of reptile hide, they all carried knives, and they all looked angry. One held a weapon that looked like a wooden spear gun. With a grim expression, Charter dropped the knife and held up his hands. Emilie held up her hands, too.

Two other merpeople dragged Daniel up the stairs, despite his resistance. He caught Charter's eye and said, guiltily, "Sorry. They just burst in through the door–" One of them poked him to tell him to be silent.

Charter said, "It's all right."

Emilie knew it was anything but all right.

The merpeople searched them first, taking the knife and the rest of Emilie's matches. Emilie thought they would be shoved into the room with the Cirathi, but instead the Nomads prodded them up the stairs. There was a door on the next landing, with a merman standing guard outside it. At a gesture from the leader, he pushed it open.

They were guided into a big room, lit by several lamps, bare of furniture except for a few clay water jars. But it was the occupants who captured Emilie's attention. Rani and an older Menaen man were facing five merpeople. Emilie started forward, only to be dragged back by her guards. She called out, "Rani! Are you all right?"

"I'm well, Emilie." Rani looked her over, her scaled brow furrowed. "These idiots have not hurt you?"

"No, I'm fine." She hoped, for the moment. Rani didn't look hurt, and her head wasn't bleeding anymore.

The older Menaen man had to be Dr Marlende. He had shaggy gray hair and a beard that badly needed to be trimmed, which kept Emilie from spotting any resemblance to Miss Marlende. He wore a rather shabby tweed suit coat over a somewhat the worse-for-wear workman's trousers and shirt. He said, "Charter, Daniel, how good to see you!"

One of the merpeople was less enthused to see them. Holding one of the translation shells, he turned to Rani and said, "You lied. You said you were alone." He was young, very handsome, wearing a necklace of polished shells and a reptile skin belt set with disks of silver metal. The others with him, three young men and one older woman, wore the same kind of finery; Emilie suspected they were looking at the Nomads' leaders. Or at least the leaders of this group of Nomads.

Rani snorted, amused. "Of course I lied. You keep dragging me and my people off by force. We are not friends, Prince Ise." To Dr Marlende, she explained,

"That is Emilie, who came here with your daughter."

"Excellent!" Dr Marlende said, and nodded to Emilie.

Prince Ise rounded on Charter, demanding, "Where are the others?"

They haven't caught them, they don't know they're aboard the airship, Emilie thought, relieved. His expression stony, Charter said, "I don't know. We split up, to look for Dr Marlende and the Cirathi."

Prince Ise spoke to the mermen guards in his own language, and three of them hurried off, probably to organize a search. Emilie just hoped no one thought to check the airship. Prince Ise turned back to Dr Marlende and Rani. "You can't expect me to negotiate with you after this. You have tried to escape, to attack my people—"

Rani eyed him with contempt. "Oh, and if you were in our position, you would sit in a cell and do nothing, and wait for your captors to 'negotiate.' Is that what you would do?"

Ise set his jaw, furious. He's young, Emilie thought. Younger than the Queen, certainly. Dr Marlende said, "Oh, I think in our position Prince Ise would be fighting quite hard to escape. And I think we can agree that it is generous of him to speak to us at all, with everything he has to deal with at the moment."

It had given Ise time to get his self-control back. He said, more evenly, "I have been generous. I offer you an alliance. If you would help us fight the Queen's forces, we would treat you as honored guests."

Dr Marlende shook his head. "My airship is for exploration, not war. And neither we nor the Cirathi have any business interfering in your disagreements with the Queen. Our involvement would cause you nothing but harm in the long run."

Ise folded his arms, his whole body communicating contempt. "I might have believed that, before the metal ship joined the Queen's fleet. Our spies say they have the same magics and projectile weapons that you do. I'm only asking you to even the balance."

"They were tricked!" Emilie had to interrupt. "They think you attacked the ship, but it was the Queen's people, pretending to be Nomads. And now they're only helping her because they think the Queen has Miss Marlende and me as hostages; they don't know I escaped with Rani and that Lord Ivers has Miss Marlende prisoner. If you let us all go, they have no reason to fight you."

"Yes, Rani informed me that Lord Ivers has my daughter prisoner," Dr Marlende said, sounding grim. "The nerve of the man."

Ise regarded her a moment in silence, and Emilie couldn't tell if her speech had had any effect on him or not. He looked at Rani and said, "She tells the same story you told."

"Of course she does." Rani was exasperated. "It's the truth."

Prince Ise paced away from them, obviously torn. But before he could say anything, another merman pounded up the stairs, calling out. He spoke rapidly to Ise, who answered sharply in his own language. Then Ise turned to Dr Marlende and said, "The Queen's forces have found our concealed cove. We'll drive them off, but when I return–" He hesitated again, but added, "This conversation is not over."

He strode out, the other merpeople following, leaving them alone in the room. The guard outside shut the door, and Emilie heard the lock thunk into place.

Rani said, annoyed, "Well, that was not a timely interruption."

"I'm not certain it would have been any different had we talked all night," Dr Marlende told her. "We might convince him, but the Nomads have many leaders, and I don't know how much influence he has." He motioned for them to draw together in the center of the room, and said quietly, "Keep your voices low, please. Prince Ise usually leaves the translation shell with the guards."

"They've made a mistake, leaving us together like this," Rani muttered. "Surely Ise will recall it and send the guards to separate us soon."

"You can't use your magic to escape?" Emilie asked Dr Marlende, keeping her voice low.

Daniel looked offended that she had asked the question, but Dr Marlende smiled at her. He said, "I can create a few rather flashy illusions, but I need access to my airship's aetheric channeling devices for anything more effective." He turned to Charter and Daniel. "Any suggestions, gentlemen?"

Charter glanced thoughtfully at the door. "There's a room above this one? Is there a trapdoor in the roof?"

"Possibly, we've never been allowed up there," Dr Marlende said.

Rani put in, "But we're three levels up, and there are guards on the ground below. This stonework is not so easy to climb." She added to Emilie, "I tried earlier. It was very embarrassing."

"We don't need to climb," Charter told her. He looked at Dr Marlende. "Cobbier, Mikel, and Seth are in the airship."

"Ah." Dr Marlende lifted a brow, and exchanged a look with Rani. "The guards will expect us to try to escape through the ground level exit, so they'll concentrate their efforts there."

Rani said, "Then what are we waiting for?" and started for the door. Charter followed her.

Daniel looked from them to Dr Marlende. "Do we need a spell, a charm? I can try–"

"They know my abilities," Dr Marlende told him. "They wouldn't be fooled by the illusion of an empty room."

"We are doing it the old fashioned way." Rani took up a position to one side of the door, and gave Charter a nod.

Charter pounded on it, and shouted, "Help, we need help!"

From the other side of the door, a merman's voice said, "Be quiet!"

"Please!" Charter kept pounding. Rani made a frantic gesture at Emilie. Emilie, interpreting this as best she could, shrieked as loudly and ear-piercingly as possible and flung herself on the floor.

Emilie kept shrieking, and Dr Marlende began to

caper around her tearing at his hair and giving a good impression of hysterical grief. Emilie wasn't sure how long they could keep it up; she felt she was already close to bursting a blood vessel. But a moment later, the door started to open.

The guard was cautious, entering spear first, but Rani moved like lightning. She grabbed the end of the spear, jerked the lighter merman through the doorway, and slung him across the room. As Emilie scrambled to her feet, Daniel hit the staggering merman with a water jar. The jar cracked and the merman collapsed.

The guard still outside tried to shove the door shut, but Charter wedged himself into the gap, holding it open. He cried out and Emilie gasped, knowing he must have been stabbed. But he held the door long enough for Rani to throw her considerable strength against it, slamming it open.

With the guard's captured spear, Rani slashed at the remaining merman, and he ducked away and stabbed at her again. Emilie reached the door and caught Charter as he slumped, staggering under his weight. The right shoulder of his shirt was already soaked with blood. Behind her Daniel reached the doorway, just as another merman charged up the stairs. Daniel was still holding the cracked water jar and, leaning down, slung it across the floor. "Oh, clever!" Emilie said, as it rolled down the first few steps, struck the merman in the shins and knocked him flat.

With a sudden lunge, Rani shoved the other guard's spear up, flipped her spear around and whacked him in the head with the butt hard enough to knock him back into the far wall.

Dr Marlende reached Charter, trying to take his arm to support him. Charter said, "No, get up to the roof, signal the airship! I can make it."

Dr Marlende snapped, "Then hurry, damn you, I'm not leaving anyone behind!" and charged up the stairs. Stumbling a little, Charter started after him.

Emilie hesitated, her first impulse to help Charter, but Rani and Daniel had plunged down the stairs, going to rescue the Cirathi. No, better help them, she thought, hurrying after them.

The merman Daniel had tripped with the jar had hit his chin on the stone steps and was dazed. Daniel snatched up his spear in passing and Emilie, about to step over him, remembered, that door is locked, we need the key. Hoping this was the guard from that landing, she stooped down to pull at his belt, looking for the key, but there was nothing there. Suddenly he grabbed her arm, and a surge of panic almost blinded her. She snatched his big knife out of the sheath and hit him across the head with the hilt. It made an unpleasant thunk as it hit his skull and he fell backward. She pulled away, breathing hard. Hitting a person was very different from trying to hit the plant-creature who had attacked Miss Marlende. She felt sick, but there was just no time for it. She hurried down the steps.

Another merman was already down, sprawled on the floor of the landing, and Rani and Daniel blocked the stairs, struggling with three others. Emilie dashed to the fallen merman, found a round metal knob attached to his belt with a cord, and jerked it free. As she stood and shoved it into the lock opening, Daniel fell backward and Rani lunged in to cover him. Gritting her teeth, Emilie forced the key to turn. The lock clicked and the door flung open, nearly slamming her against the wall. But a strong scaled hand caught her arm and steadied her as several Cirathi rushed out the door. They overwhelmed the mermen on the stairs and drove them back down the steps.

The Cirathi holding Emilie up was a young woman, only a little taller than she was. She spoke in her own language, then switched to Menaen, saying excitedly, "You are rescuing us!"

"We are!" Emilie replied.

The young Cirathi threw a worried look around. "How?"

"Oh, right! Up, we have to go up, to the airship!" Emilie said hurriedly, pointing up the stairwell. Rani shouted something in her own language that must have confirmed this, because some of the Cirathi started up the stairs, a few remaining behind to help Rani and Daniel hold off the merpeople.

Emilie followed them, past the next landing and up to the very top. They found Charter struggling up the stairs, and one of the larger Cirathi caught him, heaved him over a shoulder, and continued to climb.

They reached the landing at the top of the tower, where a doorway set at an angle opened into a large room. There was no trapdoor in the ceiling. "That's not good," Emilie said under her breath. There were windows, fortunately, big round ones with no glass panes; Dr Marlende was hanging out of one, waving a lamp that burned like a white firework. As Emilie reached him, he pulled himself back in, saying with satisfaction, "They've seen it, they're coming!"

Emilie looked past him and her heart leapt. In the light from the ground lamps, the big silvery shape of the airship was lifting above the other towers, turning toward them.

Dr Marlende said, "Where's Charter? Ah, there he is." Charter was upright and conscious though bleary-eyed, leaning on the shoulder of the Cirathi man, holding a crumpled handkerchief to his bleeding shoulder. Five other Cirathi had come up with them. All except the man supporting Charter were fairly small, scarcely taller than Emilie. Rani must have ordered the younger ones to flee up the stairs, with the one adult to take care of Charter.

Dr Marlende looked around the room, tapping his bearded chin. "Now if we can just hold off our captors until our transport arrives…" The lamp he still held was the usual sort the merpeople used, a convoluted shell hanging from a woven strap of reed or seagrass, which burned fish oil. Except this one was glowing white and spitting sparks. Emilie assumed Dr Marlende had done something magical to brighten it so that the men in the airship could see it.

Shouting, thumps, and crashes sounded from the stairwell, and Rani, Daniel, and the rest of the Cirathi hadn't appeared yet. There was no door, nothing they could use to block off the doorway. Emilie ran to the opposite window, the one above the front of the tower. Two of the young Cirathi were already there, looking worriedly down at the shadowed compound. One pointed for Emilie and she saw a group of merpeople running toward the tower. "Yes, they're sending reinforcements." Emilie bit her lip. It sounded like Rani and the others could barely hold off the guards now. She turned to Dr Marlende. "Can we do something? Go outside, to keep more of them from coming into the tower?"

Dr Marlende strode over to look out the window. He nodded grimly. "Yes, I think we'd better try a fire illusion." He glanced around the room. "If you could find me another couple of lamps..."

Emilie hurried to the doorway, taking down the lamp hanging near it. Even if it was an illusion, some of the merpeople might not be willing to test it too quickly. The young Cirathi didn't all seem to understand Menaen, but they saw what Emilie was doing and ran to collect the other lamps in the room. As they returned to the window, Dr Marlende hefted the lamp he was holding, eyeing the nomads running across the compound. As they neared the base of the tower, he flung the lamp out the window.

As it plunged toward the ground, white fire burst out of it. Emilie winced away, seeing stars before her eyes. She blinked hard, trying to see what had happened. The lamp had hit the ground, still blazing, if not quite as brightly. The nomads scattered and retreated in confusion. But Emilie couldn't feel any heat from the fire, and knew in a moment or so the nomads would realize it too. Dr Marlende said, "Now we'll try this on our antagonists in the stairwell, though I fear they'll realize it's illusory."

He started toward the doorway, but Emilie stopped, caught by the view out the opposite window.

The airship was above the tower now, the balloon huge above the smaller suspended cabin, trying to angle down to reach the window. Emilie saw Seth hanging out the open cabin door, holding a bundle of rope under his arm. Behind her, a deep voice said, "Tell them to drop a harness, this one can't climb."

Emilie glanced back. Without the lamps, the room was very dark, lit only by the dim light coming through the windows. After a moment, she realized the speaker was the Cirathi man who was helping Charter. "I can make it, Beinar," Charter said through gritted teeth.

"Of course you'll make it," Beinar said, as he helped Charter toward the window. He sounded annoyed that there was any doubt at all.

Emilie was glad Beinar was confident; it made it a little easier to ignore the tight panic in her chest. She leaned out, shouting up at the airship, "We need a harness; Charter's got a wounded arm!"

Seth waved at her and ducked back inside. A moment later, a chain ladder with wooden rungs dropped out of the airship, dangling just out of reach. It was followed by a sturdy rope with a bundle of leather straps on the end, presumably the harness. The airship angled closer, and Emilie saw the propellers at the back of the cabin starting and stopping as it maneuvered toward the tower. She stretched, reaching for the ladder. It swung toward her; she made a wild grab and caught hold of a rung.

Charter rasped, "Careful, if the ship moves up, it'll jerk you right out!"

"Right," Emilie muttered, bracing herself against the side of the window as she hauled at the heavy ladder. The airship seemed lighter than air, but it was far too heavy for her to anchor by herself.

A Cirathi girl hurried to help her, their combined strength dragging the heavy ladder up to the sill. Then Beinar propped Charter against the wall, and took the ladder, pulling it into the room. Holding on to it, he stretched out a long arm and snagged the harness.

Emilie realized Beinar couldn't help Charter into the harness and hold the ladder at the same time. She motioned frantically to the Cirathi girl that she was about to let go. The girl nodded and called out to the others in her own language. Two ran back from the doorway to grab onto the ladder, and Emilie went to help Charter.

Between the two of them, with Beinar giving quick instructions, they got Charter's arms through the loops and Emilie quickly buckled the straps. In the dim light, Charter's face was pinched with pain, and he was sweating and shaking with the effort of standing.

Beinar took one hand off the ladder to tug on the

straps, said, "Good," then hauled Charter around and shoved him out the window.

Emilie couldn't help a strangled noise of protest, though she knew this was what they had to do. Charter hung in midair for only a moment, before the ropes were hauled rapidly upward. They must have a winch, Emilie thought irrelevantly, sticking her head out the window to watch.

Mikel and Seth caught Charter as he reached the walkway and hauled him inside, then Seth reappeared, signaling wildly. He shouted, "Send the rest up!"

Emilie pulled back in, got a scrape on the cheek from the swaying ladder, and reported, "He says to come on up!"

Beinar spoke in Cirathi, and one of the girls started up the ladder, climbing quickly and agilely. As the next one started to climb, Emilie ran to the doorway. From the landing she could see bright white light glowing up the stairwell. She couldn't hear fighting anymore, though she could hear worried voices speaking in Cirathi. She called down, "Dr Marlende, Rani, we have to go!"

She heard Rani's voice give an order, and several Cirathi charged up the stairs. Emilie pointed urgently toward the ladder, and Beinar called to them. As one of the newcomers took over helping to brace the ladder, the last young Cirathi started up.

Daniel bounded up the stairs next, breathing hard. His clothes smelled of male sweat, musky, something that wasn't nearly as unpleasant as Emilie thought it should be. He said, "Dr Marlende's made a fire barrier across the stairs, making them think we've set the place alight. But he has to be there to maintain it."

"Can you do a charm–" Emilie began.

He shook his head, interrupting, "There's no way they would believe this room is empty, and they'll be able to hear us–"

"To make them think there's a door here?" Emilie finished, determined to be heard. "It's dark, and the way this doorway is angled–"

"Yes!" He grabbed her shoulders, startling her so badly she almost slapped him. "Not a door, we can't do that, but another fire barrier! It might work, just long enough."

Daniel plunged down the stairs again, calling to Dr Marlende, and Emilie waited tensely. After a moment, he reappeared again, with Rani and Dr Marlende behind him.

Emilie stepped back into the room. The only Cirathi left were Beinar and one other man, anchoring the ladder. She hadn't heard any screaming or other commotion, so she hoped that meant no one had fallen.

Rani stopped, looking around the darkened room. She was breathing hard, and Emilie couldn't tell if she was wounded. She said something to Beinar in Cirathi, and nodded at his answer, then she squeezed Emilie's shoulder and started for the ladder. "We are almost there, Emilie."

"Almost," Emilie agreed, following her. She thought there was still plenty of time for everything to go hideously wrong.

At the window, Emilie leaned around Beinar to look down. Merpeople had gathered below, agitated, obviously trying to figure out what to do about the airship. Others had climbed to the top of the nearest tower, and one tossed a fishing spear at the cabin, though it fell short. "It's too high," Beinar muttered to Emilie. "So far they haven't brought out any spear guns."

"They are probably shooting at the Queen's people with them," Rani said grimly. She spoke to the other Cirathi man, taking his place at the ladder. He started to climb.

Emilie watched anxiously. The merpeople on the other tower cast a few spears, calling out angrily, but the man climbed rapidly, all the weapons falling short. Emilie let out the breath she hadn't realized she was holding, and looked back at Daniel and Dr Marlende.

Daniel stood at the doorway, his head down in concentration, Dr Marlende standing silently behind him. "Dr Marlende can help him do the charm?" Emilie asked.

"He hopes he can. Daniel's magic is different, apparently," Rani said, watching them worriedly. "Emilie, you climb now."

"Oh." Emilie had somehow managed to ignore the fact that she was going to have to climb the ladder too. Telling herself it wasn't as bad as climbing down the narrow tube into pitch darkness, she came around to grab the rungs and start the climb.

She found immediately that the big difference

between this ladder and the one down through the island was that this one was horrifically mobile. It swayed, the chain links clicking, the wooden rungs creaking and turning under her hands. Keep going, keep going, Emilie chanted mentally. She looked down, saw the ground and the angry merpeople, and almost vomited. She looked up at the dark airship looming hugely above her and that was somehow worse. She forced herself to go on, ignoring the shouts from the merpeople on the other tower, refusing to look at them in case that somehow improved their aim or spurred them to throw hard enough to reach her.

When someone grabbed her arm she choked back a yelp, but it was Seth. He dragged her up and onto the airship's catwalk.

Emilie found herself clinging to the railing, the wind tearing at her hair, her legs trembling violently. She couldn't believe she had made it. And why weren't the others following her?

"Where are they?" Seth demanded. "What are they doing?"

Emilie shook her head. "They can't- They're blocking the room off with an illusion, but if the merpeople realize what it is–" She couldn't see the front of the tower from here, but the merpeople on the ground suddenly turned and ran around the curve of the walls. "Oh hell! Someone must have figured out the tower wasn't on fire–"

Then the ladder suddenly jerked as a figure climbed

out the window. It was Dr Marlende, followed closely by Beinar.

Emilie watched, gripping the slender railing. They were almost up to the airship when Daniel started to climb. He had his head turned, shouting back down to the window, as he climbed. Then suddenly the ladder came loose, swinging free.

Emilie gasped in horror, but an instant later she saw Rani was hanging onto the end. She pointed wordlessly, and Seth swore. He turned, leaned into the doorway to shout, "Up, lift her up!"

Dr Marlende reached the catwalk, pulled himself up, then turned to reach for Beinar. Below, Daniel had stopped climbing to cling to the ladder as it swung wildly. Merpeople hung out the window of the tower now, casting spears. They came within a hairsbreadth of Rani and Daniel, but the ladder's motion confused their aim.

Beinar reached the top, but hung on to the strut of the railing, waiting for Daniel. The airship was lifting up, slowly and ponderously, and Daniel had started to climb again.

Seth and Dr Marlende were looking down at Daniel and Rani, exhorting them to hurry; Emilie kept watching the merpeople, looking from the window to the roof of the nearby tower. It took us too long, she thought, holding them off, getting the airship over here. They've had time to- She saw the figures in the window make way, saw someone holding the long shape of one of the projectile weapons. She yelled, "Look out! Gun!

There's a–"

Daniel was nearly to the catwalk, Rani just below him. Rani ducked down against the ladder, but Daniel looked wildly around. A bolt glanced off the ladder near his hand and he jerked away, lost his grip and hung by one hand. Beinar, holding on to the strut, stretched down to make a grab for him. And the next bolt struck Beinar in the neck.

Emilie froze, a sob of dismay caught in her throat, as he slumped forward. Dr Marlende flung himself flat on the catwalk, reaching for him, but Beinar tumbled off and fell. Emilie looked down, unable to help herself, and saw his body strike the ground, far below now.

Rani scrambled up the ladder, reached Daniel and pulled him back up. Seth crouched down, and he and Dr Marlende hauled Daniel up. Rani swung up after him. The airship was well above the towers now, turning away into the dark. Seth and the others dragged up the ladder, Dr Marlende helped Daniel through the door. Then Rani caught Emilie's arm and pulled her inside.

The cabin was dark, lit only by the soft glow of small electric lights set under the windows. The floor under Emilie's feet was soft and oddly textured, like a cork mat. The Cirathi were silent with shock, standing numbly at the windows. They must have seen everything.

Rani drew the two nearest into a hug, and someone sobbed quietly. Emilie knew if she stood here another moment, she would burst into tears. She turned and started toward the bow of the cabin.

It was too dark to see much, but she made her way past a few boxes and bags of supplies, stumbled into a padded bench, then down a short corridor lined with wooden cabinets. It was very quiet, as though they weren't in motion at all. The only indication that this was a vehicle was the faint vibration traveling through the floor from the propellers at the rear of the cabin. It was very strange.

She came out into a small round room that was mostly window, the glass curving around to form a wide port looking out into the darkness. Two small side windows were propped open, allowing in a cool breath of air. There were more lights here, set low just above the consoles of knobs and dials. They were small and tilted down, to illuminate the controls but not dazzle the eyes of the operators.

Dr Marlende stood at the small wheel, with Seth and Mikel. Daniel was crouched on the floor, his face buried in his hands.

Emilie rubbed her forehead, trying to collect her thoughts. She asked, "Do you know where the *Sovereign* is?"

Dr Marlende said, kindly, "No, my dear, I was going to give Rani a moment to steady herself before I asked. Do you know?"

"Yes." Emilie closed her eyes, recalling their position when they had arrived at the island yesterday. Yesterday? She thought in surprise. It feels like a week. "When we came up to the island, the Dark Wanderer was behind us. The Queen's fleet was toward the end of the island, off the starboard side, and Rani thought she saw the *Sovereign* there, so that should be..." Eyes still closed, she pointed.

"Ah, thank you, Emilie, that is exactly what I need to know." Dr Marlende turned the wheel, and made an adjustment to one of the knobs, and the floor tilted slightly under her feet.

Emilie nodded, pushing her hair back. It was saturated with sea salt and sweat, and felt like a dry tumbleweed perched on her head. "Is Charter going to be all right?"

"He should be," Seth told her. "Cobbier took him back to the bunk room to tend his shoulder."

That was good. Daniel was still on the floor. Emilie felt she had to do something about that. She crouched down in front of him, pulled at his wrists until he lowered his hands and looked at her. She could see his face in the instrument lights, and it was tear-streaked. She said, "It wasn't your fault." It was everyone's fault; it was no one's fault. Blaming Daniel was as bad as blaming Beinar, for being brave, for being the one who tried to help all the others, for being the one Rani sent upstairs with the younger Cirathi, knowing that he would take care of them.

Daniel shook his head mutely, and Emilie felt a flash of anger. If she could take this without breaking down, he could damn well take it too. "We don't have time to coddle you," she said roughly. "We need you. Now get up, wipe your face, and do your duty."

Daniel blinked, then glared at her in outrage. He

pulled away from her and stood up. Emilie got to her feet.

Seth and Mikel were staring at her, startled, while Dr Marlende's attention was studiously on the controls. Daniel turned away, folding his arms and gazing grimly out the port.

Rani stepped through into the cabin then. "We are heading for the *Sovereign*?" she asked. Her voice sounded a little raspy, as if she had been crying. She dropped a comforting arm around Emilie's shoulders, and Emilie leaned against her solid warmth.

"Yes, Emilie's given us the last position you noted for it," Dr Marlende told her. He frowned down at a dial. "We should be passing over the outer barrier now."

Emilie heard the distant roar of falling water; they must be climbing out of the canyon. I'm flying, she thought suddenly. Another thing she had never expected to do. Maybe I'll have time to enjoy it later. "How will we contact them? If the Queen didn't take any more hostages, maybe they can just run away from her."

Dr Marlende nodded to Seth. "Try to raise them on the wireless." Seth turned, but Daniel said quietly, "I'll do it, sir." He moved to a cabinet on the far side of the cabin, opening it to reveal a small wireless set.

Seth didn't comment, but exchanged a look with Mikel, and Emilie thought they were both relieved. Daniel adjusted some dials, and the wireless began to hum. He started to tap on the telegraph bar.

To Rani and Emilie, Dr Marlende explained, "The concentration of aether in the air makes it difficult to get through over long distances, but at this range we should be able to reach them." He added, with a slight edge to his voice, "I assume Lord Ivers has returned to the surface by now, which is unfortunate. It would perhaps be more satisfying to deal with him here, out of reach of the Menaen authorities."

"Lord Engal probably thinks so too," Emilie said. "Lord Ivers kept sending men to shoot at him."

"I had no idea the philosophical community had degenerated into internecine violence, but apparently it has," Dr Marlende muttered. He craned his neck, looking out the port. "Ah, there's the Queen's fleet."

Emilie and Rani went to the side to look out. Below them in the darkness were hundreds of little flickering lights, illuminating the large oblong shapes of the big barges, and the smaller darting rafts and boats. In the faint light around the smaller craft, Emilie caught glimpses of waves and a sandy beach. "They're going ashore there."

"Yes, Ise was right," Rani said thoughtfully. "They are attacking the island."

"That must be the *Sovereign*!" Mikel said. "Here, to starboard."

Emilie went to his side and saw it immediately. The *Sovereign*'s electric lights had a steady yellow glow, completely different from the fishoil lamps of the other ships, and they reflected off its metal hull. It was one of a group of ships lying just off the concave shore of a cove area, outlined by the lights of the smaller skiffs and rafts that had drawn up along its beach. Seth said, "That cove has a passage in through the canyon wall, to a small protected harbor where the nomads leave their boats. There's a stairway down to the valley floor."

"Yes, it must be the site of the main attack," Dr Marlende said. "She must be using the *Sovereign* to block any attempt at escape. Hopefully Engal wasn't forced to give them any rifles."

Then Daniel said, "I've got the *Sovereign*!" The wireless was now clicking back at him. Seth stepped to the cabinet and picked up a pencil and pad.

"They're very glad to hear from us," Daniel muttered, his expression preoccupied as he hurriedly translated the code into words.

Dr Marlende said, "Tell them we've recovered all our companions from the nomads, including the Cirathi and young Emilie here, and that my daughter is not being held hostage by the Queen. Ask if they are free to break away from the fleet."

Seth scribbled down the message, converted it to code, and showed Daniel, who tapped it out on the wireless. The answer came quickly, and after a moment Daniel translated, "They're free to break away, if you're certain the Queen doesn't have Miss Marlende and Emilie. She was threatening to kill them unless the *Sovereign* cooperated."

Dr Marlende glanced at Rani and Emilie. Rani said, "Lord Ivers has her, we are certain."

Dr Marlende nodded to Daniel, who tapped out a brief assent. The reply was longer in coming. Seth translated it, saying, "They say if we can distract the ships around them, they should be able to break free."

"Tell them to expect a distraction in the next few minutes," Dr Marlende said, and turned the wheel.

The deck tilted under Emilie's feet as the airship turned, angling down. She managed to catch herself on a console without turning any of the knobs. She retreated to the doorway where Rani was holding on. Emilie asked, "Are you going to use magic to distract them?" She was thinking the illusory fire could be very effective dropping out of the sky.

Dr Marlende took the airship into a long dive. "I hope we don't have to. I'd like to conserve my resources for the moment. But I think the flares should suffice. Seth, could you...?"

Phosphorus flares proved even more effective than bright illusions, as Seth, Rani, Mikel, and two other Cirathi tossed them off the catwalk. They ignited directly over the Sealands' ships, lighting up the sky and causing confusion and terror. Emilie and the others watched from the windows as one long warship sideswiped another and broke off a whole bank of oars. She lost sight of the *Sovereign*, but then realized that in the midst of the chaos, it had doused its electric running lights and must be steaming for the open sea.

Emilie hurried back to the steering cabin in time to hear Daniel's report from the wireless: "The Queen's naval commander forced them to abandon the *Lathi* before the battle, and they anchored it off a small island a few miles from here. They're going to retrieve it now before the Queen's forces get re-organized enough to order a pursuit."

"Oh, I don't think they'll pursue us," Dr Marlende said, bringing the airship around for a pass over the other section of the fleet. "The Nomads should take this opportunity to counter-attack. I know Prince Ise has forces hanging back to the south. I should think they'll all be quite occupied for a while. Tell the *Sovereign* to meet us–"

The wireless interrupted with a sudden series of clicks. Daniel frowned, startled. "That's not..." He scribbled hastily on his pad, then checked the code book. He looked up. "A ship called the *Philosopher's Quest*?"

Emilie shook her head, baffled, as Daniel hurriedly transcribed another message. Then his jaw set, and he said grimly, "It's a request for assistance. From Lord Ivers."

ELEVEN

They met up with the *Sovereign* hours later, as the eclipse was passing away across the sea. The spot they had chosen was a low-lying island some distance from the Nomads' fortress. As the airship reached it, Emilie could see the Aerinterre aether current in the sky, the solid band of heavy gray cloud with the translucent column stretching up from it, vanishing high in the air.

Not having to worry about navigating shoals, the airship had arrived first. Dr Marlende lowered it far enough to drop the ladder, so Seth, Cobbier, Daniel, and a few Cirathi could climb down to the pebbly ground and secure the anchor cables to several squat but sturdy trees. The *Sovereign* was only a short time behind them, and it soon arrived, towing the *Lathi*. They waited impatiently on the beach as the steamer anchored and sent the launch ashore.

Kenar leapt out of it before the boat reached the beach and waded in the thigh-deep water. Rani met him halfway and they flew into each other's arms, and Rani swung him around and nearly knocked him off his feet. It was the most romantic thing Emilie had ever seen in her life, and her eyes welled up with tears. All the other Cirathi gathered around, waiting excitedly for their chance to greet him. Emilie knew the happy moment would end when Rani had to tell him about poor Beinar.

Lord Engal waited more decorously until the launch had actually been drawn up on the beach, before he climbed out and strode up to shake hands. "Dr Marlende, I presume."

"You presume correctly, sir." Dr Marlende greeted him gravely. "Thank you for sending young Emilie to our assistance; her arrival was quite timely."

Lord Engal eyed her with exasperation and, she was startled to see, some fondness. "At this point, it hardly surprises me."

"Now if we can just extract my daughter from Lord Ivers," Dr Marlende continued.

"Yes." Lord Engal frowned, shielding his eyes to look into the distance. "If what he said was true, which is rather a big 'if,' since the man is an inveterate liar and criminal–"

"Yes, of course." Dr Marlende neatly cut off the potential diatribe. "But if his aetheric engine has not been sabotaged, then he has no reason to linger here or contact us."

During the eclipse, as they fled the battle between the Queen's forces and the Nomads, there had been a long three-cornered wireless conversation between their airship, the *Sovereign*, and Lord Ivers' craft. He had claimed that at some point before he had left the Sealands' capital, one of the Queen's courtiers who had been aboard his airship had sabotaged his aetheric engine, leaving him stranded in the Hollow World.

"You were right, Rani," Emilie had said quietly. "The Queen didn't intend to let him go. She knew he wouldn't be able to get back, and he'd have to come to her for help, and she'd make him use the airship against the Nomads."

"Yes, but her plan would not have worked," Rani said, lifting her brows. "The airships need fuel for the engine in the back that works the propellers. Dr Marlende explained this, and all the limitations of this craft, when we first began to explore together."

Emilie snorted. "I bet Lord Ivers didn't explain his limitations to the Queen."

"But he must have explained the aetheric engine, or the merpeople wouldn't have known how to sabotage it," Daniel said. He was taking a break from transcribing the wireless, and Seth and Mikel were manning it and the code book. Leaning against the wall near Emilie, he hadn't referred to their little altercation earlier, but he did seem to be making an effort not to act awkwardly around her. It was taking an effort on her part not to act awkwardly around him; she felt she had overstepped herself quite a bit.

Rani said, dryly, "That was stupid of Ivers."

"Yes, and naive, on his part," Dr Marlende had agreed, standing at the airship's wheel. "He thought them too primitive to do anything with the information." He added, with grim satisfaction, "He's paying for his poor judgment now."

Lord Ivers had promised to release Miss Marlende in exchange for their help with his engine, though Emilie wasn't counting any chickens until that actually happened. She thought Lord Ivers would try until the last moment to double-cross them. But they had eventually arranged to meet here on this island, and now all they had to do was wait.

As they stood on the beach, Dr Barshion came up to Dr Marlende. He shook hands, saying, "It's an honor to see you again, sir. And we can certainly use your help with the *Sovereign*'s aetheric engine." He admitted, "The ship's engineers and I weren't quite up to the mark, I'm afraid."

Emilie was glad to hear him say it aloud. She didn't think it would help if Dr Barshion got stubborn about accepting Dr Marlende's aid the way he had when Mr. Abendle had wanted to ask Miss Marlende's opinion. But maybe it was easier for him, since Dr Marlende was both a man and an acknowledged expert. Dr Marlende only said, kindly, "As long as you've brought the supplies I had to send Kenar and my poor friend Jerom for. I was completely wrong about the resonance needed for the quickaether sustainers, and it contaminated the replacements I had brought along before we realized what the problem was."

Emilie missed the rest, as Kenar arrived and caught her in a hug that lifted her off her feet. His voice rough with emotion, he said, "Thank you for rescuing Rani, Emilie."

"I wish we'd been able to rescue Miss Marlende as well, but we were too late," Emilie said, breathless as he set her back down. "And they shot at us, a lot." She looked up at him and asked hesitantly, "Did they tell you about Beinar?"

"Yes, they told me." He squeezed her shoulders and she could see the sadness in his eyes. "He was a very good friend."

They waited through the morning. Dr Marlende and Daniel went aboard the *Sovereign* to get the materials needed to fix the airship's aetheric engine, and to consult with Dr Barshion and Mr. Abendle. The Cirathi spent the time checking over their ship, making minor repairs, and getting it ready for their long voyage home. "I think we have worn out our welcome in these waters," Rani said. They were in the galley cabin, and Emilie was helping her sort out which foodstuffs had gone bad and which could be saved. "We'll go back and report to our guild, and tell everyone else to think twice before they come here."

"I'm never going to see you or Kenar again," Emilie said, only realizing after the words were out how forlorn she sounded. She poked dispiritedly at a bag of meal that had something growing in it. "I mean, even if there are other expeditions, they probably won't let me come. I'm only here accidentally, after all."

"Ah, Emilie," Rani said, putting down a jar and turning to regard her. "We will never forget you. Will you forget us?"

"No, never," Emilie said, her voice thick.

"Then that will have to be enough," Rani said, and hugged her again.

Someone called out from the deck, and they ran out to see the distant shape of an airship approaching from antidarkward. "He did come," Emilie said, feeling a certain tightness in her chest ease. They would get Miss Marlende back. "He didn't lie about that, at least."

Rani nodded thoughtfully. "Now we just need to figure out what he is lying about."

Lord Ivers brought his airship in toward the far end of the island, lowered it until it was about twenty feet above the ground, then dropped a chain ladder.

Emilie waited on the beach with Lord Engal, Dr Marlende, Rani, Kenar, and Dr Barshion, along with Oswin and Daniel and half a dozen armed sailors. Most of the Cirathi were aboard the *Lathi*, and there were armed sailors on the deck of the *Sovereign*, just in case Lord Ivers made some sort of attempt on either ship.

Now that both craft were here for comparison, Emilie could see Lord Ivers' airship was a little larger than Dr Marlende's, and its two-story cabin was certainly more impressive. But the wind off the sea was strong, and the airship was having to fight it, its propellers spinning rapidly as the pilot made hurried adjustments. "They aren't going to anchor," Oswin pointed out.

"No, but I wouldn't either, in his position," Dr Marlende said. "One of the hazards of a course of betrayal and aggression is that one can never trust others. You know they have more than enough cause to betray you in turn."

Rani folded her arms, frustrated. "Which was the point I was trying to make when I suggested we simply set upon him and extract your daughter."

"If we could have figured out an effective way to do it," Lord Engal muttered, "I would have embraced your suggestion whole-heartedly."

The airship steadied finally and a lone figure began to climb down the chain ladder. From his height and his clothes, Emilie could tell it was Lord Ivers himself. "He's coming alone?" she said, surprised.

Lord Engal snorted derisively. "Of course. The man's ego wouldn't permit anything else."

Lord Ivers reached the ground and made the long walk down the beach toward them. This was the first time Emilie had seen him face to face. He was lean, with light Northern Menaen blond hair and striking blue eyes. He was about Lord Engal's age, but he had sharper features, and was more handsome. Much more the conventional image of a noble lord philosopher. Especially compared to Lord Engal, who was big and hearty and looked like he could do a good day's manual labor without suffering unduly. Emilie expected that Lord Ivers' gentlemanly appearance probably had a lot of people fooled.

He stopped a few paces away, nodded to Dr Marlende, and said, "Dr Marlende, I presume."

Lord Engal said dryly, "I did that already."

Lord Ivers eyed him, his lip curled in mild derision.

"I'm sure you enjoyed it. You've always been greatly pleased by your small accomplishments."

Lord Engal sputtered, "It's your petty competitiveness that turned this from a philosophical experiment into a race–"

"Oh, you calling anyone 'petty' has to be the ultimate–"

There was some restless movement among the others. Kenar gritted his teeth, Rani rubbed the bridge of her nose in tight-lipped annoyance, and Dr Barshion sighed wearily. Emilie was pretty certain it was Daniel who had snorted incredulously. Dr Marlende cut it off before it went on any longer, saying sharply, "Gentlemen! If this is a race, I've won it." He turned to Lord Ivers. "Now release my daughter, sir, or I'll shoot you." He rested his hand on the pistol tucked into his belt.

Now that's more like it, Emilie thought. Everyone seemed a little taken aback, except Rani, Kenar, and Daniel, who obviously knew Dr Marlende better than the others. Lord Ivers looked affronted, and Lord Engal startled. Lord Ivers said, "You would shoot a man in cold blood–"

Dr Marlende was unimpressed. "My blood is hardly cold. Release my daughter. Now."

Lord Ivers watched him a moment, then evidently decided to get down to business. He said, "I will be happy to release Miss Marlende in exchange for your assistance with repairs to my aetheric engine."

Dr Marlende countered, "Release my daughter now, and I'll forgo my desire to shoot you." He added, reluctantly, "And I'll consider not stranding you and your crew of miscreants here."

Emilie was watching Lord Ivers very carefully, and she thought she saw relief and satisfaction flicker across his face, though it was too brief to be certain it wasn't her imagination. He said, stiffly, "My engine wouldn't have failed if it hadn't been sabotaged, unlike yours and Engal's. I suggest you will benefit more from my assistance."

Lord Engal laughed. "'Your engine?' I don't know who you stole it from but–"

Dr Marlende interrupted again. "You've heard my offer. Release my daughter now, sir."

Lord Ivers' jaw tightened. "You agree to repair my engine?"

Dr Marlende didn't budge. "As I said, I'll undertake not to strand you here. Now give me your decision. I'm just as happy to shoot you and continue this negotiation with your second-in-command."

Lord Ivers said, grimly, "I see I have no choice. I'll release Miss Marlende." He turned, and lifted his arm to wave, once, at his airship.

Emilie tensed, aware that everyone else had too. The sailors moved restlessly, shifting their grips on their weapons.

But after a moment a single figure in a battered tweed jacket and skirt stepped out of the door and onto the platform, and started to climb down the ladder. Emilie's heart leapt. It was Miss Marlende.

Emilie held her breath as Miss Marlende quickly

walked all the long way down the beach, but it wasn't a trick or a trap. As she reached them, Kenar muttered something in Cirathi, sounding profoundly relieved. Lord Engal still watched Lord Ivers with skeptical suspicion. Dr Marlende just stepped forward, and said in a thick voice, "Are you quite well, my dear? I've engaged not to shoot him, but I'm happy to retract the promise if you've been harmed."

Lord Ivers looked affronted. "I beg your pardon. I've treated the girl in a perfectly civilized–"

"I'm fine, father. He's an arrogant and greedy cad, but he didn't hurt me," Miss Marlende assured him. She looked tired and a little mussed, but didn't seem injured at all. She reached Dr Marlende and hugged him tightly. "And I'm so happy to see you."

Emilie managed to wait her turn behind Dr Marlende and Kenar, but finally she could throw herself into Miss Marlende's arms. "I'm sorry we couldn't get you out too," Emilie said in a rush, aware she was babbling but unable to stop. "By the time Rani and I got back, the airship had taken off–"

"Emilie, it's all right," Miss Marlende assured her, hugging her back. "If I'd been quicker off the mark, I could have jumped into the water after Rani, but I missed my chance. There was nothing you could do."

"This is a very touching reunion, but I believe we have other more pressing concerns–" Lord Ivers began.

"Oh, shut up," Lord Engal told him, earning Emilie's approval for all time. "I want your airship anchored and your men to come out and turn over their weapons, and if they hold so much as a pocketknife back, I'll shoot you myself."

Radiating contempt, Lord Ivers agreed to everything Lord Engal asked.

Somehow, that didn't make Emilie feel the least bit reassured.

"I still feel it was too easy," Rani said, frustrated. "Ivers practically handed himself to us."

"Yes," Miss Marlende agreed. "He had to know my father wouldn't feel obligated to fulfill his end of the bargain, not after Ivers behaved like a criminal." They were aboard the *Sovereign*, in the lounge with the big windows, where Emilie and the others had spent the voyage down through the aether current. Kenar and Daniel were here too; Dr Marlende and most of the others were working on the *Sovereign*'s aetheric engine, and Lord Engal and his sailors were busy guarding Lord Ivers' men and searching his airship. Miss Marlende added, "Lord Engal intends to press a charge against him for my kidnapping. And once the magistrates begin to investigate that, I'm more than certain we can turn up some evidence that he ordered the sabotages we suffered while planning the expedition, as well as the attack on the *Sovereign* in Meneport."

Emilie was glad to hear that Lord Ivers would pay for what he had done, though she thought the punishment would probably be inadequate. She said, "He planned to strand us here – can't we do the same to him?"

Miss Marlende shook her head. "Abandoning Lord

Ivers might be the most appealing solution, but we just can't do it. If left in the Hollow World, he would probably become a pirate or worse, and with his knowledge of aetheric and conventional engines, there's no telling what trouble he would make."

Daniel added, "Dr Marlende is afraid the Queen's people would find him, and Ivers would help them invent new devices to use against the Nomads, and anyone else within range."

Kenar said, "Are we certain the airship was really sabotaged? That it wasn't a trick to allow him to contact us?"

Emilie had been wondering that herself.

But Miss Marlende said, "No, I'm certain the sabotage was real." She leaned forward on the couch. "I heard the crew talking about it. Two small but key components, including the quickaether stabilizer for the motile, were removed. Both were easily disconnected elements. I suspect the merpeople requested a tour of the airship, then removed them while Ivers and his crew were distracted or absent. They might not have known what the components did, but it wouldn't take an aetheric sorcerer or an engineer to spot them as important. I expect they thought the airship wouldn't be able to take off; when it did, they thought their plan had failed, and they pinned their hopes for overwhelming the Nomads on the *Sovereign*."

She added, "Lord Ivers' sorcerer is competent to maintain the spells, but that's all. He had no hope of effecting the repairs himself."

Emilie asked, "But what are we going to do with his airship? If we leave it here, the Queen might find it."

Kenar jerked his chin toward the door, indicating the activity on the beach. "Engal plans to destroy it. I think it's the best course." He smiled a little. "He's looking forward to telling Lord Ivers about it."

Rani snorted. "I'm sure he will like to make Ivers watch."

It was a shame; the airship was beautiful, in its way, but they couldn't leave it here. Emilie said, "Will they set it on fire?"

Daniel nodded. "With the fuel oil from the conventional engine, after they remove the quickaether and the other valuable components."

"It will take some time." Watching the Cirathi worriedly, Miss Marlende said, "I think you should go ahead and leave, if the *Lathi* is ready to sail. You've already done so much for my father, and after what happened to your friend Beinar... I don't want you to sacrifice anything else for us."

Kenar lifted his brows, and exchanged a look with Rani. Rani let out her breath, and said, "We did much for your father because we owe him much, and I don't think he would leave us, if our situations were reversed. But I feel there is little we can do for you, except help you stare suspiciously at Lord Ivers." Rani shrugged. "We will stay as long as we can, and follow you to make sure your ships enter the aether current as planned."

Smiling, Kenar nudged her with his shoulder. "Good. I know the others will agree."

Miss Marlende nodded, and Emilie could tell she was relieved. "Thank you."

The conference broke up at that point, as there was nothing much they could do, and Rani and Kenar needed to get back to the *Lathi* to continue the preparations for their voyage home. As the others left, Daniel caught up with Emilie in the corridor, and said awkwardly, "I wanted to apologize for my behavior, on the airship, after Beinar… fell. It was, uh…"

Emilie thought that "natural" was perhaps the word he was looking for. He had known Beinar personally, when she hadn't, and she felt she had been high-handed, at the least. She said, quickly, "No, it's all right. I'm sorry I was so sharp with you. I was just afraid something would happen and we wouldn't escape after all. And it was a shock."

Daniel nodded, and they continued down the corridor. After a moment, he said, "You get angry when you're shocked?"

Emilie threw a suspicious look at him. Possibly he was teasing her. "Apparently so." Partly to poke back at him, and partly from real curiosity, she added, "Why aren't you helping Dr Marlende and Dr Barshion with the engines?"

"I'm not that kind of sorcerer." Daniel shoved his hands in his pockets, though he didn't sound too disgruntled. "I just don't have the aptitude for aether mechanics. I'm learning naturalistic magic."

Emilie frowned. "From Dr Marlende? I thought he was an expert in aether mechanics."

Daniel smiled faintly. "He's an expert in both."

Emilie had no trouble believing that. Dr Marlende wasn't the kind of philosopher who wrote learned articles on other people's discoveries; he was the kind who made the discoveries. "What about Dr Barshion?"

"I don't know." Daniel sounded thoughtful. "I've seen his name in the Philosophical Society's journals, occasionally, but I don't know anything about him–"

Seth came out of the cross corridor at the end of the passage, spotted them, and waved. He said, "Come up to the wheelhouse, the doctor thinks he has it figured out!"

Daniel lengthened his stride, and Emilie hurried to keep up. Daniel called back, "What figured out? You mean–"

"How we're all getting out of here!"

On the chart table in the wheelhouse, Dr Marlende spread out several maps, with Lord Engal, Captain Belden, Miss Marlende, Dr Barshion, and Mr. Abendle looking on. Charter was here too, his arm in a sling and looking much better than the last time Emilie had seen him. He nodded to her as she and Daniel and Seth squeezed in around the table. Emilie smiled back, then looked at the maps. Except they weren't maps, but diagrams of something, covered with arrows and handwritten figures.

Dr Marlende said, "Lord Engal has been aboard Lord Ivers' airship, and removed all the aetheric components that were salvageable. It's ready to be destroyed, and

Seth and I will set that in motion as soon as we're finished here."

Lord Engal stroked his beard. "I also removed the scientific information he collected, photographic film, notes, plant and insect specimens, that sort of thing." Dr Marlende eyed him, and Lord Engal cleared his throat. "I expect you to take charge of it, of course. I've collected my own information."

But he'd like more, since it would make for an even better presentation to the Philosophical Explorers Society, Emilie thought, managing not to roll her eyes.

Dr Marlende said, "Of course." He turned back to the diagram. "With the array of spare parts and supplies you have generously brought along, I can quickly repair the damage to my own aetheric engine, but the *Sovereign*'s situation is far more difficult. The aether component that supports the protective shield, the "bubble" necessary for travel within the current, is out of balance. It can be raised to enclose the ship, but it simply will not hold its shape for the entire length of the journey. I could try to recalibrate it, but it might take several days. And with the possibility that the Queen's forces are searching for us, our time is severely limited. What I propose to do is finish the repairs to my airship, and calibrate the two vessels' aetheric engines to work together, and then extend the airship's protective bubble to include the *Sovereign*, so we can travel through the aether current together."

Everyone stared at him. Emilie thought she was following his line of thought, and the whole idea seemed dangerous. Not that traveling through the aetheric current was safe to begin with, but this seemed an even more unlikely and dubious method.

Dr Barshion leaned over the diagrams, his brow furrowed. "So both crafts will travel through the current as one?"

Emilie realized the arrows and figures must represent the Aerinterre aether current, though she still couldn't make head or tails of them. She said, "But what happens to the *Sovereign* once we get there?" She knew that once inside the current, it didn't matter what it passed through, but if the *Sovereign* went back through the volcano it would surely end up perched on the rocky mountain somewhere. And she couldn't be the only one who was wondering that. Captain Belden was listening with sharp interest.

Dr Marlende told her, "This aether current has many outlets, through fissures in the ocean bottom around the island. I only used the volcano itself because it was more convenient for my airship." He tapped the diagram. "I can release the *Sovereign* from the joining here; its protective bubble should last long enough for it to be drawn with the current straight out the fissure and to the surface. There will only be a few minutes of current travel left by that point, and my airship will continue up and exit the current through the volcano's cauldron."

Lord Engal nodded slowly, his brow furrowed with concern. "I don't see that we have much of a choice, if the *Sovereign* can't make the complete journey unassisted."

Dr Marlende said, "Very well, then." He rolled up his diagram with a satisfied air. "Now all we have to do is survive to reach the surface!"

Everyone winced.

The *Sovereign* steamed toward the Aerinterre aether current, reaching it after the end of the next eclipse. The *Lathi* trailed behind, sailing under its own power, and Dr Marlende's airship soared overhead.

Lord Ivers airship had been left behind on the island, a broken, charred ruin. The rigid metal framework of its balloon, exposed as the gas inside had been released and then the fabric covering burned away, had looked like a huge creature's skeleton. It depressed Emilie to see it, and somehow seemed to bode ill for their future prospects.

As Lord Engal had decided, Lord Ivers and his men were now locked up in one of the *Sovereign*'s secure holds. It made Emilie nervous to have them there, though there were four armed crewmen guarding the door at all times. Lord Ivers had thrown a fit and made angry threats when Lord Engal had given the order, but since he and his men had already given up their weapons, there wasn't much he could do.

Emilie thought Lord Engal and Dr Marlende had taken every precaution, at least every precaution that they could think of, but she was still uneasy. Standing at the railing with Miss Marlende, watching the giant round cloud of the Aerinterre current loom overhead, she said, "I'm just worried, that's all."

"I'm worried, too," Miss Marlende admitted. She was watching the airship move closer to the *Sovereign*, angling in to get as close to it as possible in anticipation of joining their protective spells. This seemed to be a fairly difficult and potentially disastrous operation, and it was making Emilie edgy just to watch. Miss Marlende continued, "I won't feel easy until we're steaming into port."

"We couldn't leave Lord Ivers behind on an island and come back and get him later?" Emilie suggested, only partly joking.

"It's tempting," Miss Marlende said. "But somehow I don't think travel down here is going to become all the rage. Especially if the trip through the current tends to damage the aetheric engines. Ivers admitted that after he arrived his sorcerer had to repair the aether navigator in his motile too."

Emilie glanced up at her. "That was what you thought was wrong with the *Sovereign*'s motile, wasn't it?"

"Yes, and it turned out I was right, though there were apparently a few other adjustments that needed to be made that had confused the issue. My father repaired it fairly quickly last night. But it's the protective bubble that's the real problem, of course." Dr Marlende had spent part of the night on the *Sovereign*, getting its protective spells ready to work in concert with his airship. Then he had called the airship on the wireless, had it lower a ladder over the *Sovereign*'s deck in the glare of the spotlights, and dramatically climbed it to finish the repairs and preparations aboard it.

"Why didn't Dr Barshion, and Mr. Abendle and Ricard know about that, then?" Emilie asked, somewhat annoyed. "At least we would have known what was wrong."

Miss Marlende grimaced. "I don't know. I don't think Barshion's in over his head, but I do think perhaps he was overworked, and overtired." She sighed. "But I suppose it doesn't matter now."

Her eyes were on the *Lathi*, which had anchored at a safe distance from the current. Emilie followed her gaze. They had already said their goodbyes before leaving the island, and the Cirathi were only waiting to watch them enter the current before they began their own voyage home. Emilie said, "I wish we could say goodbye again." She wished she didn't have to say goodbye at all, but she knew that was impractical.

"It wouldn't make us feel any better," Miss Marlende said, sounding glum, and gave Emilie a hug.

It took some time, lots of maneuvering, and various people with megaphones shouting warnings from the *Sovereign*'s decks, but they managed to lower the airship down over the water, so its cabin was level with the *Sovereign*'s second deck. Emilie watched this process from the deck above, in the enclosed promenade with Miss Marlende, both of them braced to run inside if the propellers swung their way. The rigid balloon was bigger than the *Sovereign*, blotting out their view of the sky.

Mikel stepped out onto the catwalk and tossed a line

across to the waiting sailors. "Just attach it to the railing!" he called.

Lord Engal motioned for the man to go ahead, and he looped the line around the metal railing. Oswin, who had just come up from below, said worriedly, "If the wind changes and pushes the airship away, it'll take that railing with it."

"It's not meant as an anchor. It's a symbolic connection between the two vessels, for the spell." Engal turned to the nearest hatch and called to a waiting sailor, "Tell Barshion we're ready!"

A few moments later, a deep vibration shuddered through the deck; the *Sovereign*'s aetheric engine engaging. Emilie gripped the railing nervously, remembering how the deck had heaved last time, but Miss Marlende said, "It's considerably smoother, isn't it? My father must have made some adjustments."

There was an answering roar from the airship that made Emilie jump; before this it had been relatively quiet. Then the gold barrier rose up, cutting off their view of the water, streaming upward to enclose the airship and the *Sovereign* together in a giant bubble. The noise of the two engines rose and fell, and Emilie saw the airship's propellers had stopped spinning.

She followed Miss Marlende down the stairs and out onto the open deck. As they arrived, Dr Marlende and Mikel were dropping a set of metal stairs down from the catwalk over the *Sovereign*'s railing to the deck. It was at a steep slant, but at least the airship was still now, steady as a rock, held in place by the protective bubble.

"We're ready when you are, My Lord," Seth called from the catwalk, and stepped back into the airship.

On the deck below, Lord Engal told Oswin, "Get down to the engine room. Notify me immediately if there are any problems supplying power to the aetheric compartments." Oswin bolted off and Lord Engal turned and strode inside.

Miss Marlende pushed away from the railing. "Let's watch from the wheelhouse."

They hurried through the corridors, reaching the wheelhouse as Lord Engal was ready to give the command. The big ports around three sides of the room were filled with the golden light of the bubble, except for the one to starboard, where the bullet-nose of the airship's balloon was visible. Emilie could just make out the sea past the barrier, though the glare of the sun made it difficult. Captain Belden and the other two sailors looked suitably stoic, but Emilie thought they were sweating. Lord Engal saw them and said grimly, "Better hold on."

Miss Marlende and Emilie braced themselves against the cabin wall. Lord Engal nodded to Captain Belden who took the lever of the engine telegraph and pulled it down, sending a "full ahead" message to the engine room.

The entire ship shook, metal screeched. Then Emilie felt the deck push up at her feet. Her stomach lurched and she gripped the railing more tightly. The aether current drew both vessels up out of the water; she could see the surface dropping away below. Somehow this sensation hadn't bothered her aboard Dr Marlende's airship; maybe because Dr Marlende's airship was actually supposed to fly.

They went up and up, faster and faster, until the sky darkened and they could see nothing past the protective bubble. Lord Engal let out his breath and said, "That's that. All we have to do now is wait until we reach the surface, and the rift in the ocean floor."

Oh, that's all, Emilie thought, but everyone relaxed a little, breathing again.

TWELVE

Emilie found this return journey much more tense than the trip down, which didn't seem to make much sense. Maybe it was the fact that now she knew just how difficult and dangerous traveling in an aether current was. The first time it had just seemed like magic, the easy powerful magic of fairy stories. Now she knew it was really the hard uncertain magic of philosophical sorcery, and that it might fail at any moment and kill them all.

It didn't help that she felt as if these short days in the Hollow World had aged her at least ten years.

She spent the time with Miss Marlende, sitting in a couple of hard chairs in the chart-room. It would have been more comfortable to go down to one of the lounges, but neither of them did. It eased Emilie's nerves a little to be here, watching Lord Engal check the aether navigator and his copies of Dr Marlende's diagrams. Sometimes he sent a sailor down to take a message with hastily scribbled figures to Dr Marlende on the airship, or below decks to Dr Barshion with a question.

But nothing went wrong, and tension started to segue into boredom. Emilie and Miss Marlende got up to stretch their legs, and walked around the ship a little. It was oddly quiet; everyone in the crew who wasn't manning a station had been told to stay in their quarters. It was eerie, and something of a relief to get back to the wheelhouse.

After a few hours, Mrs. Verian served a brief meal of sandwiches and tea, which Emilie helped her carry up from the galley. Having a full stomach made it harder to stay awake, at least for Emilie, and she dozed off and on for a bit, waking whenever she almost fell out of her chair.

She straightened up finally, blinking the sleep away, to see Lord Engal pacing back and forth in front of the wheel, rubbing his hands together briskly. He called a sailor in and sent him off with a hurried message for Dr Marlende. "What's going on?" Emilie asked Miss Marlende.

"We're almost there." Miss Marlende stretched and rolled her shoulders. "It's getting close to the time when we'll break off from the airship and make our way out through the fissure in the ocean floor."

Emilie hugged herself, breathing out in relief. "We made it."

Miss Marlende said, preoccupied, "I'll feel better when we're out of the current." She glanced at Emilie. "What will you do when we get back, Emilie? Did you want us to drop you off at Silk Harbor?" She hesitated. "Or did you want to go home?"

Emilie frowned at the polished wooden floor, which was marred by sandy footprints and sandwich crumbs; it had been a few days since anyone had had time to think about things like sweeping the floors. Realistically, she knew her future at Silk Harbor was uncertain. Karthea would be hard-pressed to be able to provide her with any other wage than a place to sleep. You don't even know if she'll let you work for her. But if she won't... I'll think of something else. She said, "Silk Harbor. I still want to see if my cousin will let me help with her school." She added tentatively, "Perhaps I can see you and Dr Marlende again, when you're in town?"

Miss Marlende watched her, her brow furrowed in concern. "Are you certain? I'm sure whatever difficulty you had with your family- Perhaps I could help-"

"I can't go home." Telling Kenar had been much easier, probably because he hadn't really grasped the full implication of what she had said. When she had first arrived on the boat, telling anyone else, especially Miss Marlende, had seemed impossible. But Miss Marlende knew her better now. Emilie glanced around, making sure the men in the wheelhouse were too busy to overhear, then reluctantly wrestled the words out. "Even if you and your father and Lord Engal gave me letters explaining what happened, even if you came with me and lied and swore that I'd been chaperoned the entire time, it wouldn't do any good. That's why I left."

"Chaperoned? Oh." Miss Marlende's frown deepened. "I think I see. There were accusations without basis?" She read Emilie's expression accurately. "And perhaps some threats of punishment for things you hadn't done, or didn't contemplate doing?"

"Yes." Emilie felt a tightness in her chest ease. "My mother ran off to become an actress, and although she got married..."

"You would think, in this day and age..." Miss Marlende's mouth set in a grim line. "You don't believe there is any chance of reconciliation?"

"Not now. Especially not after I ran away," Emilie admitted. "Maybe later. Years later." The situation between the Sealands Queen and the Nomads had given her some perspective. She thought too much had been said on both her part and on her uncle's part for anyone to back down.

Miss Marlende said slowly, "Well then, perhaps, if the situation with your cousin doesn't work out, you'd be interested in a position as my personal assistant?"

"What? Yes." Emilie blinked. "Doing what?"

Miss Marlende smiled. "I do a great deal of work for my father, writing letters, monographs about his work, plus traveling and meeting with members of learned societies, that sort of thing. I could use some secretarial help. And perhaps, if I have a younger woman in tow, I'd look a bit more matronly to some of the men I have to meet with, and they would be less inclined to treat me like a frivolous debutante." She shrugged wryly. "Probably not, but it's worth a try."

Emilie nodded rapidly. "Oh, yes. Thank you." It sounded less like adventuring and more like a junior social secretary, but still... Social secretary to adventurers would be far more interesting than schoolteacher. It was a fabulous opportunity.

Lord Engal interrupted then, stepping out of the wheelhouse, frowning distractedly. "Evers? Where's Evers?"

"You sent Evers with a message to my father," Miss Marlende reminded him.

Emilie thought she might as well start being useful immediately. "Do you need someone to take a message, My Lord?" She had remembered to call him "My Lord" that time; she hoped he had noticed.

He said, "Yes, to Dr Barshion, if you don't mind. I asked him to send me the adjustments for the aether navigator we'll need to make for the Aerinterre surface current. It's not urgent at the moment, but I don't want to waste time once we break through to the surface."

"I'll be right back." Emilie went down the stairs, glad for a chance to work off the excitement. Her heart was pounding a little. She found herself looking forward to getting back a great deal more now.

She went all the way down to the lower deck, just above the engine room, and down the aetheric compartment corridor. The air was hot and damp. She passed the room with the device that kept the air clean inside the bubble. It had the same mist, earthy smell, and bemused operator as the first time she had seen it.

She reached the doorway of the aetheric engine room, where a sailor stood on guard. He nodded to her, smiling, and she recognized him as one of the men who had helped search the island where they had found the

Lathi. "Hello. I've got a message for Dr Barshion."

Ricard poked his head out. He looked tired, and sweat was beaded on his forehead, but his expression was cheerful. It was another sign that things were going well down here. "Hello, Miss Emilie. He's not here. He went up to the wheelhouse to see Lord Engal."

"No, he's not there," Emilie told him. "That's where I've come from. Lord Engal wants the adjustments for the aether navigator for the Aerinterre surface current."

Ricard stepped back and Mr. Abendle came to the doorway. Behind him, Emilie saw the copper dome on its plinth, connected to all the pipes and tubing. It was humming loudly and hissing a little as wisps of steam escaped from its pipes. Mr. Abendle had a bandana tied around his head like an old pirate. He said, "That's odd. Oh, I bet he went to Dr Marlende first. I'll get the figures for Lord Engal and send someone up with them."

"All right, thank you." Emilie started away, feeling sweat already sticking her shirt to her back. She hoped she would have time to take a bath after they reached the surface.

She reached the cooler air of the stairwell, and stopped. The stairs that led down to the main engine room and the boilers were at the opposite end of the aetheric room corridor. This stairwell led down to the forward hold, where Lord Ivers and his men were held prisoner.

It wasn't that she was suspicious... But this was an odd time for the *Sovereign*'s aetheric sorcerer to go missing, even temporarily. If, just say if, Lord Engal sends a sailor with a note, asking for the figures, she thought, Dr Barshion pretends it's asking him to come to the wheelhouse, and no one knows where he is. That would be one reason for Lord Ivers to put himself in Lord Engal's power, if he had a man on the inside, someone who could help him... Do what? Escape after we get to the surface? she wondered.

You've read too many novels, Emilie. But now the thought was like an itch in a place you weren't allowed to scratch in public. I'll just take a look at the guards to make sure everything is all right.

She went down the stairs. There was a short corridor at the bottom, but only one open hatchway along it. She headed toward it, prepared to say that Lord Engal had sent her to see if everything was all right. Though that was a little unlikely. Maybe she could say...

Emilie froze in the hatchway, staring. The four crewmen left to guard the hold lay sprawled on the floor, and the door behind them was wide open. They were wearing only their shirts and drawers; their uniform jackets and trousers were missing.

It took her a full minute to believe her eyes. Especially since Dr Barshion was also sprawled on the floor near the crewmen, a bloody gash in his forehead.

He stirred and moaned a little, and Emilie hurriedly knelt beside him and patted his cheek, demanding, "Dr Barshion, are you all right? What happened?"

Barshion groaned, his eyelids fluttering. He said, "I told him I wouldn't do it. Sabotage, slowing Engal down, that was what he paid me for, not murder. I'm not–" His eyes opened and he focused on her. He grabbed her arm, hard enough to hurt, and gasped, "Stop him. Separating the vessels, it could kill everyone aboard..."

Dr Barshion slumped back, his eyes closed, and Emilie shot to her feet. She ducked back out to the corridor and tore up the stairs. She wanted to shriek at the top of her lungs for help, but if the escaped prisoners were nearby, they could catch her, stop her from warning the others. Lord Ivers had had a crew of nine besides himself, though only four would have *Sovereign* uniforms; it was mainly those four she was worried about.

She ran down the aetheric compartment corridor, reaching the startled sailor guarding the engine. She stepped into the doorway, where Ricard and Mr. Abendle were checking dials and writing down the readings. She said breathlessly, "Lord Ivers' men escaped! You have to lock yourselves in until they're caught."

They both looked up, incredulous. Mr. Abendle said, "What? Escaped?"

Already backing away, Emilie said, "The guards were drugged, knocked out, I have to warn everyone– No, you stay there!" she added as the sailor started to follow her. "Guard the engines!" Running for the stairwell, she hoped he listened to her.

She ran up the stairs and paused on each landing to look down the corridors, but she didn't see any other crewmen to alert. She reached the second deck and hesitated, torn between running up to the wheelhouse to give the warning and going immediately to the airship. No, better go to the airship first. She would alert them and then take the word up to Lord Engal. The airship was far more vulnerable than the wheelhouse.

Emilie ran lightly down the corridor, her bare feet making little noise. Losing her boots was standing her in good stead now. The ship was still quiet except for the distant engine noise, but now that seemed sinister rather than serene. As she reached the outer corridor, the one that ran parallel to the deck, she saw the nearest hatch was partly open. *Uh oh*. She was certain Captain Belden had ordered all hatches be kept closed. It was possible whoever had taken the last message to Dr Marlende had left it open. Possible, but not likely, Emilie thought grimly. She flattened herself against the wall and peered through the opening.

The first thing she saw was Daniel, standing on the airship's catwalk above the steps that led down to the ship's deck. A sailor in the dark *Sovereign* crew uniform was just starting up toward him.

Emilie's eyes narrowed, then she swore in recognition. It was Cavin, the man who had guarded Rani's prison cell in the Sealands city.

Emilie shoved the hatch open and ran onto the deck, and shouted, "Daniel, stop him, he's one of Lord Ivers' men!"

Daniel looked toward her, startled, and Cavin charged up the stairs at him. Daniel stepped forward to block the stairs, ducked a punch from Cavin, and grappled with him.

Seth came out of the door behind him, shouted a warning to the men inside, then dove forward to help Daniel fight off Cavin. The other escaped prisoners ran out of a hatch at the stern end of the *Sovereign*'s deck, Lord Ivers among them, and Emilie ducked back into the corridor. Now she had a clear path to warn the wheelhouse.

She ran back to the cross corridor and nearly slammed into the chest of a crewman. She stumbled back, saw his face and his ill-fitting jacket over a stained shirt, and yelled, "They know you've escaped, I've warned everyone–"

He grabbed her shoulders and snarled, "Shut up or I'll–"

That was as far as he got, as Oswin loomed up behind him and cracked him across the back of the head with a pistol butt. He fell away from Emilie and collapsed onto the floor. Emilie gasped in relief. She told Oswin, "There are more of them, outside, I tried to warn the airship–"

"We know; Mr. Abendle sent Ricard to the wheelhouse." Oswin brushed past her, followed by six large sailors. They ran back to the outer hatch and charged out onto the deck.

Emilie started to follow them out the hatch, but jerked back as gunshots rang out. She peeked around the edge of the hatch more cautiously, saw men fighting in a confused scramble toward the end of the deck. Then the attackers retreated back through the hatch there, leaving a couple of men lying unconscious or dead on the deck. Emilie heard them pound down the corridor toward her. Alarmed, she darted out onto the deck and slammed the hatch behind her.

Oswin and his men pursued the prisoners back into the ship, obviously determined to protect the wheelhouse and the engine rooms, but Emilie saw the door to the airship hung open. Oh, no. She ran forward to the end of the stairs that led up to the catwalk, trying to see inside. Figures fought in the dimness inside the cabin, but she couldn't tell who they were, who was winning.

Then Daniel staggered out of the cabin onto the catwalk, struggling with another man. The other man was bigger and Emilie didn't think the outcome looked certain at all. She looked around desperately, spotted a pistol lying near the hand of one of the fallen attackers. She grabbed it up, finding it unexpectedly heavy.

But as she turned back to the airship, Daniel got in a hard punch to the man's chin that made him stumble back until he fell over the railing down onto the *Sovereign*'s deck. He struck the wooden surface hard, and Emilie stepped hastily away. Daniel saw her and grinned triumphantly, despite a bloody nose.

Then Lord Ivers stepped out of the cabin door behind him. Emilie pointed, yelling, "Look out!" but as Daniel swung around, Ivers pointed a pistol at him. Daniel froze.

Ivers strode down the catwalk, seized Daniel's shoulder and turned him around, pressing the pistol to his head. He said, "Cooperate or I'll blow your head off."

Gripping her pistol tightly, Emilie bolted up the stairs. "Let him go!"

Lord Ivers turned on the narrow catwalk and dragged Daniel with him, the barrel of the pistol pressed against his temple. But as Ivers saw Emilie, his expression went from furious to amused. "Sorry, but I'm afraid I need him. Dr Marlende has locked himself inside the steering cabin and I can't get him to open the door without a hostage."

He didn't look worried at all. Oh, that's not a good sign, Emilie thought. "Don't move. I'll shoot." She pointed the gun, trying to project an aura of deadly certainty. If she could have fired, she would have done it already. She had never held a pistol before and she didn't know if you had to do anything before pulling the trigger; she was afraid if she fumbled it, Lord Ivers would shoot Daniel. Also, she knew it might kick, and she was terribly afraid of firing a bullet into the airship. She wasn't sure one bullet would hurt the balloon, but they were right down near the engines and it might go through the glass. She couldn't count on any help from inside the airship; she could hear violent fighting still going on in the cabin.

"You won't," Ivers said confidently. "A well-brought-up young lady like you."

"I'm not a well-brought-up young lady," Emilie said, projecting confidence. Ivers knew nothing about her, after all. "I'm a stowaway, and a thief, and a lookout for a dock gang that steals mail bags." And an accomplished liar, she almost added, then decided against it.

Daniel's eyes widened. She had convinced him, at least.

Ivers stared, his brows drawing together in consternation. But he tightened his grip on Daniel. "Nevertheless, I'll kill him if you don't get out of my way."

"Why should I?" Emilie countered. "I don't like him; he's been terribly rude to me."

Daniel glared, clearly offended. At least she was distracting him from the gun at his temple.

"You don't like him?" Lord Ivers dragged Daniel forward. Emilie held her ground, though she had the feeling this wasn't going to work out for the best. From Lord Ivers' sneer, he clearly knew she was bluffing. "A handsome boy like him?"

"I'm impervious to physical attraction," Emilie tried.

"It's true," Daniel managed to gasp.

Emilie pressed her lips together. No, the stalling wasn't going to work. But she saw something out of the corner of her eye, on the *Sovereign*'s railing, behind Lord Ivers.

It was Miss Marlende. She was leaning out on the railing, aiming her pistol at Lord Ivers, obviously trying to find an angle where she wouldn't hit the airship or Emilie.

Emilie's heart leapt but she controlled her expression and made herself focus on Lord Ivers' face. "If you let him go I'll drop the pistol," she offered.

It was the wrong thing to say. Lord Ivers' expression twisted and he muttered, "Sorry, my dear, I've no more time to waste." Gripping Daniel around the neck, he pointed his pistol at Emilie.

Emilie yelled and dropped into a crouch, covering her head, though she knew that wouldn't help. The gun went off with an ear-shattering bang, but it was Lord Ivers and Daniel who jolted forward and collapsed onto the catwalk.

Emilie scrambled forward to grab Lord Ivers' pistol out of his nerveless fingers. Ivers was half atop Daniel, and neither man was moving, and there was blood splashed on the metal beneath them. Emilie shoved both pistols down the catwalk and turned back to the men, struggling to lift Ivers off Daniel without dumping either one off the walk.

Footsteps clattered on the steps behind her and she threw a wild look around, but it was Miss Marlende. She shoved her pistol into her belt, saying, "We have to get them inside! The protection spells are about to separate."

Emilie got a grip on Lord Ivers' arms and put all her weight into dragging him off Daniel. Miss Marlende stepped around her, grabbed his belt, and heaved him off. To Emilie's relief, Daniel groaned and stirred, lifting his head. "You had to shoot them both?" Emilie asked, breathlessly, helping Lord Ivers along with a shove as Miss Marlende hauled him down the catwalk. "Not that I'm complaining–"

"It was the only angle I could get that didn't include the airship," Miss Marlende explained, her voice rough from effort. "When you ducked, I was able to take the shot. Hopefully, I just winged Daniel."

"I think so," he groaned, trying to push himself up. "Ow."

Emilie got his free arm and pulled it over her shoulders, and helped him shove to his feet. They staggered after Miss Marlende. Emilie said, "I think someone's still in the cabin. Seth was–"

The airship's door flew open and Cavin came staggering out. Seth lunged after him, delivering a punch to the head which knocked Cavin down the stairs to sprawl on the deck.

"That's the last of them," he gasped to Miss Marlende. His glasses were askew, his knuckles bloody, and he looked more like a prizefighter than a scholar. He reached for Lord Ivers and helped Miss Marlende drag him through the doorway.

A young crewman ran out of the third deck hatch, calling over to them, "Ma'am, the ship's secure, and Lord Engal says we need to go now!"

Miss Marlende told him, "Get those men and yourself inside, then shut the hatches!"

The crewman went to the rail, spotted the men lying on the deck, and waved an acknowledgment. Emilie helped Daniel toward the door into the airship, saying, "If splitting the bubbles doesn't work, will it matter if we're inside or out on the deck?"

Miss Marlende gave her an admonishing look. "Hush, Emilie."

Daniel groaned again. On the deck below, several crewmen ran out of the hatch, seized Cavin and the other fallen men by their jackets, and dragged them inside. As Emilie helped Daniel through the doorway, she saw Cobbier and Mikel sprawled unconscious on the airship's deck, with another one of Lord Ivers' men. Charter was leaning in the doorway to the steering cabin, looking gray around the mouth. The fight couldn't have been very good for a recently wounded man. Seth dumped Lord Ivers beside the other escaped prisoner, Charter tossed him a coil of rope, and he hurriedly began to tie them up. Emilie looked back out the door and saw Miss Marlende hadn't followed them inside, but had run down the steps to the deck, starting to untie the line that formed the symbolic connection between the two ships.

Emilie deposited Daniel on the first bench seat, and ducked back out again as Miss Marlende climbed back up to the airship. Together they lifted the end of the set of steps where it was hooked onto the catwalk and dropped it down to the *Sovereign's* deck. As they stepped inside, Miss Marlende slammed the door behind them and shouted, "Tell father we need to go now!"

Seth bolted for the steering cabin and Charter just slid to the floor. Emilie took a step toward him, then stumbled when the airship shuddered. The deck slammed up and hit Emilie in the face. At least that was what it felt like. Sprawled on the cork floor, she lifted her head. Miss Marlende had fallen too, and Daniel had been knocked flat on the bench.

Emilie shoved herself upright, using the bench as a ladder, and leaned over Daniel to look outside. The

Sovereign was gone. She could see something past the golden glow of the bubble, and realized it was rocky walls, stretching up.

Beside her, Miss Marlende staggered to her feet, and gasped, "I think we were a bit late on the release."

"A bit?" Daniel said, still trying to struggle upright.

"What does that mean?" Emilie asked.

Miss Marlende began, "It means—" Outside, the bubble shivered, going almost translucent, before it solidified again. Emilie flinched, and Miss Marlende finished, in a smaller voice, "We might not have enough power."

"Oh." Emilie bit her lip, watching the rock stream rapidly past the fading glow of the bubble. "It was Dr Barshion. He was in Lord Ivers' pay."

"That explains a great deal," Miss Marlende said, her voice tight with anger. "I hope he hasn't killed all of us."

The airship shuddered, metal squealed, then a powerful jolt threw them all to the floor again. Sprawled there, Emilie saw the gold glow of the bubble vanish. "Oh no," she gasped, "I think—"

We're dead, she meant to finish, but that was daylight streaming in. Real daylight, surface daylight.

The pressure vanished and the airship jolted and shuddered again, but this time the force came from the side, like a strong wind. Emilie struggled to her feet and knelt on the bench to look out the window.

They were rising above a vast rocky cauldron, the top of the volcano. Clouds streaked the blue sky and wind whistled around the cabin. It pushed the airship over the rim, and they drifted above the outer slopes. They were rocky and bare at the top, sliding down amid boulders and old rock falls into a forest of short wind-twisted trees. Miss Marlende called out, "Father, we're losing altitude!"

"Yes, my dear," Dr Marlende answered from the steering cabin. "I believe we've lost a number of gas cells."

"Are we going to crash land?" Emilie craned her neck for a better view of the slope. If they were, it looked as if they were going to do it very slowly. Now that the bulk of the volcano was blocking much of the wind, the airship was spiraling slowly down. At least they were on the surface, out of the aether current.

"Yes," Miss Marlende said, "But we still have enough gas cells left so it will be more of a thump than a crash." Her brow furrowed with worry, she added, "I just hope the *Sovereign* made it."

"Can someone help me up?" Daniel asked from the floor.

"Oh, sorry!" Emilie helped Miss Marlende haul Daniel back to the bench. When they had him sitting up, Emilie turned back to the window.

"Can you see it?" Miss Marlende asked anxiously.

They were past the tree-covered slopes and over flat grassy fields, and Dr Marlende was guiding them gently down in a wide spiral. As the airship turned, Emilie caught sight of the sea, past low rocky bluffs. She leaned close to the glass and squinted against the glare off the water. She saw light glinting off something, something coppery. "Yes, there it is!" she cried out.

It was the *Sovereign*, steaming toward the island shore.

THIRTEEN

"Now, you do know the way to your cousin's house?" Miss Marlende asked, looking a little worried. "It's going to be dark soon."

They were standing on the dock at Silk Harbor, under a cloudy early evening sky, near the *Sovereign*'s slip. This spot had been crowded with journalists and onlookers earlier, but by the dinner hour the furor had calmed down, and now there were only the usual dockworkers, off-duty sailors, and a few passengers making their way down the wooden boardwalk above the boat slips.

Dr Marlende's airship had attracted the attention as it was towed in this morning on a large pontoon barge by a tug boat. It had taken a few days to get the tug and the barge from the port on the far side of the island of Aerinterre, load the airship, and then travel here, so the word had flown ahead of them on the wireless. Emilie wasn't sure what had caused more sensation, the news of the successful expedition, or when Lord Engal had formally given Lord Ivers in charge to the magistrates.

He had also had to give Dr Barshion in charge, a moment of considerably less satisfaction for everyone.

Somewhat recovered from his injury, Dr Barshion had admitted that he had been in Lord Ivers' pay from the moment Lord Engal had hired him. He had given Lord Ivers copies of Dr Marlende's notes, and research that Miss Marlende had shared with Lord Engal, had committed some small sabotages and spied on everything Engal, Miss Marlende, and Kenar had done to prepare for the expedition. Barshion had apparently hoped to stop the *Sovereign* from ever making the attempt, leaving Lord Ivers to rescue Dr Marlende and take all the credit and acclaim. Once they were down in the Hollow World, he had started to regret what he had done, but he had still put the sleeping spell on the guards, so Ivers and his men could escape. But he had refused to help them destroy the *Sovereign*, and Ivers had bashed him in the head and left him for dead.

Emilie felt a little sorry for him. A little. She would have felt considerably more sorry for herself and the rest of the crew if Ivers had managed to take control of the airship and destroy the *Sovereign*, and all the witnesses to and evidence of his wrongdoing. They were just lucky that no one had been killed in the escape attempt. Some of the crew, including Mikel and Charter, had been left behind temporarily in the town hospital at Aerinterre, and would have to be retrieved later.

"I'm sure I know the way," Emilie told Miss Marlende now. The others would be leaving with the *Sovereign*, which was preparing to set out for Meneport tonight to arrive in the morning and meet the representatives of the Philosophical Explorers Society. The airship would be remaining here for repairs to its balloon, because Silk Harbor had one of the only weaving factories in Menea that could produce the special fabric. "It's on Caveroe Street, on Tamerin Hill. Karthea's letters said it's not a far walk from the port." She felt considerably more prepared to present herself to her cousin than she had before. For one thing, she had new clothes: a skirt, shirtwaist, and jacket, plus a cap, stockings, and a set of walking boots suitable for town or country. There was also an extra set of under things and a nightgown, and a shoulder satchel to carry them and what was left of her old clothes. On Miss Marlende's request, Mrs. Verian had run out to a large drapery shop not far from the harbor and purchased all of it for her. Emilie could now arrive at Cousin Karthea's looking respectable, with something to wear until the package with her own things arrived in the post.

The Marlendes would be back here in two weeks, to collect their airship and Emilie. She had decided to take the time to stay here and visit Karthea, so she could explain to her why she had left home, so Karthea would know the truth and be able to pass it along to the more far-flung members of the family. It would also be a good chance to write letters to her brother in the navy and her friend Porcia, to let them know she was all right. Emilie expected she would be spending much of her time at Karthea's studying up on just what it was a lady's assistant and social secretary did.

"All right, then, as long as it's not far. I'm going to give you some money–" Miss Marlende began, taking a small purse out of her jacket pocket.

"Oh no, I couldn't accept it!" Emilie said. She hadn't started her new position yet. "I'll be fine, really."

"Emilie," Miss Marlende eyed her. "Do you even have the money to buy dinner, if you had to?"

"Well, no." The last of her money had been pinned into the pocket of her bloomers, and it had been lost at some point, probably one of the times she had had to jump into the water.

"Isn't that how you got into this situation?"

"Well, yes," Emilie admitted. "Maybe I'd better take it."

"Besides," Miss Marlende said, handing her the purse. "You've already been acting as my assistant and as an auxiliary member of my father's ground crew, so we probably owe you back wages for the voyage."

"Oh, that's true." That was different than taking charity from a friend.

Miss Marlende continued, "I've also put in a note with the addresses for our townhouse in Meneport and my father's workshop. If you get into any difficulty in the next two weeks, please write to us or send a wire. Do contact us," she emphasized. "Don't try to stow away on anything to get there. I can send someone to get you, or I can wire you passage money for a ferry."

"I'd be a much better stowaway now than I was before," Emilie had to point out.

"Yes, I'm sure you would." Miss Marlende smiled,

and hugged her again. "We'll see you soon, Emilie. Try not to get into trouble."

"I'll try," Emilie promised. She had already said goodbye to the others, and even given her direction to Lord Engal, who had said that he might need to contact her for her account of the voyage. But even knowing that she would see her again before long, it was still hard to walk away from Miss Marlende, waving goodbye.

Emilie managed it, heading down the dock toward the stairs that led up to the walkway, and the streets above it where the gas lamps were being lighted as dusk fell. The houses and shops of Silk Harbor were spread out over the low hills above the wide sweep of the port, the streets dotted with trees. She could see people on the paved walks, and house lights coming on. She took a deep breath, filled with the sea, boat tar, and the scents of grilled fish and beef from the nearest chophouse. It wasn't as busy a place as Meneport, perhaps, but much less easy to get lost in.

Footsteps pounded behind her and she glanced back, surprised to see Daniel. He was dressed in a much more respectable jacket and trousers than she had last seen him in, and had shaved recently. He carried a satchel over his good shoulder, and his other arm was still in a sling. Miss Marlende's bullet had torn his shoulder, but hadn't hit bone. It had done quite a bit more damage to Lord Ivers, though he would still recover.

"Hello," Daniel said breathlessly as he caught up to her. "Miss Marlende said you were going this way."

"Hello." Emilie lifted an inquiring brow. "What are

you doing here? Aren't you going to Meneport with the others?"

He explained, "My family lives in a small village a few miles outside of town. I was going to stay over here tonight and then head out to see them in the morning. I'll catch up with Dr Marlende when he comes back to get the airship." He looked a little bashful. "I thought I'd walk with you. Maybe your cousin can tell me where there's a good rooming house."

"I see." Emilie smiled, turning to head for the walkway. "Maybe she can." And they walked up into the town together.

LAURA LAM

PANTOMIME

Somewhere, there's a place for everyone

STRANGE CheMIStRY

"Who hasn't dreamed of
running off and joining the circus?"
BRIAN KATCHER, AUTHOR OF ALMOST PERFECT

SUCH WONDERS IN STORE FOR YOU...

EXPERIMENTING WITH YOUR IMAGINATION

strangechemistrybooks.com
facebook.com/strangechemistry
twitter.com/strangechem